2016

D0455269

KEEP ME IN MIND

JAIME REED

Point

All rights reserved. Published by Point, an imprint of Scholastic Inc., *Publishers since 1920.* SCHOLASTIC, POINT, and associated logos are trademarks and/or registered trademarks of Scholastic Inc.

The publisher does not have any control over and does not assume any responsibility for author or third-party websites or their content.

This book is a work of fiction. Names, characters, places, and incidents are either the product of the author's imagination or are used fictitiously, and any resemblance to actual persons, living or dead, business establishments, events, or locales is entirely coincidental.

Library of Congress Cataloging-in-Publication Data

Reed, Jaime, author.
　　Keep me in mind / Jaime Reed. — First edition.
　　　pages cm
　　Summary: Sixteen-year-old Ellia Dawson wakes up in the hospital with retrograde amnesia, unable to remember Liam McPherson, the boyfriend who insists that they are in love—Liam is devastated, and, desperate to reawaken her memories, begins to write the story of their relationship, convinced that it will somehow recreate their relationship.
　　ISBN 978-0-545-88381-8 (jacketed hardcover)　1. Amnesia—Juvenile fiction.　2. Memory—Juvenile fiction.　3. Falls (Accidents)—Juvenile fiction.　4. Interpersonal relations—Juvenile fiction. [1. Amnesia—Fiction.　2. Memory—Fiction.　3. Love—Fiction.　4. Interpersonalrelations—Fiction.]　I. Title.
PZ7.R252314Ke 2016
813.6—dc23
[Fic]

2015031159

10 9 8 7 6 5 4 3 2 1　　16 17 18 19 20

Printed in the U.S.A.　　23

First edition, May 2016
Book design by Abby Dening

*To my family and friends and to He who knows me
better than I could ever attempt.
Thank You.*

CHAPTER
ONE

LIAM

UNTITLED | Page . . .

At that hour, the beach was deserted save the fishermen manning their posts on each of the twin piers. The sun hid just behind the mountains in the east, and a purple sky hovered over the Spanish rooftops beyond the dunes. To the west lay darkness, rolling waves and a half moon, but no view could compare to the one jogging by my side. She was a living, breathing celestial event and the closest star I would ever reach.

The she in question was none other than the Ellia Renée Dawson, a girl so gorgeous, so gloriously epic that it bordered on the absurd. Some celebrities went by one name, like Oprah or Madonna or Bono—they were just that iconic. But Ellia had achieved a level of awesome where she could be identified by a simple pronoun. To this day, legends of her reign echoed the halls of León High School and inspired a number of copycats, but Ellia was a force with no equal. One seriously had to wonder what she saw in a lanky bookworm like me.

That question had crossed my mind hundreds of times and it surfaced as I looked over my shoulder to see her struggling to keep up with me. Her rich brown skin shimmered with sweat and a thick puff of black curls bobbed at the top of her head. She wore running tights and a cut-off sweatshirt that hung off one shoulder. The words I'M NOT LAZY, I'M A STAY-AT-HOME CHILD *were printed across the front and summed up her workout ethic perfectly.*

Though she exploited the many miracles of spandex, the poor girl couldn't run to save her life. Horrible posture, flailing arms, and her refusal to control her breathing made our fitness routine a work of comedic genius. It also showed she wasn't the flawless deity her reputation had led everyone to believe. At the end of the day, she was just a girl. My girl. And she loved me enough to sneak out of the house to keep me company.

Her participation dragged my regimen out an extra hour and did zilch to improve my sprint time for track season, but who cared? It was a small price to pay for a few more minutes alone with her before the sunrise forced us to part ways.

"I won't make it! Go on, save yourself!" Ellia gasped and clutched her chest, then collapsed on the sand and pretended to be dying.

"I'm not leaving without you!" I called back in my best action-star voice. "We're in this together!"

"Don't be a hero, you fool! You've got too much to live for! It's too late for me, but you still have a chance!" She fell back down and began twitching.

Laughing, I trotted to her side and towered over her sprawled form as she began to make snow angels in the sand. "Your acting skills are terrible, babe. Don't quit your day job."

She stopped and glanced up at the stars, which were still visible this early in the morning. "Liam, I don't know how you can do this in and outside of school and not demand combat pay. All this running has to be bad for your joints. I can hear my bones crying. And that runner's high you keep talking about is a straight-up myth."

"It's not a myth; you just have to keep at it. Running's good for you. It gives you stamina and gets the blood flowing."

"That might be how things go on your home planet, but us earthbound folk need a legit reason for strenuous work. Either you're running from something or running to something. Whatever the case is, it better be worth all the huffing and puffing."

"Quick, someone put that on a T-shirt," I quipped. "It'll fit well with the rest of the Ellia Dawson Smart-Mouth Fall Collection."

"Ooh! That's actually a good name for a clothing line." She patted the spot next to her. "Come sit and take a break with me."

"A break?" I dug in my pocket and checked the running app on my phone. "We just started five minutes ago."

"Yeah, I need to stretch some more. I think I pulled something." She pouted.

Oh, she was pulling something all right, but then she looked up at me with her big, round eyes that always reminded me of a Pixar character. Saying no to her was close to impossible.

I sat down on my bent knees and captured one of her legs in my hands. "Aw, my poor wittle baby. Where does it hurt?" I gave her slim ankle a light squeeze. "Here?"

"Nope." She smiled and bit her bottom lip.

My fingers encircled the soft calf. "How about here?"

"Close, but not quite."

I moved in for the kill and tickled the sensitive spot on the back of her knees.

Squealing, she wiggled and tried to scoot away, but didn't get far. "Ah! Stop! Stop! I'm sorry!"

"Had enough?"

"Yes!" she cried out, giggling. "Stop!"

"Good." I let go and then lay long-ways in the sand beside her.

She was still laughing and I kissed her through her smile. Her lips were full, soft, and carried the faint taste of toothpaste and cherry lip gloss. She raked her fingers through my hair and returned the kiss in earnest. All at once, everything became this great emergency where we couldn't get close enough, but we were willing to die in the attempt.

Then it occurred to me that I should probably breathe soon, so I pulled my mouth from hers. Forehead on forehead, we rested against each other for balance; we were too dizzy.

"We should get going on that run. The sun will be rising soon and people will be getting up," I warned.

"Nuh-uh. Don't wanna." She shook her head, making our noses rub together. *"I could be home, sound asleep in my warm bed where I'm supposed to be, but* nooo. *I'm out here before the butt crack of dawn, messing up my hair and getting tortured by you."* Her lips dabbed around my cheek and jaw. *"The things I do for you, sir."*

I lowered my head and planted a kiss on her bare shoulder. *"I thank you for your sacrifice, ma'am."*

"As you should." She shifted her body so she lay on her side to look at me fully. *"My dad would kill me if he found out I snuck out here."*

"You mean he would kill me," I corrected her.

"Whoever he could get his hands on first." She shrugged, but her frown and the loud click of her tongue told me that something was bothering her. *"It's not fair having to sneak around like this, like we're outlaws. It was cute at first—it was giving me all kinds of Romeo and Juliet, Bonnie and Clyde,* On the Run *realness. But now I'm just over it. I love you, you love me, and this shouldn't be a part-time gig. We need to upgrade."*

I could understand her frustration. Her dad was a mean battle-ax and all of my visits to her house were heavily supervised and often cut short if I so much as kissed her cheek. Any real quality time was spent over the phone or online. Even in school, our meetings were brief, what with classes, teachers, and learning and all. Privacy was a rare and expensive piece of merchandise that we'd been forced to steal to keep from starving.

"Why does your dad hate me so much?" I asked after a long bout of silence. *"You sure it's not because I'm white?"*

"*Yeah, sure, play the race card.*" She snickered. "*You're a boy—and a cute one—and I'm his only daughter. That's enough for him. It's nothing personal.*"

"*Well, it's* personally *affecting me,*" I replied. "*I can't wait until we graduate. We can finally do what we want.*"

She watched me carefully then reached out to stroke the side of my face. "*Hey, hey, cut that out. Stop brooding.*"

I leaned into her warm palm. "*I'm not brooding.*"

"*Yes, you are. You're doing that bottom-lip thing and you got a line between your eyebrows. That's definitely brooding. I sense another poem in the works.*" She draped an arm over her eyes in a show of dramatized angst. "*Life is so bleak and not my own / For my parents hound and gripe and moan / That only sports will pay off college student loans / Thus my dream to write is but a seed unsown / I am now and shall remain forever . . . alone.*"

I glared at her. For the record, my writing was better than that, but my prose did lean on the dark and moody side. Only Ellia knew about that; she was the only one I ever allowed to read my work. Unlike my parents, Ellia could see my true calling and, by her own edict, her opinion was the only one that mattered.

"*Ha-ha. Real funny. You're in the same boat as I am, Miss Project Runway,*" I replied, effectively wiping the smirk off her face. "*Have you broken the news to dear old dad that you vetoed the whole engineer idea? I'm sure he was devastated to hear that his only child won't be taking over the family business.*"

Trash talk had always been our shtick, but my comment must've struck a nerve because she rose to her knees in a burst of movement.

"All right, that's it!" she yelled and brushed the sand off her tights. "We are staging a coup! I refuse to spend the rest of our junior year hiding in shadows. We have a year and a half to convince our folks that we want different things. We are not puppets or avatars to live through vicariously."

I lifted a power fist in the air. "Word."

She cut her eyes at me. "Please don't do that. You make it weird." Then she continued, "Let's form a pact, a promise right here, right now that from this point forward we live our own lives and pursue our own dreams, and, no matter what, we will never be as uptight with our own kids. Promise?" She reached out her hand for me to shake, but I threaded her fingers between mine instead.

"I promise," I said.

Her slender fingers closed over my hand and squeezed. "We won't stop until your novel hits the New York Times *bestseller list and a hot supermodel is wearing my gown on the cover of* Vogue. *If one of us gets lost and veers off the pathway, the other has to pull them back. Deal?"*

"Deal. No matter what." I nodded, knowing she meant every word and that alone gave me a valid reason to try. To hope.

If I had an answer to the question of what she saw in me, it would be the recognition of a person lost. We may have been from different backgrounds, but we spoke the same language and we each bore the weight of family expectations. Ellia hid it well with humor and sass, but those sad brown eyes pleaded for someone to set her free. I understood that feeling, and whether she knew it or not she held the keys to my freedom, too.

"Okay. Now that that's settled, I've got a second wind, so on with the cardio! I'll race you to the pier. Ready? One, two, three—go!" She dashed across the beach before I could even get to my feet. With her typical clumsy strides, she headed to the winding bike trail leading up the hill. The path had a high peak that overlooked the beach below and served as the quickest route toward the docks.

She threw her head back with a wicked laugh of certain victory and then spun around and gestured for me to follow. Dusting the sand from my shorts, I took my time catching up with her. I could outrun her by miles and it seemed only fair to give her a decent head start.

Little did I know that these would be the last few minutes we'd have together. If I had known, I would've stopped her or told her to wait for me. That one small error in judgment would cost me dearly. The penalty came by way of a piercing scream ringing in the air.

"Ellia?" The name ripped from me in a startled breath and served as both a question and answer. It had to be her. My adrenaline spiked, and unleashed the darker parts of my imagination.

I poured all my energy into running at the sound, my heart pounding in my chest, my leg muscles burning from the rising incline. Ellia couldn't have been too far ahead, but it was enough for me to lose sight of her. As I neared a bend in the path, it then became apparent that she hadn't cried out again. There was no sound from her at all; the only footsteps I could hear were my own.

"Ellia!" I called out into the darkness again, but only crashing waves and my pounding heartbeat replied.

Panic quickly set in as my ears strained to pick up any sign of life: a whimper, a curse, another bloodcurdling scream; anything other than the eerie quiet that made the hair rise on my arms. I begged for just one footprint, one small flash of movement to help me find her. I'd never begged for anything so hard in my life . . .

I lifted the pen from the page and ripped my reading glasses off my face. My eyes began to prickle and burn and I pressed down on the sockets with my knuckles. The tears came anyway, and kept coming as I tried to pick up the pen again. Even with blurry vision, it was obvious that what I'd written down was absolute gibberish. The letters dipped past the blue lines of the paper in squiggly waves and then trailed off at the margins. Not one single word was legible.

Every night this week had produced the same results. No matter how hard I tried, I couldn't get past this exact point in the narrative. These thoughts couldn't stay locked in my brain, and for the sake of my physical health, I had to find rest at some point. For the past month, sleep came to me in three-, sometimes four-hour spells before I was up at my computer or scribbling in my notebook for the rest of the night. Now my old standby was working against me.

I closed my notebook and dropped it on the floor by my bed, resigning myself to the fact that I wasn't going to get any coherent writing done this morning. My thoughts were skipping around again and had completely jammed once I decided to commit that painful memory to paper.

My head fell back against the headboard and my stare bounced to various points around the room until it settled on my desk clock. I had an hour before I needed to get ready for school and a hard run would help to clear my mind.

I threw on some running shorts and a T-shirt, then laced up my sneakers. Charging my phone, grabbing my keys, and ruffling my hair was the extent of my pre-workout ritual. I tiptoed downstairs so as not to wake up Dad and, after chugging down a bottle of water, I headed out through the back kitchen door.

Thin purple streaks in the sky let me know dawn was approaching. The air was a bit cold for February in this part of California. Hopefully, the rapid blood flow would keep me warm. I headed west and ran like my life depended on it. The air sawed in and out of my lungs and I enjoyed the burn, craved it. My arms swung back and forth, propelling my movements like blades slicing through air. Once I attained a comfortable rhythm, my brain could finally shut down and my body operated off-line. It was good not having to think for a while. I was aware that hard pavement lay under me, but my feet barely absorbed the impact and all I could see ahead was my destination.

The bad part about mental autopilot was that the body was left to follow its original flight plan. Repetition had programmed popular commands and navigation points into its system. The only way to override it was to make a conscious effort to change course, but that involved thinking, which would defeat the purpose.

This was the excuse I made for stopping at the curb across the street from Ellia's house once again. It was simply a reflex. It couldn't be helped.

My eyes drifted up to the second window to the left and, in a true act of self-torture, I waited in hope for my girl to appear through the curtains. I knew she wouldn't, but I liked to think that at any minute she'd turn on her lamp and signal that she was on her way down to join me. I could picture her scurrying around the side of her house, crouched low under her parents' window, then racing across the grass to meet me at the corner. Wishful thinking can create a mirage of the highest caliber and the amount of power the mind wielded never ceased to amaze me. If pushed hard enough, it could make you believe almost anything.

CHAPTER

TWO

ELLIA

There he goes again. Same time, same place, every morning for the past week without fail. At exactly 5:30 A.M., he'd emerge from the dark and unkempt foliage of my neighbor's yard across the street, cut across the high grass, then commandeer the sidewalk as his personal gym. The streetlamp served as both a spotlight and warm-up bar as he stretched, flexed, and shook loose his limbs before taking off toward the beach at a run.

He'd leave for about forty minutes then return to the same spot, dripping with sweat, seawater, or whatever made his running shorts stick to his body like shrink-wrap. Then he'd reclaim the walkway for the cooldown portion of his workout. On a good day, I'd catch a flash of ripped abs whenever he lifted his shirt to wipe his face. I'd be lying if I said that the view wasn't worth the price of admission—the dude was hot. But if he wanted to take this show on the road, he should lose the T-shirt and maybe pick up some dance moves.

He embodied the typical California boy—sandy blond hair, lean build, and an allover tan. But unlike the rest of the beach boys of Quintero, he gave off a sad and gloomy aura that seemed to pour off him in waves as he glanced up at my window. The lights were off in my bedroom, but the intensity of his stare made me wonder if he could see me through the sheer curtains. Unless this boy had mutant X-ray vision, it was highly unlikely. Even still.

That stare . . .

The funny part was, his morning vigil didn't scare me—I was just confused as to why I'd wake up at the exact same time he'd come around. 5:30 A.M. Every day.

Looking down at the black screen of my phone, I made the decision to break the ice and finally talk to him. We hadn't spoken since I was released from the hospital a week ago and by now he probably thought I was avoiding him, which was only half true.

The past month had been an adjustment to say the least, integrating who I used to be into who I was now and relying on photographs and secondhand accounts to fill in the rest. One of those accounts happened to be the sweaty boy now doing jumping jacks across the street.

I pulled on a sweatshirt then crept out of my room with my sneakers dangling in my hand. I went full ninja, tiptoeing past

Mom and Dad's room, skirting around creaking floorboards, slinking down the stairs, and slowly unlocking the dead bolt on the front door. Only when I was safely outside and felt the cool morning air on my face did I finally let out the breath I'd been holding. My folks had canine hearing and hawk vision when it came to me these days, so one wrong step and it was a wrap.

I was on the porch steps, sliding on my shoes, when he finally spotted me. He made a move to come forward, but I communicated through hand signals that I would go to him. Looking left to right for witnesses, I dashed across the street and jumped onto the sidewalk with only a square of concrete between our feet. The silence that followed was immense.

Seeing him face-to-face, outside of the world of tubes and beeping monitors, was a bit surreal. When you're lying down or in a reclined position on a bed, everyone's taller than you. Now that I was vertical, my head just barely reached his shoulders—and I was five foot seven. I'd clock him in at about six two, and he maybe weighed a buck fifty. He was slim, but shredded with muscle, probably from all the running.

The overall framework looked even better up close, but it wasn't the first thing you'd notice about him. The square jaw, the faint cleft in his chin—they were the supporting cast to the star attraction. Those blue eyes invited you to stay and linger for a while. Inside those eyes was a cloudless sky or a still lake, a serene and quiet place to daydream.

He broke the awkward moment with a whisper. "Ellia."

I tipped my head in a slight bow. "Liam."

"You're up early."

"Yeah, I'm usually up at this hour. No matter how late I go to bed, my eyes will just pop open around five, like clockwork. No idea why."

He nodded thoughtfully as his gaze lifted to a spot just over my left temple. "How's your head?"

My hand shot up and touched the gauzy material wrapped around my head in a turban. Part of that area had been shaved bald to make room for the Frankenstein stitches that ran from the crown to the corner of my left eyebrow. It itched like crazy, but it was either walk around with a medical do-rag or try to figure out how to style three-fourths of my hair. As it was, I barely had strength to shower.

"It's fine. I'm fine." I kept my eyes busy with random points of noninterest. The telephone wires overhead. The parked cars that lined the curb in both directions. The slope of the street that plunged past the vanishing point and met the ocean at the bottom of the hill. His sweaty T-shirt with the arms cut off and the words LEÓN HIGH SCHOOL TRACK AND FIELD on the front in bold varsity font.

That actually explained a lot.

He dipped his head until his face was in my line of sight, his voice soft and full of concern. "You still getting those headaches?"

"Yeah. I got a big one right now—that's why I'm out here. I need your help with something," I said, all too ready to change the subject. "How are your hacking skills?"

His thick eyebrows rose, clearly not expecting that question. "Um . . . nonexistent. Why do you ask?"

"Well, you said we were close, right?" I began speaking quickly, feeling uncomfortable. "You seem to know a lot of stuff about me. I was just wondering if you could help me unlock my phone. I've been trying for a week and I can't figure out the code. It's six characters and no one in my house knows it and I didn't write it down anywhere, because why would I? And what's worse is the list to all my other codes, like the user account on my laptop, are stored inside my phone as backup and I don't have a backup for the backup, so . . ."

He stared blank-faced at me.

I pushed out a long breath, my shoulder slumping in defeat. "Never mind. Forget I said anything."

I turned and walked away, my phone in hand. All my contact numbers, pictures, and possible clues of my missing life hid inside an overpriced piece of plastic. It could be the meds talking, but being at home for a week without electronic stimuli was causing physical withdrawal. I felt naked. My thumbs were now unemployed. Texts and voice mails were trapped in limbo while cobwebs collected around my last status update.

There was nothing else I could do—the life I knew and what I tried to know were gone. My only hope was not to trip and do a face-plant on the pavement in my rush to flee the scene. That would be a really messed-up streak of karma.

His voice stopped me in the middle of the street. "Vivian."

I turned back to him. "What?"

He stared off to the trees, looking pensive. "You wouldn't use numbers unless you had to. You'd want something simple, something not many people would know about. A name. V-I-V-I-A-N. Six letters. That should work."

He had a point and I was blown away by his observation. I was terrible with numerals and all my passwords in the past were an inside joke. Which brought me to my next question. "Who's Vivian?"

He dismissed the inquiry with a small shake of the head. "Just try it."

My thumbs flew over the keypad, and, with a musical chime, the home screen lit up with icons.

"Oh my god! It worked. Thank you!" I wrapped my arms around his neck and hugged him tight. I could tell the gesture surprised him, but eventually he hugged back. As soon as I pulled away, I was nose-deep in my phone, sifting through apps and checking for Internet access. "How did you know that?"

"Lucky guess. At least this explains why you never called me," he said.

I lifted my head and met his steady gaze. "Uh, yeah. Sorry. I just have a lot going on right now and . . . whatever this is with us, I just don't know."

He rubbed the back of his neck and glanced down at his sneakers. "No, it's cool. I'm glad to know you're okay."

"I am. I just need to take this all in," I said, for lack of a better response.

This was the other half of what I wanted to avoid—the expectation, the longing, the hope for everything to go back to normal, to feel things that were once there. It was one thing to wake up from a three-day coma having no memory of the past two years of my life. It was another thing to have a tearstained boy hovering over my bed, calling me "babe" and declaring his undying love and devotion.

I suspected my response was no different from what most people would have said in that situation. And at the time, I had no clue the devastation three little words could cause. *"Who are you?"*

"Ellia, it's me, Liam," he'd said, leaning over my hospital bed, his blue eyes wide. "Your boyfriend."

The doctors told me that I was missing part of my memory, but this? I'd never seen this dude a day in my life. I was already in a bad mood, and having him roll up to my hospital room while I was trying to sleep had me ready to fight.

I shook my head at him, unsure if he was lying or just crazy. "How can you be my boyfriend?" I asked, my voice hoarse. "Do we go to the same school? You don't look like a freshman."

"That's because we're juniors. You don't remember meeting me?" He'd reached across the bed for my hand, but I pulled it away.

For a stranger, he was getting way too familiar, and I was tempted to call the nurse. He seemed harmless enough, but my internal panic button stayed locked in case some foolery was about to jump off.

"I'm not a junior," I'd argued. "I just started high school. Look, I think you got the wrong hospital room. You can't really see my face with all the bandages, but I don't think I'm the person you're looking for."

His expression was one of disbelief and worry as he drew away from the bed. "Yeah, you are."

That look on his face was haunting, like someone had died. I was embarrassed for him. And then I was embarrassed for freaking out the way I did. Then when I later found out from a friend that he was telling the truth, I could only imagine how embarrassed he felt for putting his heart out on the line like that. It was all one big ten-car pileup of mortification. Meanwhile, in the back of my mind, I was thinking, Do my folks know I dated a white guy?

So yeah, I'd been dragging my feet on this little reunion. I couldn't be responsible for destroying something that beautiful.

"Listen, I'm gonna run for a bit then get ready for school. You wanna come with?" Liam asked as the silence began to choke us both.

I cut my eyes at him. "Sorry, but aside from zombies, flying bullets, and wild dogs, there's no legit reason for anyone to run voluntarily." The comment won me a grin that animated his entire face.

He took a step back and then another. "You underestimate yourself. You'd be surprised what you can do."

"Oh yeah? Like what?"

He turned in the middle of the street then began to walk backward. "You're into fashion and you like to sew. You're always making up weird outfits and dressing up that creepy mannequin in your room."

I laughed at the thought of my ridiculous room, which I hadn't recognized when I came home from the hospital. I apparently now owned an old sewing machine and there were folded scraps of fabric piled on my desk. Hundreds of glossy magazine pages doubled as wallpaper and there was a life-size mannequin by the closet wearing nothing but an eye patch and a hot-pink feather boa. That dummy scared me every time I got up to use the bathroom. Yeah, that thing definitely had to go.

"Anything else I should know?" I called after him.

"The pictures on your phone should help fill in some of the blanks for you," he said. "By the way, the mannequin—her name's Vivian." He spun around, broke into a jog, and disappeared down the hill, leaving me with a fresh batch of confusion.

I should've been used to it by now, but more bizarre occurrences kept showing up every day, much like the boyfriend I couldn't remember. Liam. Weird, gorgeous, cardio-junkie Liam. The most confusing thing of all was that on some subconscious level I looked forward to seeing him tomorrow. Same time. Same place.

CHAPTER
THREE

LIAM

I wasn't breaking any new ground by saying I hated high school. The hours were ridiculous, the work was tedious, and there was no reward save the hope of early release.

The learning part, however, I actually liked. I excelled at storing up useless information. I also found twisted delight in observing the student body. It was better than any nature show and taught me more about human behavior than whatever weird medical trivia my mom threw my way. I'd always been more of a spectator than a participant, a wallflower soaking up the atmosphere and gathering material for a future story. Everything made for a future story.

This morning, I parked my car in the school lot, bracing myself. Ever since the accident, my day couldn't start without getting harassed by the Ellia supporters: friends, classmates, frenemies, haters, girls who wanted to be her, and guys who wanted to date her. I'd barely climbed out of my car when I was greeted by one of her biggest fans.

Kendra Bailey was Ellia's replacement on the dance team. Just under five feet, this brown-skinned windup doll usually said the first thing that came to her mind with no censoring capacity or off switch. For that reason, I fumbled with my backpack hanging off my shoulder and pretended to look busy.

My front pouch was covered with buttons, mostly concert souvenirs, except for the big black button in the center that read TALK NERDY TO ME. Ellia had given it to me as a joke. But the *zing* that zapped my fingers when I touched it wasn't funny. It could be just static electricity coming off the metal, but it felt like an ominous prelude to another craptastic day.

"Hey, Liam," Kendra said, and kept pace with me as I walked.

I reluctantly looked up from my backpack. That one glance was all the prompting she needed before jumping right into her long-winded monologue.

"So this whole Ellia thing's got me trippin' about life and how short it is, 'cause there's no guarantee that we'll live long enough to get old. I mean, just last week, a guy cut me off on the freeway and I could've died and I was thinking, *The last thing I told my dad was I need twenty bucks for gas.* The lamest final words you can tell someone you love, and now I'm trying to make every word count for something, just in case my number's up." She twirled the ends of her hair as she looked up at me for feedback.

My response was a sideways glance that I hoped conveyed the full measure of my disinterest.

The drama seekers at school all wanted me to perform, to play the role of the grief-stricken widower without having had any of the perks of a real marriage. They'd watch me in class or in the halls, waiting for some emotional outburst they could sigh or coo over. I wasn't that guy, and, more to the point—of which I had to remind everyone, including Kendra—Ellia wasn't dead.

"I know she's alive, fool, but it really makes you think," Kendra replied with a smarmy expression. "I just chatted with her that night—I told you that part, didn't I?"

"A few times." I kept walking through the grid of old vehicles riddled with bumper stickers and Hawaiian-print seat covers. Oddly enough, most of these cars belonged to the faculty.

Kendra's short legs kept my pace with hurried strides. "But it's trippy though, right? To think the last thing I told Ellia was 'see ya at school.' So generic. It's like something you write in a yearbook to someone you don't know that well."

This could go on for weeks if I didn't put my foot down. "Kendra, do you waste time thinking of what your life was like inside the womb? No, because it doesn't matter anymore. You can't go back there and too many unknowns lay ahead of you to even care. After you die, the last thing you said or did won't matter for the same reason, so stop stressing."

Kendra threw up her hands. "See? That's what I'm saying! You can make the simplest stuff sound deep."

"Um, thanks." I tried my best not to roll my eyes, then left her to her existential crisis.

I followed the masses under a wide, flat, roof canopy as they migrated toward the main building. Backpacks bounced in stride with the power walk of the punctual. Car keys dangled from hands, a status symbol of maturity, the freedom to leave at any time. Rushing feet trampled the burgundy floor mat at the entrance, the words HOME OF THE CONQUISTADORS faded under dirt and tread.

It all had a flow, like marching ants or blood vessels channeling through valves and passageways. The major clog in this circulatory system was the presence of the not-quite-popular girls, who traveled in packs and were known to do a lot of giggling whenever a boy walked by.

"Hi, Liam." Four girls greeted me in a strange musical chorus. I couldn't tell if they were freshmen or upperclassmen. They all seemed similar to me—the same messy braided hair and tight jeans, the same inflection in their voices that made everything sound like a question, the same duck-face pose for every bathroom selfie.

I waved and kept walking. I didn't want to invite more conversation that I wasn't awake enough to endure. I'd caught a three-hour nap last night and the energy drink I chugged down after my run was a liquid placebo.

I turned onto another hallway and, as practiced, averted my

gaze from anything wall-related, from the bulletin board to the happy-cutesy couples who made out in front of it. Every square inch of León High School seemed to be a memorial in *her* honor, a kind of Graceland where visitors could relive the Ellia Dawson experience for themselves. There was the display case by the main office where her achievements were preserved behind glass. Assistant captain of the dance team. Chief organizer for student council. Costume manager for drama club. Editor of the social column of the student newspaper.

My girl was everywhere, so getting over her was not a realistic goal. The most depressing artifact in this museum, the part that choked me up every time, was walking past her locker. All of her stuff had been cleared out. The stickers were scraped off, but the gummy adhesive left tacky gray smudges on the tan door, like phantom fingerprints on a window. No one had been assigned to it yet.

"Liam!" called a voice from behind me, followed by a hard punch on my shoulder.

I turned and saw Wade McPherson wearing an angry frown on his face.

Wade was on the track team, too, but he was by far one of the slowest people on and off the field. He had the rugged, muscle-bound jock image down pat, whereas I was more on the skinny side.

I rubbed my sore arm. "What was that for?"

"You took off without me," he complained. "You were supposed to wait for me this morning and you left before I got out of the shower. I had to take the bus. The *bus*, Liam!"

"Well, that ought to teach you to wake up on time. I'm not going to be late for school on behalf of your vampiric sleep schedule."

"We all can't get up at oh-dark-hundred to run like you do. Some people actually have lives," he said, reviving the argument we'd had countless mornings before.

Wade lived with us three weeks out of the month. This way, he wouldn't have to be uprooted again while his mom worked in Chicago at a PR firm, or however gold diggers kept busy between husbands. I had a hard time explaining exactly who Wade was to new people, despite having the same last name being a dead giveaway. If you squinted hard enough, you could see the family resemblance.

"You better show up on time after school or else you're going to get left again," I said as we climbed the steps to the second floor. The top floor was for seniors and AP students only, but Wade remained stuck at my peripheral. His shaggy brown hair and the peach fuzz on his chin hid under a maroon hoodie that he'd worn every day for the past two months. Since the breakup with his online girlfriend, he'd been in full mourning without all the black.

He shot a quick glance around then leaned in and

whispered, "All right, look, me and a couple of guys on the team were wondering if you could give us some tips."

I stopped in front of my first-period class, then turned to him. "On?"

"How you did it. Ellia and the other girls she hangs with are all stuck up. Got a whole bunch of attitude, doing that neck thing when they talk." He rolled his neck in a circle to show his point. "But then you walk by and they're all 'Hey, Liam,' knocking each other down to get your attention. It's like Black Friday and you're the last flat screen on sale. So how'd you get her to go out with you? No offense, but you're too quiet and your game is weak."

I would've found this insulting if I hadn't had the same question myself. There were a bunch of interracial couples on campus—that wasn't an issue. People just had a hard time figuring out how I snagged a girl like Ellia Dawson. The black kids were indignant, the white kids were intrigued, the Asian kids were confused, and the Hispanic kids hailed me as their hero. For Wade to be interested in this old issue meant that his mourning period was finally over.

"All I did was talk to her. Like a person," I explained in the simplest terms I could find.

His crossed arms and club-bouncer stance would've been intimidating if he wasn't four inches shorter than me. "Nah, there has to be something, though. There's a secret recipe behind all this and I'm gonna find out what it is. Did you promise to do her homework for a year?"

"She's smart enough to do her own homework." Unlike some people I knew. "It's good to know that you're no longer grieving over an imaginary girl."

"Natalie's not imaginary! She lives in Vancouver." He searched around as if afraid his voice could carry across the border to reach his ex's ears.

Wade and this girl named Natalie had a summer fling that should've ended with the season. Their attempts at a long-distance relationship couldn't keep her faithful during winter formal. No Dear John letter, no phone call, but a picture of her with another guy on her timeline marked the end of their affair. My girlfriend almost died, yet Wade was the one crying at random, wearing that ugly hoodie, and blasting Coldplay in his room for three weeks straight.

"Back to you and Ellia," he said. "She's been out of the hospital for almost two weeks and you don't go to see her and you don't talk about her. Your dad won't tell me what's going on, so . . . what gives, *nephew*?"

I shuddered at the title, which he knew I hated. Most people assumed we were cousins, but the truth was *far* more messed up than that. Just admitting it out loud had all the makings for a trashy talk-show segment. Here's the thing: Wade is my dad's baby half brother—the product of my deceased's Grandpa's late-in-life second marriage—which, technically, makes

Wade my uncle, even though I'm five months, thirteen days, and eleven hours older than he is. That never stopped him from ragging me every chance he got.

As for this Ellia controversy, I had to choose my words carefully around Wade. He despised secrets, but he couldn't keep one to save his life. And once my involvement with Ellia's accident hit the airwaves, my peers would pounce. I stuck to my default answer. "It's no one's business."

His wary blue eyes narrowed in a way that reminded me so much of Dad, it freaked me out. That was another thing about Wade—he looked old in the face, with lines around his eyes and on his forehead. It might be because his own dad had been prehistoric. "Okay, I'll just sneak into your room and read your diary instead."

"I don't have a diary."

He smirked knowingly. "If you say so."

"They're called writing journals, Wade. You know, for converting *thoughts* to word format."

"Uh-huh," he replied. "Either way, the truth's going to come out. You can just tell me, or I could find out on my own. And you *really* don't want to leave me to my own devices."

The warning bell rang. "Whatever," I said. "Catch you later."

I ducked inside my classroom before he had a chance to respond or say something that could result in both of us getting suspended. I knew he was going to make good on his promise.

I just had to be extra careful around him and lock my bedroom door from now on.

I slid into my usual seat in the back row of English class and replayed the conversation. Why didn't I just tell Wade that Ellia was hard to reach? It wouldn't be a lie. She couldn't remember who I was, she was out of school for the rest of the semester, and I wasn't allowed anywhere near her house. She was, by definition, unreachable. She had my number and email address, yet my in-box remained empty. This kind of avoidance made you wonder where you stood in a relationship. We never officially broke up, but amnesia had a way of declaring matters null and void.

Somewhere in the background, Mr. Hardgrave went on about the parallels between *The Picture of Dorian Gray* and Edgar Allan Poe's *The Tell-Tale Heart*. Wearing his standard plaid shirt, tan blazer, and jeans, he zipped across the room on an obvious caffeine kick. His booming voice made it impossible to get any decent sleep first period.

Was it weird to have class with a bunch of seniors? Not really. They're pretty cool for the most part. They had too much on their minds for pettiness, like SATs, getting into the right college, and figuring out what to do with the rest of their lives.

"Come on—look alive, people!" Mr. Hardgrave coaxed us groggy students with a high-octane energy usually saved for pep rallies. "What do these two stories have in common?"

On its own accord, my hand shot in the air while the rest of the class was still trying to wake up.

He stopped and pointed to me with hope in his eyes. "Yes! Liam!"

"Guilt," I said as heads turned in my direction. "Both stories deal with evil deeds, and no matter how hard you try to cover it up, you can't really get away with anything. Either with your freedom, your youth, or your own sanity, a penalty has to be paid."

"Good answer!" he bellowed, as if I'd just won myself a new car, then scribbled on the dry-erase board with renewed enthusiasm. The words GUILT and PENALTY filled up the white space and bore into me with their own brand of judgment.

I tore my eyes from the board and pulled out my notebook. English was my best subject, but I'd filled my quota of the Q&A portion for this period. The rest of the class would have to go at it alone.

Words flew from my pen as if they were being chased while my knee knocked Morse code underneath the desk. My eyes stayed focused on the lined paper, not once glancing up at those accusatory words written in all caps on the board.

I'd suffered enough *guilt* to last a lifetime and I didn't need a beating heart under the floorboards to remind me of my wrongs. I just needed to think of her face. Replay the voice mails I'd saved on my phone. Look down at my textbook at all of the cartoons she doodled on the paper-bag cover. Stand in front of her house every morning and walk the hallways at school that were haunted by her absence. That was *penalty* enough. But at least it was something to do.

CHAPTER FOUR

ELLIA

The technical term for what I had was *retrograde amnesia*, which was the inability to recall past events because of severe head trauma. It could be physical trauma such as a brain tumor, or, as in my case, a hard blow to the head. It could also be psychological trauma, something that would mess you up for years, if say, you witnessed a grisly murder. It all really depended on the brain and how it coped and repaired itself. And I didn't feel repaired yet at all.

Still in my pajamas, I'd worked up the energy to trudge downstairs and join my family at the dinner table, but only in a physical way. My mind was decidedly elsewhere. Not that anyone in the room was altogether present.

Mom stood by the stove and prepared yet another organic fish-and-veggie dinner that tasted like dirt and ocean floor. The woman had *no* chill and possessed the talent of taking an idea and running with it. This served her well as an interior designer. But as a cook? Not so much. She read *one* health article about the healing powers of spinach and kale, and now our fridge contained enough plant life to warrant its own ecosystem. Even after my ordeal, my requests for buffalo wings and bacon continued to be ignored.

Dad sat across the table with a permanent scowl while he read from his tablet, which seemed fused to his arm. I could count on one hand how many times I'd seen him without a device in his hand or within reach. It's a wonder how the man showered.

"Still can't get your phone to work?" Mom asked me as she set down a platter of theoretical food and pulled out a chair next to Dad. Even this was done with the grace of a model—straight posture, rolling wrists, dressed to impress—a product of her Savannah pedigree and years of charm school.

Dad set down his tablet then dropped a dinner cloth on his lap. In contrast to Mom's willowy frame, Dad had a stocky, bulldog build suited for tackling offensive lines, but his potbelly spoke of the inactive hours he spent sitting in front of a drafting table.

I set my phone down and picked up my fork. "Actually, I got it open. I was just checking to see if Stacey's still coming over later."

Dad leaned forward with notable interest. "Really? You

figured out the password? That's a good sign. Do you recall any-thing else?"

I figured it was best to not tell them *how* I recovered my password. Sneaking out of the house to see some random guy wouldn't go over well with this crowd. "No." My answer came out more bitter than I'd intended, but I didn't want to get their hopes up.

My neurologist, Dr. Whittaker, said that adapting to everyday life would be an adjustment. If he meant constant crying, disorientation, and suspicion, then yeah, it was quite the adjustment. I'd never been one for scary movies, but amnesia brought out the haunted-house paranoia in me.

It's like returning to a familiar room and noticing objects had been moved while you were gone—a chair here, a picture frame there. Items that were once brand-new were suddenly broken in and worn from age. It was all very subtle, but enough to suspect paranormal activity or a cruel practical joke. When no one else saw what you saw, the freak factor really kicked in, because you were singled out and left questioning reality.

A part of myself was missing—a theft, a violation of time and effort. I was starting from scratch. So yeah. Me. Bitter. Just a tad.

I'd been told that this type of amnesia was usually tem-porary and memories would resurface once the swelling went down. But there were those rare cases where the memory loss would be permanent. Doctors always had to bring up the worst-case scenarios, which kinda sucked for them as professional caregivers and whatnot. Nobody wants to be the bearer of bad news. Maybe that's why they made the big money.

Nevertheless, my folks weren't trying to hear that noise, hence me being forced into a raw-food diet and placed under a microscope. It also explained why my parents served me a double order of side-eye to go with this flavorless meal.

"How are your headaches? Are they any better?" Mom asked me.

"I guess. I get them like once a day now," I muttered and used my fork to poke at some mushy gray substance on my plate.

"Is the medicine helping at all? I can call Dr. Whittaker and change your prescription," Dad offered, his cell phone already resting in his hands.

I'll admit that the drugs helped with my anxiety attacks and kept me sane, but so did sarcasm. Unfortunately, my brand was a bit harsh for the public and not FDA approved. "The Relpax has me feeling like a zombie as it is. I'll be flat on my back if I take any more," I said.

To his credit, Dad actually paused for a full minute before proceeding to dial. "I should call him anyway just to double-check."

Now this part of my life I could definitely remember. The discussion *about* me that didn't really *include* me. The talking *at* me, but not *to* me. That would involve feedback or, heaven forbid, an opinion.

The Dawsons were doers, fixers, movers, and shakers from a

long line of overachievers with the title *Dr.* or *Prof.* in front of their names. Words like *impossible*, *fail*, and *can't* were considered cuss words in our household. Any attempt at angst or a pity party quickly led to a rundown of our family tree, stemming back to the British Crown and the sugarcane fields of Barbados. Wars and adversity we could handle. Mental illness and the like, however, were another story.

Dad left a message for Dr. Whittaker and then set down his phone to frown at me. "So, Ellia, we need to discuss rehabilitation."

I looked up from my plate and dropped my fork. "Why? The physical therapist said my speech and motor skills are fine."

"Yes. Thank heavens for that, but Dr. Whittaker believes it's time for you to begin cognitive therapy," Mom replied. Her big doe eyes softened with sympathy.

"Ellia, you knew your recovery would be a long process," Dad added. "You may be fine physically, but we need to determine if anything aside from your memory is impaired."

I shook my head, not really knowing what that entailed, but hating it anyway. From the moment I opened my eyes in the hospital, I'd been poked, prodded, had bright lights shined in my eyes, rolled into a giant tube that looked like a tanning bed and sounded like a clothes dryer. I'd endured a number of exams—X-rays, EEG, CT scans—and I was sick and tired of being a specimen.

"I don't think that's going to do any good," I said.

Mom shook her head. "We need to hit this at every angle, and Dr. Whittaker has recommended several psychologists in the area—"

"Oh here we go." I rolled my eyes. "*Dr. Whittaker this, Dr. Whittaker that.* You talk about this guy so much he might as well live here. How about what *I* think? You know, the person with the actual memory problem? I just got out of the hospital and I'm not ready to see another doctor. I don't need any more drugs thrown at me."

"It has nothing to do with medicine. This is a *psychologist,* dear." Mom drew out *psychologist* in a long drawl designed for no other purpose than to make me feel stupid. She tended to do it a lot. "They specialize in reasoning skills and behavioral methods. They can't prescribe you drugs. That would be *psychiatry.*"

"I don't care what it's called—I'm not going. I'm just trying to get a handle on my living situation, master the art of washing my hair with sutures nailed to my scalp—oh, and figure out what grade I'm in, because as far as I know I'm still a freshman. How about we handle these little problems first before we get to the big ones?" A sharp pain in my temple brought my outburst to a halt. I covered my head with my hands to try to push back the pain from traveling to my left eye.

Mom reached over and touched my shoulder. "Baby, are you all right?"

I squeezed my eyes shut and pinched the bridge of my nose. "I'm okay. I just need some time and space, that's all."

"Fine," Mom said, though the clipped tone of her voice suggested the opposite. "We'll discuss this later. Go upstairs and take your medication before it gets worse." She collected my half-eaten plate then got to her feet.

I glanced at Dad, who simply raised an eyebrow at me. *You heard your mother*, the look said.

I'd been properly dismissed and, though there would be a round two in the near future, I was thankful for the delay. I wondered how long I could milk my headaches to avoid uncomfortable dinner topics.

On the way to the stairs, a rhythmic knock came from the front door.

"I'll get it!" I called out and made my way to the foyer.

I opened the door and smiled in relief at the familiar face.

Stacey Levine was one of the first people I saw when I rejoined the conscious world—and I'd recognized her right away. Stacey had been my best friend since forever. It was only the past two years of our lives together that remained a blank slate.

Stacey had been visiting me every day, always equipped with progressively stranger tales of our adventures that I could no longer remember.

I used to call Stacey *Jersey Shore Barbie*. She was naturally gorgeous, with tan skin underneath generous applications of bronzer. She was also loud, opinionated, and outrageously comfortable in her own skin.

So I shouldn't have been all that surprised at what she was wearing. She stood on my porch in red pumps and a short, white button-down dress that looked too tight to breathe in. I could only guess from the matching Red Cross nurse's cap that the getup was supposed to be a nurse's uniform.

She smiled and shimmied her shoulders to a soundless beat as she delivered the most disturbing singing telegram I'd ever witnessed.

I heard—that you—were feeling ill,
Headache, fever, and a chill . . .

I lifted my hands to stop her. "What are you doing?"

"Oh come on. *Please* tell me you remember that scene. It's like your favorite movie." When she got nothing but rapid blinking as a reply, she swept a hand over the length of her outfit. "The naughty nurse telegram? *Ferris Bueller's Day Off*? Eighties Day, freshman year? You dressed up as Tina Turner? I was Madonna—'Lucky Star'? The twenty-four-hour John Hughes Netflix marathon? None of this is ringing a bell?"

"Sorry." I winced, hating the disappointed look on her face.

Her shoulders dropped and her happy bubble burst. "It's really gone, isn't it?"

"Yep. Is this your way of trying to jog my memory?" I took in her outfit again. She clearly put a lot of thought and, um, *effort* into this little performance. But I also had strict parents and nosy neighbors, so this show needed to happen elsewhere. "Just so you know, real nurses wear hospital scrubs. Where did you get that outfit anyway?"

Her blood-red lips pulled into a wicked grin as she shook her head. "You don't wanna know."

And I believed her.

"Well, come inside before someone calls the cops." After closing the door, I turned in the direction of the kitchen. I could hear Mom washing dishes and Dad talking on the phone, no doubt with the all-powerful Dr. Whittaker.

"Mom, Stacey's here! We'll be upstairs," I yelled. Then I led her to my room by the arm before Mom could reply, make small talk, or ask me about my headache again.

Upstairs, I locked the door and rested my back against the wood. Dinner with the folks shouldn't make people exhausted, but I needed a breather. Stacey was nothing if not a breath of fresh air.

"Well, since my powers of persuasion don't work anymore, I might as well get comfy. This fabric's itchy anyway." She tossed off her nurse's cap, and an ombré of brunette and blond waves fell to the middle of her back.

"I can't believe you drove to my house dressed like that."

"What? This?" She scoffed. "Girl, please. I've gone to school in worse. But that's another story for another day." She dropped her ginormous shoulder bag on the bed and headed toward my dresser.

While she paraded around my room as if she lived here, my gaze floated around the papered walls and the strange fashion paraphernalia. My attention fell on a magazine ad for gold platform stilettos. Cute style, but nowhere close to functional. Kinda like me in that respect. "Was I trying to be a model or what?" I asked her.

"Nope, you're not tall enough," she said as she pulled out a baggy T-shirt and shorts from my drawer. "You prefer to make the dresses, not wear them."

"When did this happen? Last time I checked, I wanted to be an engineer like Dad."

"No, *Dad* wanted you to be an engineer like *Dad*," she rephrased and tied the drawstring of the shorts. "It's all in the proper nouns, snookums."

I flinched in sudden horror. "Does he know that?"

"Look at your room, El." She swept a hand across the open space. "It's not exactly a cold case for the FBI. Maybe he thinks it's a phase and that part of your memory might stay lost. I, for one, hope it doesn't. I want free shoes." She winked at me.

I shook my head, but smiled at the normalness of it all. After I'd woken up in the hospital, people I'd known for years suddenly appeared thinner, older, fatter, taller, with subtle nuances in their faces that displayed the progression of time. Even I had changed, with curves I didn't recall, though I was still too skinny to be in a music video. These modifications brought on countless hours of staring. I'd traveled two years into the future with no way to get back.

Everything else around me might have changed, but Stacey stayed exactly the same—no kid gloves or avoiding the obvious. Even before the accident, I relied on that consistency. It was a solid central point that I could focus on while the world spun around me.

"God, I'm so glad you're here," I said.

Stacey pulled a T-shirt over her head then paused. "Uh-oh. What happened now?"

"Can't I be happy to see my best friend?"

"I don't know. Could you actually smile when you say that?" she replied. "What's wrong?"

"It's nothing. Just the same old crap, different day. And now my parents want me to go to cognitive therapy," I said in my mother's yawning drawl.

"Is that like meditation or something?"

"I wish. It's sitting in a cold, sterile office with fake plants, clipboards, and paperwork, and people asking me a bunch of stupid questions I don't know the answers to." I closed my eyes and drew in a deep breath. "Why can't they let me figure it out on my own?"

"That would mean thinking for yourself, and we simply can't have that in the Dawson household." She spoke in a deep voice in a bad parody of Dad.

I tried to crack a smile, but a molten-hot blade of pain had embedded itself into the left side of my skull. My body locked instantly and I took quick, shallow sips of air as I waited for this episode to end. In reality, my migraines ran in ten-minute bursts, but this kind of eye-watering agony held no concept of time. My brain had a heartbeat, each pulse shooting fire to every nerve ending in my body, until finally, mercifully, I would pass out.

"Here. Open up." I heard Stacey's voice as if it were from a parallel dimension, then came the rattle of a pill bottle, followed by the *snap*, *twist*, and *hiss* of a carbonated drink she'd brought with her.

I opened my eyes a sliver and found her standing in front of me, holding two orange tablets in one hand and a bottle of root beer in the other. I had three prescription pill bottles sitting on my bedside table, but Stacey managed to find the right one. She also had the foresight to close the curtains so the room was in semidarkness. Noise, light, movement, and human interaction were sworn enemies of the dreaded migraine. Pain had a huge ego and it wouldn't settle for less than your full attention. No distractions. No escape.

I opened my mouth and allowed her to feed me my meds and the soda like I was a helpless infant. Keeping my eyes closed, I let her lead me to the bed. I hated for her to see me so weak, but it was hard to act proud when pain robbed you of speech.

I lay on my back across the bed with a pillow over my face until the worst was over. And Stacey, bless her heart, remained at my side the whole time. After twenty minutes of welcome silence, the pain had become less acute and had begun to distribute evenly around my entire skull. She waited another five minutes before asking if I was feeling better.

"Getting there," I grumbled through the pillow.

"Okay, this sucks. We need to take your mind off the pain." I heard her rummaging inside her purse.

I poked my head from my hiding place as she pulled out a white paper bag covered with greasy stains. Upon seeing the restaurant logo on the front, my eyes lit up. "I love you."

"I know." She passed me the bag. "You want me to feed you again?"

"I'm good." I unraveled the top of the bag and the mouth-watering scent of onion rings filled my nostrils. During the past month of practically living off nuts and berries, I would've killed for anything like this—deep-fried and swimming in hot sauce. This was what heaven smelled like.

Stacey grabbed her own bag and lay on her back next to me as I shoved a donut-sized ring in my mouth in one bite. No further medical weirdness was discussed.

As we ate, Stacey played soft music from her phone while I tried to figure out how to operate mine. It was frustrating, not to mention annoying, since the thing would chime every time someone posted on my Facebook wall and I couldn't remember how to turn off the notification.

"Here, give me that." Stacey snatched my phone and then, with a few taps, the phone was silent.

She frowned at the post that I'd written that morning: *I'm still alive, y'all. Chill.*

"Really? That's all you wrote?" Stacey asked. "No one in school has heard from you in weeks, and that's your only response?"

"I don't know what else to say. And what they're all dying to know is none of their business."

"Hmm. The price of fame, I guess," she muttered, then popped an onion ring in her mouth.

I had over three hundred friends on Facebook and could only point out twelve of them. There was Stacey, of course, and eight other girls I'd met in elementary school. A girl I couldn't stand in junior high was now a friend and had posted encouraging messages on my wall. *Get well soon* and *Hope you're okay* were splashed all over my timeline from people who believed I was dying or on life support. I must've been pretty popular to merit this much attention, but then tragedy could make people a celebrity overnight.

"Anyway, back to this eighties thing." Stacey pulled up Facebook pictures on her own phone. "We have the Decades Celebration in school every year in the spring—fifties, sixties, seventies, eighties, nineties—all week long. Everybody dresses up and there's a bunch of parties around town based on the theme.

Here's last year's Seventies Day." Stacey pointed to a picture of me wearing bell-bottoms and an afro so big it covered my eyes. The best part was my hair, unstraightened, with the curls picked out.

In the photo, Liam stood behind me with his arms around my waist. He was also rocking bell-bottoms and a disco shirt that busied the eye with psychedelic colors.

Who were these happy people? How exactly did their paths cross? And what was *Lessthanthree*? Liam had posted those three words—mashed into one—in a comment under the picture.

I consulted my own photo albums and found shots of me posing for school activities and games, none of which I could remember. Then I came upon one of me, Stacey, and Liam in another set of weird outfits, standing in front of a row of lockers at school and making faces at the camera. I wore a sideways ponytail with bangs that were teased to the heavens and . . . Were those stonewashed jeans?

"Hold up. What am I wearing and why, and how come you let me go out of the house looking like that? I need answers." I showed the image to Stacey.

"The nineties, El. What'd you expect? We dressed up like the cast from *Saved by the Bell*. You were Lisa, I was Kelly, of course, 'cause I'm awesome, and Liam was Zack. You had to pin him down and load a gallon of gel into his hair to get it to look like that. He was not a happy camper."

"He looks happy," I said, more to myself than to Stacey.

Liam had a nice smile, bright and playful. And, wow, he wasn't kidding about us being close. He and I were in nearly every picture together.

As I swiped through the slide show of hugs, smiles, and kisses, I began to feel like I was reading a stranger's diary. It felt personal, intimate, and I had no business spying on someone else's life.

Stacey's next comment interrupted my thoughts. "Yeah, Liam's always happy when *you're* around. Any other time, he's all like, 'Dude, life is like an empty can of suck. It makes a bunch of noise, but there's nothing in it. No one else feels and thinks and bleeds like I do and I use big words so I can be even more misunderstood. Wah, wah, wah,'" she mocked, and I couldn't help but smile.

"You plan on talking to him sometime this century?" Stacey went on. "Your phone works now, so you can't use that excuse anymore."

"Why do *I* have to do the calling?" I stuffed more onion rings in my mouth and tried to ignore the shocked look on Stacey's face.

"Yeah, because touching base with your boyfriend is *so* weird," she muttered.

"Boyfriend? That title doesn't really suit a total stranger, now does it?" My thumb busily swiped the screen until her heated glare became too intense to ignore. "Stop looking at me like that. I'm not ready to go there with him, okay? And he's not exactly beating down my door to talk to me either."

Shaking her head, she gathered our trash and stuffed it into her purse. Normally, she would've tossed it into the wastebasket, but I couldn't risk Mom finding greasy fast-food bags in my room. One benefit to carrying superlarge purses: They were great for smuggling contraband.

When Stacey got to her feet and headed toward the door, I asked, "Wait, are you going to help me sort through these pictures or not?"

"Can't stay long. My parents are making me go to Kevin's school play tonight. Family support or whatever."

The boy version of Stacey with big gray eyes and rosy cheeks popped in my head, an image that I realized was outdated. "He's like eleven now, right?"

"Twelve and about to go missing," she grumbled.

"Don't be like that. Kevin's so cute. I wish I had a little brother." I smiled at the idea of a house full of siblings.

"Really? 'Cause I'll be more than happy to pack his stuff and drop him off later. A lot has changed while you've been out, Sleeping Beauty. You've got some catching up to do. Liam could help you with that if you'd let him." She grabbed her nurse dress and red pumps and cradled the load in her arms. "Oh, and go watch that Ferris Bueller movie. It's on Netflix. I'll call you later."

"Wait—"

"Good luck." She blew me a kiss and waved.

"Stacey!"

"Buh-bye now." Still wearing my T-shirt and shorts, she closed the door behind her and left.

Too lazy and drugged to chase her down, I called out again, to which she replied in song, *"Danke schoen, darling, danke schoen . . ."*

I recognized the song from somewhere, maybe a commercial. But the melody faded then disappeared upon the closing of the front door.

I was once again alone with my thoughts, which was the last place I wanted to be. According to the calendar, I was sixteen now, so that meant Stacey and I had been joined at the hip for almost a decade. That is, if you included missing two years that were unaccounted for. Just like that—learning how to drive, my sweet-sixteen party, all of my ninth- and tenth-grade class credits—*poof!* Gone. These were supposed to be the best years of my life, and I couldn't recall most of them. What other experiences had been stolen from me? What other friendships, bonds, and trusts had been stripped away?

One person came to mind. His sad blue eyes watched me every morning, neither advancing nor retreating, but waiting for the return of Ellia Dawson. It seemed that everyone was waiting for her grand comeback, including me. My life wasn't the only one that was at a standstill, and it was hard to tell what was worse: forgetting or being forgotten.

LIAM

The double doors swung open and more students filed into the library. Lifting my eyes from my notebook, I inspected each face that cut between the bookshelves. None of them matched the person I was waiting for. Sighing, I leaned back in the chair and reread the only words I'd written on the page.

"Either you're running from something or running to something. Whatever the case is, it better be worth all the huffing and puffing."

Ellia always had something snarky to say about my fitness routine and then ended up running with me anyway. But this particular sentiment had haunted me for weeks. It could be because it was one of the last things she said to me before the accident. Or it could be because it was absolutely true, at least in my case.

I'd been active all my life. As a kid, I would race around the grocery store or the waiting room of the doctor's office. You know that toddler who was led around the mall by a leash and harness, or that hyper five-year-old who kept kicking the back of your airplane seat for the whole flight? That was me. Eventually, I found a way to channel all that pent-up energy through sports: Little League, football, soccer, tennis, and track and field.

The overall theme here was motion, in that it always had to be happening. It's the only truth I could understand. Living things moved. A pulse. A breath. A purpose. Movement was a life condition.

The only thing that ran more than my body was my mind, which was why I was rarely seen without a notebook in my hand. My notebook was my best friend, my first love, and the mother of my children. Our offspring: the award-winning screenplay that sounded better in my head, the next great American novel that wasn't finished, a bunch of emo poems, that messed-up dream I had last night, or some superdeep quote I'd thought up on the drive to school that morning. They were just minor fixations, a practice run to what would be my grand achievement.

I was going to write the story of me and Ellia, how we met, how we fell in love—the whole nine. It would be an epic tale of love found and lost—the real, raw accounts that were always glossed over in romantic comedies. And what better muse for my creation than the most fascinating girl I'd ever met?

I smiled at the picture of her I drew in my head—small features with an elfin impression, a halo of thick black curls, and warm brown eyes that held your gaze even when you had nothing interesting to say. Delicate as she might appear, she pulled no punches. If she didn't like you, she would not only tell you to your face, she'd also list examples to help you understand why you sucked as a human being. An encyclopedia's worth of text couldn't capture the world that was Ellia Renée Dawson, but I would try my best in 30,000 words.

This was what kept me busy while waiting for Stacey Levine to show up for our revision session after school. I promised Stacey that I'd help with her book report, but the girl was the queen of tardy. Patience was not one of my greater virtues, and I would've bounced fifteen minutes ago if I wasn't being extorted.

I'd been hounding Stacey for updates on Ellia's recovery for weeks, and Stacey felt that her new role as an informant deserved compensation.

"What's up, Hemingway," came the high-pitched voice from over my head, followed by the slam of a duffle bag posing as a purse on the table. You'd think she was running away from home with all the junk she had in that thing.

My gaze lifted from her bag to a curvy brunette who had given up the pretense of being a natural blond. She pulled out a chair across from me, plopped down, then proceeded to scrutinize my attire. "Dude, you ever heard of beauty rest? You look like roadkill in the microwave set on high."

"And you look like something made by Mattel," I replied, immediately jumping into our usual pleasantries. "You do know we had a study group at three o'clock, right?"

"Yeah," she answered and pulled pens and highlighters out of her bag.

"And you do know that three o'clock happened like forty minutes ago, right?" I pointed to the clock over the checkout desk. "I can't even give you the second-grade, little-hand-on-the-three, big-hand-on-the-twelve bit, because all the clocks in this school are digital. You could *not* have missed the number three and two zeros."

"I'm sorry, okay? I had to do something real quick and I ran late and then my phone died and I had to find somewhere to charge it, so I couldn't call you," she explained in one breath.

I shook my head. "What's with you girls and your phone issues? I saw Ellia the other day, and she needed help with hers."

"Really? You actually worked up the nerve to finally visit her? About time!" she cheered, much to the annoyance of everyone reading in the library. "Does this mean I'm no longer your mole?" she asked.

"Aw, but you make such an adorable rodent." I sighed. "And no, you're still on retainer. I didn't go to see her—well, not formally. I was out for my jog and she came out to meet me."

Stacey threw her head back and let out a loud groan. "Liam, Liam, Liam. Why don't you just go over to her house and talk to her?"

The memory of a front door slamming in my face popped into my head. I recalled the brass knocker clattering against the wood, leaving a delayed echo in my ears. I shook the painful memory away. "I can't."

Stacey's gray eyes narrowed at me. "Can't or won't?"

"Either one of those options will work. I don't want to upset her. It's just best that I stay away from her. She's in a fragile state right now, and the last time I went to visit her, things got soap opera-ish and weepy, and I hate expressing myself in liquid form," I explained in a rush.

The last person I wanted to have this discussion with was Stacey Levine. If I needed to bare my soul, I'd do so on paper. Writing was the safest way to bleed without breaking the skin. With Stacey involved, she would make sure to hit a major artery.

Elbows propped on the table, she cradled her chin in her laced hands and leaned in as if to disclose some juicy gossip. "So what did you say when you saw her?"

I shrugged. "Not much. I was kinda shocked she showed up. She needed help unlocking her phone, that's all."

"So *you're* the one who figured out that stupid code? Thank God. She was going nuts trying to open that thing. She called the store and they told her to buy a new one—can you believe that? Total rip-off. And she was willing to do it, but I was like, 'You better get your man to go MacGyver on that thing, rub some wires together and hotwire that bad boy. What's the point of dating an AP-class brainiac if you can't get him to hack into the motherboard or something?' "

Assuming that *any* of that made sense, I asked, "Why would you think academic merit was comparable to cybercrime?"

"It's your glasses." She reached across the table and used a long, rainbow-colored talon to push the frames back to the top of my nose. "You've got that sexy nerd, tech-support thing going on." She wagged her eyebrows at me.

I rolled my eyes. "Can we *please* get started?"

"Sure." She dug into her enormous bag, dropping random items on the table. Among them were combs, hair clips, compacts, several tubes of lip gloss, a curling iron, and a worn copy of *Wuthering Heights*.

After reaching the bottom of her cargo hold, and with an entire cosmetic line cluttering the table, she presented a wrinkled and coffee-stained printout of her essay. I dove right in, red pen at the ready, and immediately felt the beginnings of a headache as I read the second paragraph aloud.

"Heathcliff and Kathy grew up together and had this love-hate thing going on. He was broke and dirty and didn't think he was good enough for her and she married a rich guy just to make him jealous. Heathcliff was all butt-hurt about it and left town to make some bank. Then he rolled up years later and used his mad cash to get back at everybody who called him a bum."

Wow. I had my work cut out for me and the weight of the task grew heavier with each new paragraph.

"Okay, I don't think your teacher will accept 'psycho jerk-face' as a proper reason for Heathcliff's cruelty." I showed her the passage circled in red ink.

Stacey's head was buried in her jewel-encrusted phone, her thumbs flying over the keys in a blur.

"That's what you're here for—to pretty it up for me. Do your thing, Hemingway." She batted her eyes, her false lashes fluttering like butterfly wings. "Anyway, I was reading that book and I think you're a lot like the Heathcliff guy. When Kathy died, Heathcliff cursed her to walk the earth as a ghost just so he wouldn't be alone. He didn't care what form she took, he was willing to take her any way he could get her. So this dude's running around moors and stuff talking to some wind and spirits. Cray-cray."

"And how does that remind you of me?" I asked, but really didn't want to know the answer.

"If you're not careful, you'll get all bitter and creepy because you don't know how to accept things as they are now. Ellia doesn't remember you and she may never get that part of her memory back and might never feel the way you do again. So you got two options: make a fresh start and build something new, or go around chasing ghosts."

It was easy for her to say—Ellia still had memories of their friendship. Stacey didn't have to suffer whispers about her or looks of sympathy, or accept blame for what happened to Ellia. She didn't have dreams about sharp rocks, bloody sand, and a body that shouldn't be lying so still. She hadn't had the pleasure of a door slamming in her face or having the voice of Ellia's father stuck in her head on repeat. *"Do not come here again. You've done quite enough, young man."*

No, Stacey didn't know the whole story. No one did, and that was what had to be set straight. I was tempted to tell Stacey about the book I planned to write, but I didn't want to jinx things.

"You're saying I should give up on her?" I asked.

Stacey tapped away at her phone. "I'm saying you can't build this immortal shrine to the old Ellia and shut out the new one. Her not wanting to be with you in that way doesn't mean she doesn't care at all. I just don't want you to—"

"Hang on to false hope," I finished. Which was a stupid expression, by the way. Hope can be foolish or misguided, but there was no such thing as *false* hope. Hope was always true, even when there was no evidence to support its claim.

Finally, Stacey's bedazzled phone was set to rest and she gave me her full attention. "Look, if you love her like you say you do, then be there for her. None of that stalker business where you're staring at her house every morning. Knock on her door and pay her a visit like a sane person. If you can't help get her old memories back, make new ones. Give her a reason to know who you are or leave her alone."

The table went silent for a long beat as we stared at each other. I was stunned on two counts: that she knew what I did every morning and the possibility that she might actually have a point. Maybe I *was* chasing a ghost through the moors. Either you're running *from* something or running *to* something. Right now I was just running in circles.

I stood up, collected my notebook and her paper, and crammed them into my backpack. "I gotta go. I'll rewrite your essay and give it to you before first period tomorrow."

"Okay, cool. But don't use too many big words—Mr. Hudson won't believe I wrote it. Just add enough to make him think I'm trying," she instructed, then resumed texting.

"Yeah, sure. I'll even write in pink crayon to keep it authentic." I made a beeline for the exit before she could give a snide comeback.

I flung open the library door with my mission clear and my resolve absolute. I'd have to prove to everyone, including Ellia, that I was more than some guy she used to know, that what we shared had and still mattered. She may have forgotten the promise we made on the beach, but I hadn't, and it was up to me to back up those words with action. Memories and ghosts were for the dead. Living things moved, and I was never one to stand still.

ELLIA

A ll right, Ellia, I have a few worksheets I need you to complete," Dr. Kavanagh said in a low, soothing tone that made me drowsy. All of the specialists here spoke with their indoor voices, and it was giving me story-time flashbacks to kindergarten.

"This part of the assessment isn't time-restricted, so there's no pressure to work quickly. Just answer as many questions as you can. You can work in the waiting room if you feel more comfortable and return it to the desk when you're done, okay?" She handed me a manila folder and a number two pencil.

The thickness of the folder made it clear that I was going to be here for a while. As it was, this appointment was running close to the three-hour mark, and I knew those worksheets would follow the same pattern as the rest of my evaluation. Endless repetition.

For over an hour, Dr. Kavanagh had used old home videos and photos as flash cards and I had to identify each image with wires taped to my head. Then she read off a long list of words and made me recite the ones I could remember. Then came another list and then another and then back to the first one, on and on until my brain felt like ground hamburger meat. Now I was in the puzzle and matching phase of the testing, and if I wasn't mental before, I would be by the end of the day. I was once again being poked and prodded just to reach the obvious conclusion that something was wrong with me. All of this could've been explained over the phone, but no, my disorder had to be exposed to the open air and dissected by anyone in a lab coat.

With a polite nod, I took the folder then shuffled my way to the sitting area. There were several round tables and plastic chairs, but I chose one of the beanbags by the window. The glass reached from floor to ceiling, welcoming ample sunlight and providing a panoramic view of the courtyard below. A weird crop circle design that I couldn't make heads or tails of was raked in the sand. Old people did *chi kung* on the grass, their motions graceful and controlled as they stretched in a synchronized dance.

Serenity Behavior Health Center lived up to its name by trying not to look like a hospital. It had trickling fountains and a koi pond to soothe the mind. Plants and rock formations lay everywhere, and I'd bet a year's allowance that the furniture was set in feng shui. The only thing that kept me from mistaking the place for a day spa or a botanical garden was the PSY.D. on the staff's name tags.

The center treated a number of health issues: drug rehab, Alzheimer's, autism, ADD, OCD, PTSD, and other behavior problems that went by acronyms. I was on the fifth floor with the learning disabled and mentally challenged. Along with the counseling sessions, I'd be assigned to a tutor here twice a week to help me catch up on my missing classes so I could attempt to graduate on time.

As I flipped through the pages of my worksheet, I considered various ways to better waste my afternoon. I could be watching Vines and YouTube videos. I could be catching up on the last two seasons of my favorite hip-hop housewives reality show. I could finally learn how to thread my sewing machine, or create a collage out of all the get-well cards people sent me. The possibilities were endless, and the question that had plagued me all morning came to mind: *How in the world did I get roped into this?*

The answer was simple: coercion. I'd put up a good fight, but Mom and Dad had laid down the law and dragged me, kicking and screaming, to my first appointment. On the plus side, my folks agreed that I could go outside and even go to Stacey's house in exchange for my participation. It was a hard sell, but cabin fever was one heck of a motivator.

Since I wasn't on the clock, I decided to walk around a bit to stretch my legs and scope out the rest of the place. Outside of the open sitting area were halls lined with closed offices and conference rooms. My nosy side wanted to catch a drooling patient in a straitjacket roaming the halls, and yet a part of me was relieved I hadn't seen any.

I turned down one hallway then another, and stopped dead in my tracks at the glorious sight before me. There, stationed between the drinking fountain and a wooden bench, was a fully stocked vending machine. Cookies, chips, sticky buns, and sodas stood within reach. I floated toward it, praying that this mirage wouldn't disappear. My hand stroked the glass and I marveled at the buffet of carbs and sugar at my disposal.

So many choices and not enough change: a fact I quickly discovered when I dug into my pocket. Forty cents, a raggedy hair tie, and some dryer lint was all I had to my name. I pulled my wallet out of my other pocket only to find six pennies.

I spread my arms wide, collapsed onto the machine, pressed my face against the cold surface, and wailed to the ceiling in utter despair. Insufficient funds and a sheet of plexiglass kept me from sugary paradise. My gaze shifted to a small box under the pane of buttons, and my hope was renewed. This bad boy took debit cards!

I fingered through the compartments of my wallet and fished out a prepaid card that my parents gave me for emergencies. And by God, this was an emergency!

After a swipe and the push of a couple buttons, chocolate-covered pretzels dropped with a chorus of an angelic choir.

From the outside, my behavior could be viewed as a bit

excessive, but starvation and low blood sugar were serious business. It brought on uncharacteristic behavior, like dancing in the
middle of the hallway or hugging a vending machine.

"Do you two need a room?" a voice called out behind me.

I glanced over my shoulder and saw a boy staring open-
mouthed at me from the end of the hall. He looked about my
age and stood at average height and build. His faded black
T-shirt appeared to function as both business casual and sleepwear. He also had a folder of paperwork tucked under his arm
and a phone in his hand.

I must've looked all kinds of cray with both arms and
one leg wrapped around something the size of a refrigerator.
Then again, we were in a mental health facility, so what did
he expect?

I dropped my leg, stood up straight, and smoothed down
my sweater as best as I could. "Sorry. I was having a moment."

He stepped closer. The frayed hem of his jeans covered his
sandaled feet, and dirty strings dragged across the floor as he
walked. "I see. So, when's the wedding?"

"Haven't set a date yet." I gestured to the machine. "I was
thinking springtime. An outdoor ceremony with a bunch of
flowers made of candy wrappers. Or maybe a carriage ride to
the service with some doves flying as I walk down the aisle."

He grinned. "A fairy-tale wedding, huh?"

"What can I say? Bridezilla always gets what she wants." I
smiled back.

"I'm sorry, I gotta capture this." He aimed his phone at me.

"No! Please don't!" I covered my head with my arms. I was not prepared for pictures, especially with a scarf on my head and no makeup. Most importantly, I didn't know this kid or what he would do with those photos.

"This is too good to let pass," he said and kept snapping. "Not all crazy is the same, and you're a rare breed."

"I'm not crazy! I'm just malnourished—and would you stop clicking? That's an invasion of privacy."

"So is making out with the snack machine. Imagine how *it* feels. Poor thing might need some counseling after this." He stretched the phone away from him to get a better angle. "Don't worry. I'm not a creep or anything. I use pictures as memory cards. It helps me remember if I'm on the right floor, in the right building, and so on. I got lost on my way to the bathroom and ended up back in the lobby."

"Sounds like something old people would do," I said, then stooped down to collect my snack from the machine.

"Short-term memory loss often follows gray hair. But I'm ahead of the curve—not a single silver strand." He ran a hand over his wavy brown hair, which immediately fell back over his forehead.

I tore open the pretzel bag with my teeth then spat out the ripped piece of plastic. Ill-mannered? Yes, but so was taking pictures of strangers. "Do you have dementia or something?"

"Nope. Amnesia," he replied and fiddled with his phone.

He shared this news so casually that I couldn't help but be amazed. I'd never met an amnesia patient, and I was curious. Maybe he could give me some pointers.

"Really? So do I," I admitted. "You can't remember your past either?"

"More like the past hour. It's the new memories that are hard to keep, not old ones. I've got anterograde amnesia. I can remember my tenth birthday and all that, but ask me what I ate this morning and I have to look it up." He consulted a list on his phone. "If I see it enough times, it'll sink in. I need repetition and routine."

You'll get plenty of that here, I thought. "Wow. That sucks." The reply slipped before I considered how insensitive that sounded, though he didn't seem offended.

"Tell me about it." He shrugged and walked with me back to the waiting room. "So what are you in for?"

"Retrograde amnesia. I'm missing twenty-six months of my life, including my time in the hospital, but I *do* know that I had oatmeal and yogurt for breakfast."

He stopped and consulted his list again. "Hmm, Pop-Tarts and turkey bacon for me."

The thought of bacon made my stomach growl. "You know Pop-Tarts are bad for you, right? The preservatives alone will stay stuck in your system for years."

"At least *something* will stick," he muttered and began walking again.

I noticed the folder clamped under his arm. "You have one of those stupid worksheets, too, huh?"

His eyes stayed glued to his screen. "Yeah. I got reassigned to a new doctor and they want to see how I'm doing. You'd think he would *know* how I'm doing with all the notes my other doctor took. All hour long, he's taking notes, talking, and watching me solve puzzles, and then more notes. I forgot his name, but the boredom is ingrained in my memory."

I could relate, but I was stuck on one little part. "An hour? That's all you stay for?"

His brown eyes, warm and bright with humor, met mine. "From what I understand, all of the therapy sessions last one hour. It's just the evaluation that takes years from your life you can never get back."

My shoulders relaxed as if a boulder had been lifted from my neck. "Oh good! I couldn't go through this every week." I shoved more salty chocolate in my mouth. "So how often do you have to come here?"

"Twice a week after school."

"Do you go to León?" I asked with my mouth full and not caring. No point in being ladylike now.

"Nope. Saint Pedro. It's an all-boys academy, so any chance to hang with a pretty girl is fine by me. Good to brush up on my people skills." He smiled.

A part of me was relieved that he didn't go to my school, so word of my therapy sessions wouldn't travel back to my peers.

I may not remember high school, but I knew how the social hierarchy worked and being labeled a head case was a hard stamp to peel off.

I wondered if the boy next to me had a horror story to tell. "Do kids mess with you at school?"

"Can't say. Saint Pedro has a hardcore zero tolerance rule for bullying. If so, they do it behind my back. But then again, I wouldn't really know, now would I?"

Seeing his point, I asked, "Does it bother you at all, not being able to remember stuff?"

"It did at first. It's scary not knowing things or who to trust. It's hard to figure out who's telling you the truth or who's jerking your chain."

Oh yeah, I knew that feeling. My first few weeks after waking up in the hospital were like that—the fear, the helplessness, the paranoia of being lied to, and having adults talk down to you. The frustration alone felt worse than the migraines. Too bad there wasn't a pill for that.

By the time we made it back to the waiting room, I was halfway through my bag of pretzels and was tempted to go back for more goodies—maybe some Cheetos this time. Then I saw him staring at me, amused.

"Hey, can I ask you something? It's kinda personal, but I'm really curious." When my warning didn't faze him, I asked, "How did you get like this? Did you have an accident?"

He stopped to look at me fully. "Oh. Is that it? I thought you were going to ask me if I had a girlfriend."

I stopped chewing. "Why would I ask you that?"

"Don't know. Why would you fondle a defenseless snack machine? But hey, I'm not here to judge. This is a safe environment where people can express themselves freely," he explained, sounding like the doctors around here. "To answer your question—I drowned. I was surfing with my brother and got sucked down in the riptide. I would've died if he didn't pull me out of the water. I stopped breathing for too long and they had a hard time reviving me. Who would've thought the lack of oxygen causes brain damage? It's weird, you know? Brains need to breathe?"

So he was a beach boy. That explained the "chill bruh" drone in his voice, but I didn't find it as annoying as I usually would. His golden skin spoke more of genetics than sunburn and there were tiny freckles running up the length of his arms. He had nice arms—thin, but cut. Maybe he worked out.

"Were you surfing here in Quintero?" I asked.

"Nope. Rincon Point. My brother's got a place in Ventura and I went to visit him this past summer." His dark eyes fell on me. "Anyway, what about you? What's your story?"

I searched around the sitting area for a good answer. The truth was I really didn't know the specifics of my accident. Mom and Dad were pretty tight-lipped about it, some ish about my delicate state, but I knew there was more to it than a simple tumble and fall. Dodging scandals and unpleasant subject matter came from my Mom's bougie Southern side of the family.

"I fell and bumped my head," I answered finally. "I got a cracked skull and brain swelling."

"Cool," he said then corrected himself. "I mean not cool, but it's an interesting story to tell people, especially if you have a wicked scar. Scars are souvenirs of battles won. Plus, it makes you look more dangerous." His eyes darted to the scarf on my head and then back to my face. "You know what? I'm gonna call you Jason Bourne, like from the action movies. He couldn't remember his past either, yet that didn't stop him from being a total badass."

I sucked my teeth at his corniness, but on the low, I found it endearing. He didn't need to know all that, though. "Okay. In that case, I'm going to call you Dory, that fish from *Finding Nemo*. Her memory lasts five minutes at best. How long does yours last?"

His head teetered as if balancing the weight of his answer. "An hour, give or take."

"And you won't remember this conversation after we leave?" I had no idea why that disappointed me, but it did.

"Oh I'll definitely make a point to remember you." He smiled innocently enough, but his intent stare left no doubt that some serious flirting was happening here. Then the moment passed and he pulled out his phone again.

I covered my face. "Don't. I look hideous."

"Hey, quit with the crazy talk. You're gorgeous." He logged the photo to his database—his handheld brain, as it were. "Met a cute girl at therapy today. She's funny, eats like a guy, and is blessed with not remembering high school. You think she's cool," he recited while he typed his notes into his phone. "Head trauma, amnesia equals Jason Bourne, also known as . . ." His eyes lifted to mine and waited.

"Ellia. Ellia Dawson."

"Nice to meet you. I'm Cody, by the way. Cody Spencer." He entered the information. "So does Ellia Dawson have a phone number?"

"Why? Are you trying to get with her?" I sucked the chocolate off my thumb slowly.

His dark eyes followed the movement. "Maybe."

Yep, there was definite flirting going on. Why did dudes try to come at me when I wasn't on my A-game? And make no mistake, I looked a hot mess. I already had a boy on deck waiting for my call and I couldn't even begin to deal with *him*. Until I figured things out, I was off the market.

"Well, Cody—I mean Dory—I should probably get to work. I'm not trying to be here all day." I gave him a quick scan from head to toe, then turned away. My head tilted back so the crumbs at the bottom of the bag fell into my mouth.

"Well, it was worth a shot. Have fun, Jason Bourne," he called after me.

"Uh-huh." I could feel his eyes on me as I walked away. I didn't need to look back to check—a girl just knew these things.

I returned to my beanbag and cracked open my folder, but with less enthusiasm than before, if that were possible. Word association and matching games ran ten pages deep into the test. I had to point out which shape, number, or vocabulary word didn't belong in a sequence, but the only odd item that stood out to me was the boy wandering around the waiting room.

Cody had stopped in front of one of the wall fountains, taking pictures of the swimming fish in its base. Then he ambled to the window and snapped more pictures and jotted down notes. For nearly thirty minutes, he roamed around the sitting area like a fascinated tourist, and the movement was becoming distracting.

Every now and again, I'd look over and catch him staring. Then I'd smile and look away all tee-hee and giggly only to peek up again to see if he was still checking me out, which of course he was. On and on it went, shy smiles, stolen glances, liking what I saw and not knowing what to do about it. I'll admit, the pursuit made me feel pretty, something I hadn't felt in a while. This matching game was more challenging than the ones on my worksheet, but it fit the theme of this entire therapy session. Endless repetition. Cody said that it helped with memorization, and that may be true, because he seemed like a hard person to forget.

CHAPTER SEVEN

LIAM

locked myself in my room, armed with earbuds, my trusty
notebook, and a red pen to begin a hardcore editing massacre.
I'd gotten stuck debating over a title for chapter two. I'd considered titles like *Fate* or *Destiny*, but that sounded lame. And
my first encounter with Ellia freshman year didn't involve any
of that sappy melodrama where two people locked eyes from
across the room as cheesy music played in the background. Most
phenomena arose from a simple, uneventful beginning, such as
running into a pretty girl in the hallway. Literally, running
smack-dab into her . . .

UNTITLED | Page 12

*On my way to the library, I'd gotten a text from Dad saying he
would pick me up after school. He was usually on chauffeur duty
in the mornings—I had a personal aversion to yellow buses and*

bully-initiated brawls inside moving vehicles. Dad wanted me to man up and tough it out, but scrawny freshmen such as myself were easy prey. Considering that I had been rezoned to another high school where none of my friends attended, I was dead on arrival. I'd explained this already, but Dad needed a reminder and yet another excuse to address my lack of testosterone. If I wasn't involved in an aggressive "look at me, I'm an alpha male" activity, then I was considered a wimp. The dispute over my manhood continued via text as I hurried blindly toward the lower commons.

My head was buried in my phone until my face made contact with soft skin. I jumped back and was at eye level with a smooth brown midriff. Her waist was a narrow hourglass that fanned out to wide hips encased in blue denim. She had a combination of an innie and an outie belly button, which flashed like peekaboo as the hem of her wool sweater rose and fell with her movements.

This was the closest I'd ever been to a girl and the sight left me dumbstruck. Even as I pulled back, I could still feel her warm skin pressed against my face and smell the peach scent of her perfume.

"Hey! Watch where you're going!" The shriek that came from above shattered my trance.

The voice confirmed that this adorable midriff did indeed belong to a girl, a very cute and irate girl who was now glowering down at me from a step stool. Her arms lifted over her head to attach a chain of pumpkin streamers to the wall and also, I suspected, to keep herself from falling. I was tempted to reach out to hold her steady, but I resisted the urge.

Her head poked out between her arms and served me a look of malice. "What are you, blind?"

No, I definitely wasn't blind and I'd never been more thankful for the gift of sight. In order to adequately describe her, one would have to apply all five senses at once, and activate those that science had yet to identify.

"Sorry. I-I didn't see you there," I stammered.

"Obviously. That's why I asked if you were visually impaired. You would have to be to not see all this junk laying around on the floor. Normal people would just step aside."

"I'm not normal. But then again neither are you."

She blinked at that. "What?"

"You have an innie-outie belly button. The area itself is concave, but there's a slight nub of scar tissue that pokes out on the side. About ten percent of people in the world have outie belly buttons and you kinda have both, which makes you even rarer."

She just stared at me. "That was the weirdest thing I've heard all week."

I shrugged. "Well, it's only Thursday. Give it time."

She let out a little snort then stepped down from the stool. "Are you one of those guys who knows random information for no reason?"

"There's always a reason for knowledge."

"Only when it's useful," she countered.

"And you're saying my knowledge of umbilical scar tissue isn't useful?"

"Not unless you deliver babies for a living. Is that why you were in such a hurry? Did a girl suddenly go into labor in the locker room, and you were called in to assist in the birth?"

I smiled. *"They'd be better off calling my mom for that. She's the obstetrician, not me. I just recite random medical facts to impress pretty girls."*

"Smooth." Pursing her glossy lips, she crossed her arms over her chest and waited. *"Well, let's see it."*

My smile fell. *"See what?"*

"Your umbilical scar. You saw mine and offered unsolicited commentary, so I should at least do the same for you." She motioned for me to lift my shirt.

I did as commanded and revealed my stomach to her open appraisal, trying not to blush. She took her time, tilting her head from side to side, examining the art on exhibit.

"Hmm . . . A classic innie—oval shaped, lint-free, nicely tanned and just a tiny bit fuzzy. Not bad." She nodded in approval. *"Well, now that we're both familiar with each other's torsos, it's only proper that we formally introduce ourselves. Ellia Dawson."* She reached out her hand.

Her small, delicate fingers felt warm to the touch as I gathered them in mine. Her hand felt good in my palm, like it belonged there, so I held it a few seconds longer than what would be deemed appropriate. She didn't seem to have a problem with the extra contact. I could tell she was struck in that moment, too, that rare cosmic event when premonition takes root. Somehow, whether *good or bad, sometimes you knew when a person was going to change your life.*

"Nice to meet you, Ellia. I'm—"

"Liam! Get your butt down here now!" Dad bellowed from downstairs.

Whatever path my imagination had taken now struck a brick wall and shattered at the sound of his voice. There was nothing worse than being interrupted while in the creative process. Few people understood how hard it was to get to that mindset and stay there long enough to complete a whole thought.

"Hurry up, boy! I need you to see this!" Dad called again.

I saved my document, closed my laptop, packed up my notebooks, and set the load on my desk. I stepped into the hall and remembered to lock my door at the sound of music flooding from Wade's room. He usually slept in all weekend, but the Valentine's Day dance was tonight and he spent the day getting dolled up for the ball. He didn't have a date, but he'd probably be dancing with some girl by the end of the night.

I trotted downstairs and found Dad sitting in his favorite armchair in the living room. Lines bunched around his forehead and eyes, as usual—I had never seen him wear any other expression. Dad was a six-foot-three semitruck of a man. With light-brown curls, ice-blue eyes, and a strong superhero jaw, he encapsulated the thick-necked jock who played rugby and crushed beer cans with his forehead. Grizzly chest hair sprouted from the red Hawaiian shirt he always liked to wear. All the male McPhersons looked like mink coats, but I seemed to favor Mom in every way except for height.

Some home improvement show played on the flat screen. Since Dad retired from the Navy, he'd been on a mission to renovate the kitchen and den. Instead of just hiring a contractor, he took on the task himself. I figured he needed something to keep busy while he figured out what to do with himself now that Mom was gone. Whatever the reason, the ten-day project turned into a two-year crusade and the house was left cluttered with lumber and paint buckets.

"Come take a look at this." He waved me over and spread out a stack of pamphlets and brochures across the coffee table. "Pick a card, any card."

I sat on the couch beside him and eyed the papers with caution. "What's this for?"

"Summer volunteer work," he said. "You're going to need more than grades to get into UCLA, something to beef up your resume. Colleges like their students to be well rounded and active in their communities, so it's time to roll up your sleeves and get involved. We have the Big Brothers Big Sisters program at the rec center. There are other mentorships, too. Little League, volunteer work at the homeless shelter . . ."

I was overwhelmed, as was usually the case around Dad. Not because he resembled a two-hundred-pound lumberjack, but because his hands-on approach always left me in a mental choke hold.

"Dad, it's too soon to talk about this now," I said. "I have another year of school before I have to think about college."

"Applications open up in the fall. That means you have the entire summer to fatten up your resume and prove you're more than a pair of legs. Given your track-and-field stats, it's gonna be tough to get you in on athletics alone."

"It's a good thing they also have academic scholarships. You know, for good grades," I deadpanned, a mannerism I'd inherited from Mom, which I knew he hated.

"It's good to have something to fall back on, but you need to up your sprint time. Wade said you've been a bit sluggish lately."

I groaned inwardly. Wade gossiped more than old ladies at bridge, and Dad often pumped him for info on my progress, or the lack thereof. It was February. Track season started five minutes ago, and he was already getting on my case.

Don't get me wrong, Dad was my biggest supporter. He went to all of my competitions, but he took his involvement to angry-soccer-fan extremes. You know those kids at Little League games who watched in confused horror as their parents brawled in the bleachers? That pretty much summed up my athletic career from the first time I picked up a ball. After the second police raid at a peewee football game, I had taken up a less aggressive sport to keep the peace.

"Been getting enough sleep, son?" Dad asked after many attempts to recapture my attention.

I shook away my wandering thoughts. "Sure."

"Really? Because the bags under your eyes say something else. I see the light on in your room at two in the morning. What's going on in that head of yours, Liam?"

"I got tons of homework this semester. I have to keep up my GPA if I'm going to get into college."

"You sure it's not something else keeping you up? A certain girl, perhaps?"

I glared at him and his tacky flowered shirt. "No."

"Have you been sneaking off to see her again?"

"No," I lied.

I must not have done a convincing job because Dad went on to say, "It's bad enough I lose sleep worrying if Wade will burn the house down—I don't want to have to worry about you, too. I will not have you going to jail for a childhood crush. You remember the agreement, don't you?"

I knew better than anyone what the stakes were. Every day crossed out on the calendar made my options painfully clear. "I do."

"Then what's the problem? Why can't you just move on?" Dad asked.

Off the top of my head, I could think of a hundred activities I'd rather be doing than having a heart-to-heart with my old man. Talking about our feelings was like a breach in the buddy code. It was just Dad, Wade, and me now, and we'd agreed to certain ground rules while living together. Replace whatever you drank. Change the empty toilet paper roll. Call if you're staying out. And never discuss ex-girlfriends or, in Dad's case, ex-wives.

And yet the words flew out of my mouth anyway. "Because she's The One."

Dad blinked in confusion. "The one what?"

I shrugged and dropped my gaze to the floor. "Just . . . you know, The One."

Dad searched the walls of the living room as if lost. "Where are we? In the Matrix? Was there an ancient prophecy about her?"

"It's like you and Mom. You married her four months after you met because you knew, deep down in your bones, that she was the only girl you'd ever love. Your own words, Dad."

"Whoa, whoa, now, cowboy." A beefy hand rose in the air to stop me. "I was in the Navy when I met your mother. I'd seen the world, met a ton of people, and had real experiences before coming to that conclusion, and look how well that turned out. You're only seventeen and haven't traveled any farther than Disneyland. So do you really want to follow our example?"

Grandma had said for years that my folks' marriage was doomed from the start, so the split was a shock to no one, not even me. It was kind of hard to stand on a love based on a John Mellencamp song. There's this little ditty by the singer called "Jack and Diane," and wouldn't you know it, that happened to be the same names of my parents, so of course their fate simply had to be written in the stars, right? They essentially lived out the lyrics in real life: two kids falling in love, running off against their parents' wishes, and scraping through life as a result.

Too bad the song didn't mention the part where Diane left Jack so she could "find herself." Divorce papers were signed, Mom joined a private practice in Santa Barbara, and 625 Highland Drive was now a bachelor pad. And where did I fit into all of this? Sitting with Dad inside a partially gutted home that might never be completed and trying my best to ignore the symbolism. That was best saved for my writing.

"So you're saying I'm too young to be in love?" I asked Dad.

He guffawed. "'Course not. Any idiot can fall in love."

"Gee, thanks," I grumbled.

"Falling is easy, but it's what you do when you reach the ground that matters," he continued. "It's all hearts and flowers in the beginning, but will you stick around when that new car smell wears off and it stops being exciting and it starts feeling like work? Love is not for thrill-seekers, dreamers, or children with short attention spans. And you, son, fit into all three of those categories."

On that inspiring note, I pointed to one of the brochures for *lifeguard* and got to my feet. "I'll go with that one."

"You need to pick two of them," Dad said.

"Baseball," I called from over my shoulder as I made my way to the kitchen.

The place was a mess: old take-out boxes, crushed soda cans, drop cloths, and ceramic tiles stacked on the counter. I swept up some of the garbage and filled two Hefty bags. I hauled the load through the side door, opened the garage, then rolled the plastic trash bin onto the curb, mumbling curses the whole time.

There was nothing worse than being told how to feel, as if my own emotions weren't enough. I was tempted to call Mom for a sympathetic ear, but that didn't go well the last time I tried it.

"You kids are so angsty these days," Mom had said, unimpressed with my plight. *"I get it. You honestly believe that you invented loneliness and being misunderstood. Everyone is so fake and they don't know just how complex the universe is, and we have to experience everything right now or else perish into the abyss of our own wasted potential. You, Holden Caulfield, are no different than any other kid on the planet and your philosophy is as insipid as your social life. Now go outside and play!"*

Bear in mind I was fourteen at the time, and I hadn't had a sit-down with her since—not with that attitude. She saw too much of herself in me, and if you didn't like your reflection you tended to avoid mirrors. I was her overbite, the mole on the left side of her chin, and the cesarean scar below her navel, all of which she had fixed or removed one way or another. I swear, Wade's mom and my mom needed to have brunch and swap notes on how to mess up their kids in the cleverest way possible.

I tried to close the trash lid, but the overflow wouldn't allow it to shut. Bags tumbled to the pavement, their contents spilling out in an odorous burst. I kicked at the side of the bin, slinging trash and hating everything about everything. I was so involved in my tantrum that I didn't realize I had an audience.

A girl wearing a pink hoodie and a matching bike helmet watched me from the corner. She'd stopped pedaling and waited by the curb. A tan cruiser bike stood between her feet—the kind with a basket on the front that old people and annoying hipster kids would ride on the promenade.

I knew that face, and that height and shape, as well as my own. My brain locked up, caught in the logistics of her being this far from home. Standing on my street. At this time of day.

She wasn't an illusion or some manifestation. She was real, and above all, *she* came to *me*. It wasn't exactly a song with our names, but it was a sign nonetheless, wasn't it?

Ellia flashed a lopsided smile and offered the most profound and evocative greeting in the entire English language. "Sup?"

Showing off some fancy vocab of my own, I was like, "Hey."

Her stare bounced from me to the driveway. "Are you okay?"

"Getting there," I replied in all honesty.

"I, um . . . I'm allowed to go outside now, so I wanted to ride around and see if anything's changed in the neighborhood. Not much, apparently. Stacey said that you lived close to the park, so I figured I'd, I don't know, do a drive-by."

I smiled. "On a beach cruiser?"

"Hey, don't be jealous. This baby can pick up some speed going downhill." She patted the wide handlebars affectionately. "Since I can't drive, it beats the heck out of walking."

"You're not allowed to drive or you don't know how anymore?" I asked.

Her attention fell to her feet. "Both."

"I can fix that," I offered. "We can go to an empty parking lot and you can practice with my car." I turned to the black Ford Escort parked in the driveway and cringed.

The thing was twice my age and it only went forty miles per hour before it got the shakes. All the hubcaps were missing. Cotton and foam poked out of the seats and no matter how many tree air fresheners I hung in my car, the interior always smelled like nachos and ranch dressing. Plus, Wade had already called dibs on it tonight, and to avoid getting shanked in the shower tomorrow, it was best that I kept it parked.

Ellia wasn't really up for the idea anyway. She was shaking her head.

"No, I'm good. I like riding around. I haven't seen the outdoors in a while and I want to enjoy it." She tipped her chin toward my house. "So what were you just doing in your driveway? You salty or nah?"

Great. Of all the times I wanted Ellia to come to me, she caught me in the worst light. "I'm not salty."

"You looked salty to me. Thought you were gonna break your mailbox next."

I could feel the blood rise up my neck and settle into my cheeks. "It's nothing. Just my dad getting to me again."

"You got one of those too, huh? I get it." She teetered from foot to foot as she rotated the bike in the opposite direction.

I knew my staring was freaking her out. I couldn't help it. So many questions ran through my head, I didn't know where to start. I had to say something, anything to keep her around a little while longer.

Unfortunately, I heard the front door open. His heavy footsteps drew closer, but I didn't look back. I stayed focused on Ellia's face, her expression changing from playful curiosity to caution. Dark curls that peeked from her helmet had caught on the breeze and danced over her face. I had to remember everything because there was no telling when I would see her again after this confrontation.

Dad stepped in front of me. "Run along, young lady. You got no business being here."

Ellia's eyes darted between me and Dad in confusion. "Why?"

"My son's in enough trouble dealing with the likes of you people, so hop on your bike and don't come back."

"Dad!" I yelled from behind his wide shoulders, but I had better odds fighting a brick wall. I knew this was coming, knew seeing her would upset him, but Dad had no right to treat her this way.

Confusion quickly morphed into indignation as Ellia repeated his words. "*You people?*"

"Go on home before I call the cops." Dad shooed her off. "Go on!"

She flinched. With watery eyes, she began to pedal away. Not once did she look back, her anger palpable as she struggled to steer herself to gain speed. By the time she reached the corner, she was nothing but a mirage on the horizon, the afternoon sun casting her in a halo of orange light. And then, like in every dream I'd had since the accident, she was gone, leaving no proof that she'd ever been there.

"Clean that mess up before you come inside," Dad barked and headed back toward the house.

CHAPTER EIGHT

ELLIA

W ait, slow down." Stacey's hand shot out to stop me.
"Liam's dad's a what?"

"A *raaaciiiist*!" I dragged out the word and
hopped on one foot on her porch.

My leg muscles throbbed, sweat soaked through my
hoodie, and I'd probably pulled a ligament pedaling to Stacey's
house. Tears had stung my eyes the whole way.

I'd already called Mom and told her where I was headed, as
was part of our agreement for letting me outside. I could only
go to familiar places and I knew Stacey's address better than
my own.

Limping back and forth on her porch, I told Stacey everything that happened when I went to see Liam, including the
thinly veiled hate speech that led me to her doorstep. When

I finished, I let out a long, purifying breath and with it, all the anger that had built up during the half-mile ride over.

"I didn't do anything wrong and I got treated like trash. This is what I get for taking your advice." I sat on the top step of her porch and unhooked the chin strap to remove my bike helmet. I patted the silk scarf that I used as a headband to make sure it had stayed in place.

Stacey stepped out and closed the front door behind her. A black maxi dress fit her figure with precision, but the jumbo rollers in her hair killed the wow factor. Maybe she was going on a date.

"El, you might be reading too much into it," she said, sitting down beside me.

"What other way should I read it?" I sniffed. "I don't even know that man and he just yelled at me for no reason. He doesn't want me near his son and the only reason I can see is because I'm black."

"Oh come on—"

"That would explain all the sneaking around Liam does," I spoke over her. "I told you he watches my house in the morning, but he never knocks on the door or visits me during the daytime. You should've seen his face, Stacey. He didn't want his dad to know he was dating *us people*, as his dad called it. Liam's ashamed of me. I'm a dirty secret!" I wailed.

"Oh my goodness." Stacey rolled her eyes skyward. "Sweetie, are you trying out for Broadway? Because you're bringing nothing but drama. Look, Liam may get on every last one of my nerves, but he's never been shy or quiet about how he feels about you. He's done everything but post your dating status on the stadium billboard at school."

"Then why didn't he defend me?" I wiped my nose on my sleeve. "He was standing right there and he didn't say anything."

"I don't know. Maybe he was caught off guard. Or maybe— and this is just a shot in the dark here—but maybe you should ask him yourself."

"Uh-uh. I'm done. I tried it your way and went to see him and got told off. I'm not doing that again. Let's talk about something else, anything else, like why you're all gussied up. Are you going out?"

"In a bit, yeah. We were getting ready for the Valentine's Day dance."

"Oh, that's tonight, isn't it?" I'd completely forgotten that Valentine's Day was this coming Monday. Stacey had told me about the dance going on at school tonight, but it slipped my mind what with all the bigotry and discrimination going on. "Who's 'we'?" I asked.

"Trish Montego, Kendra Bailey, and Nina Hahn." Stacey knew it was helpful to use full names to remind me who our friends were. "They're upstairs getting ready." She got to her feet and scooped me up by the arm. "Come in and say hi. They'd love to see you."

I rapidly shook my head. "I don't think—"

"Good. You think too much anyway. Now come on." She opened the door and dragged me inside.

Stacey's house looked the same as I remembered: gold beveled mirrors with leaves and curling designs, intricately carved furniture, and embroidered cushions. It was smaller than mine, but her folks made up for it in excessive décor. The color scheme alone would've given my mom a stroke, but at least the Levines actually used their living room for its intended purpose. Living.

Stacey led me upstairs to her room and I instantly felt nervous at the sound of female voices behind the closed door. I hadn't had much social interaction and I worked better with one-on-one exchanges. Would I ever get out of that phase, the shy child who hid behind her mother's legs when confronted with new visitors? There was only one way to find out.

Stacey opened the door and three girls waited on the other side. A thin Asian girl stood in front of Stacey's vanity putting on makeup. A tall white girl with auburn hair sat on the floor, sliding on strappy shoes. The final one lay across the four-post bed, her bare feet swinging in the air. She was about my complexion, and even laying down I could tell that height was a weak trait. I recognized all of them, vaguely, from Facebook. But not from life.

"Hey, guys! Guess who's here?" Stacey swung her arms toward me like I was part of a magic trick. A chorus of squeals and shrieks filled the room as the group huddled close and trampled all over my personal space. Voices overlapped and words poured out in a jumble of confusion.

"Oh my god! Ellia!"

". . . It's so good to see you—"

"How've you been—"

". . . Girl, it's been a minute—"

". . . What have you been up to?"

". . . Are you okay?"

"You look good!"

I was getting whiplash from trying to see who was speaking. The volume spiked my anxiety and I prayed that my migraines didn't kick up.

"We were so worried about you." The redheaded one— Trish—rubbed my shoulder.

The contact freaked me out, but it was something I needed to get used to. "Really?"

"Yeah. Everyone was talking in school about how you were all disabled and crippled." The short one, Kendra, was cut off with a jab to the elbow by the Asian girl, Nina.

"Oh sorry," Kendra muttered sheepishly.

Soon I was being dragged deeper into the room and onto Stacey's bed. The next twenty minutes contained more rapid catch-up and nostalgia trivia.

"Hey, you remember that time we snuck into that frat party during pledge week and almost got hazed?" Trish asked with a mischievous grin.

"You know that bonfire on the beach at spring break?" Nina asked. "That was wild. I'll never stay up for thirty hours straight again."

"I'll never forget that time when you broke into a run-down department store and stole a mannequin. You almost got arrested for trespassing and told the security guard you were an undercover cop," Kendra jumped in, her dark eyes full of wonder. "Priceless!"

So I was a party girl *and* a criminal? Great. Of course, I couldn't recall any of this, but at least now I knew where Vivian came from.

"Those were some crazy times." I tried to play it off while glaring at Stacey for putting me on blast.

Stacey mouthed the words "I'm sorry." No one else knew about my amnesia and I wanted to keep it that way, at least for now.

It's funny how being surrounded by a group of friends could leave you detached. I wasn't *in* the moment, but was watching the scene play out as if on TV or from outside of a window. No matter how hard I tried, I couldn't get myself to wake up from this daydream and join in. Their heads flung back and their eyes watered with laughter as their teeth flashed. I envied every wink, playful shove, and innuendo that was lost on me.

"You should totally come to the dance with us," Nina suggested, and the others cheered at the idea. "You can get a ticket at the door."

"Nah, that's okay. Maybe next time." I offered a good-natured smile.

"Well, you have to show up for the Decades Celebration in March. It's going to be off the chain this year," Kendra said.

"No doubt." I slowly slid off the bed to make my escape. "I better get going. Have fun at the dance."

"Wait. We can use your expertise." Trish stood and twirled around, her beaded dress flowing around her knees. "Does this look okay?"

The room went quiet as they waited for my opinion, like it mattered. I was the last person to give someone fashion advice. After all, I was partially bald and was probably sporting helmet-hair. However, they *did* ask, so they couldn't fault me for telling the truth, and a true friend would not let another friend leave the house looking ratchet.

"Trish, your whole situation is too much, starting with the makeup. You look like you're about to announce this year's Hunger Games. Dial it back. Also, red is *not* your color, so switch dresses with Nina. She looks about your size. Kendra, wear some heels for height and it'll show off your legs better. Stacey, wear your hair down, but away from your face and lose the bangles. They're too bulky. And change clutch bags; yours doesn't match anything you have on." I covered my mouth to stop, but only after the words flew out. Where did all that come from?

None of the girls seemed offended and made quick work of the alterations while Stacey looked on with impish glee.

"There she is." She winked.

"She who?" I asked.

"The confident, take-charge Ellia. Not the sniveling ball of indecision that showed up on my doorstep. Welcome back." She curtsied.

I was horrified. "I didn't mean to do that."

"Maybe the 'old you' is coming back to the surface. This is a good thing, right?" she whispered.

I wasn't sure about that. And going by my outburst, the rude, bossy, fashion-cop Ellia with a possible criminal record didn't seem like someone I wanted to be tight with. The more I knew about her, the less I cared to know.

By the time the clothing changes were made and pictures were taken and posted with the proper filter settings, we all piled up in Stacey's Volkswagen Bug. My bike wouldn't fit, but Stacey promised that she would come get me tomorrow to pick it up. The commute to my house held all manner of clown-car absurdity, complete with reckless driving and cackling maniacs in the backseat. None of the girls seemed bothered about being an hour late to the dance, so I figured they were going for a grand entrance. I had to admit they all looked hot, so why were they going stag?

"Don't you guys have dates?" I turned around to face the girls in the backseat.

"No way! We playas can't be tied down. We like to keep our options open. It's you who decided to settle down, Mrs. McPherson," Trish teased.

I scoffed. "Please don't call me that."

"Ooh, trouble in paradise? Is married life not going like you hoped?"

"Shut up, Trish," Kendra chastised. "I think it's sweet that you found your soul mate, Ellia. I always thought you had to be old for that kind of thing, but I guess not. Kinda like arthritis. And *death*." She whispered the word as if the Grim Reaper would hop onto the windshield.

I glanced at Stacey behind the wheel, silently pleading for some backup. She quirked the side of her mouth and kept her eyes on the road. It was best that she focused on her stunt car maneuvering since stop signs were just a suggestion for her.

After she parked the car in front of my house, I climbed out and wished the girls good luck. In return, they promised they would *definitely* fill me in on the events tonight, and we would *totally* hang out later, and they *absolutely* would call to set things up and other adverbs, which implied that no such thing would happen. And I was *completely* cool with that. These girls were a trip and a half, each playing a key role in the wildest chapters in my life. Though I wasn't equipped to delve into the story just yet, I mentally bookmarked the pages to revisit at a later date.

"By the way . . ." Kendra poked her head out the window and said with theatrical flair, "*When someone shows you who they are, believe them.*"

That was random. "Um . . . thank you?"

"It's Maya Angelou. See, the last thing you say to someone is important, and what I told you before your accident was pretty weak. So now I have to think of something deep so you can remember, because who knows if I'll ever see you again."

"Kendra, she isn't going to die," Nina chided.

"You never know, though," Kendra insisted.

Nina pushed Kendra aside and climbed into the front seat. "I never understood why your head is so big. I mean, there is nothing in there."

"Hating me won't make you pretty," Kendra said.

"And talking won't make you any smarter," Nina shot back without missing a beat, which told me this bickering was something they did often.

"Oh my god, someone put a muzzle on them, please!" Stacey yelled.

"On it." Trish, who was still in the backseat, took out a tissue and stuffed it in Kendra's mouth.

"Later, El." Stacey blew me a kiss and burned rubber to the next block. I stared mystified as the compact car turned the corner, while laughter and screams of joy echoed into the night. How that girl got her license was a true act of witchcraft.

I reached the porch, unlocked the front door, and then paused at the sound of jingling. I had more junk on my keychain than actual keys—miniature toys and plastic tags with silly slogans printed on either side. I noticed that a particular item was missing: a brown dog collar with two metal tags in the shape of paw prints.

A cold snout, big brown eyes, and reddish fur flooded my senses with a rush that made me sway. For a moment, I saw it as a sign that my memories were returning, but my cocker spaniel, Babette, had died when I was in middle school, way before the memory gap. It amazed me how little things can trigger dormant memories, and I wondered what became of the dog collar.

I walked inside and bristled at the house's cold emptiness. No music, no TV, and my footsteps against the marbled foyer left a hollow echo as if entering a museum. Everything was showcase perfect and either pristine white or gold, and it was a mortal sin to step into the living room, much less sit on the imported leather couch. I was a pampered child raised in a mausoleum, surrounded by beautiful things that weren't alive.

I found Mom in the kitchen, playing with her new toy: the food processor. I glanced at the closed door off the side of the kitchen. The band of light underneath the door let me know that Dad's location hadn't changed. He'd been locked in his office all day working on a development project and likely wouldn't resurface until morning.

Mom dumped something into the juicer that had no business being liquefied. Big curls fell past her shoulders and framed a skillfully painted face that showed no emotion. The woman made poise look effortless and exhausting at the same time.

"You missed dinner," she said without looking up.

Oh, that was a real shame. "That's fine. I ate at Stacey's."

"Here. Drink this." She shoved a glass of something green and thick in my face.

I sniffed the contents for toxins. "What is it?"

"It's a fruit smoothie loaded with vitamin D, omega-3, and antioxidants to help with brainpower."

I took a timid sip. It wasn't so bad once you got past the chewing. "Thanks, Mom."

I pulled out my phone and saw that I had two voice mails from Liam. I deleted both without listening to them. Then I erased all five of his "I'm sorry, please call me" texts. I watched Mom wipe down the countertop and remove all evidence of the slaughtered, innocent produce.

"How come Liam doesn't come over?" I asked.

Mom dropped her dish towel and turned to me. "My guess would be guilt or respect for your need for space. Can't say I'm at all disappointed."

"Why?" I asked. "The doctors said that he was the one who found me on the beach."

"Yes, and it was a miracle that he found you when he did, but that's not to say that the boy doesn't have problems."

This was news to me. "What kind of problems?"

"From what you told me, he didn't have a very happy home life. His parents had recently divorced and I supposed he was lashing out in rebellion. And his father . . . well, he's a piece of work."

Tell me about it, I thought.

"I'm not one to talk ill of people, but that boy is not exactly who I would've chosen for you," she said, and continued cleaning. "He's smart and charming, but he's also troubled and doesn't seem to have any vision for himself. He'd already influenced your behavior, causing you to have trouble in school and stay out late. I was concerned about his attachment; it was a bit extreme."

The word *rebellion* swirled around my tongue before I swallowed it down. Maybe Liam used me to get back at his dad. What better way to stick it to your parents than to date someone they didn't approve of? That rule also applied to me, and going by what I learned tonight, I wasn't exactly Miss Goody Two-Shoes, either.

I thought of all the pictures of us on my phone and computer that I was tempted to get rid of, but couldn't bring myself to delete. Most were candid, unscripted moments of smiles and adoring glances. Two years was a long time to fake a relationship. No matter the motive in the beginning, genuine feelings had to have developed over time, enough to cause Mom concern.

I wished I kept a diary or a blog so I could know for sure. I couldn't get an accurate story from anyone and every new piece of information had to be processed and vetted for authenticity.

"Why do you ask? Did you see him today while you were out?" Mom asked.

"Um . . . nope." I finished the last of the smoothie then set the glass in the sink. "I'm just getting a head count of all my friends from school. It's hard keeping track of them all."

Mom dropped her dish towel on the counter and placed her hands on my shoulders. "I know this is tough on you, but look at this as a new chapter in your life with new opportunities. A chance to start over without having to backtrack or regret past mistakes. A clean slate."

"Sure, Mom."

I went to my room with too many questions and a growing migraine. As I chased two painkillers with a glass of water, I surveyed the area. I felt like a convict in my own home—no pardon, no plea bargain. Sixteen years of imagination crammed within thirty square feet and four walls, boxing me in to what I should know and what was expected of me.

I had friends fan-girling over my criminal past, a dude stalking my house, classmates blowing up my timeline with foolery I couldn't remember, and girls looking up deep-sounding quotes and asking themselves, "What is life?" That's a lot of pressure to put on a kid with head trauma.

I had to give Stacey props—she may be a maniac driver, but she never took her eyes off the road or got distracted by the craziness in the car. Right now, I envied that kind of focus, because I kept looking back and reaching behind me for something I couldn't even hold. Time moved in one direction: forward. It might be a good idea for me to do the same.

CHAPTER NINE

LIAM

oul was not the proper word to describe my mood. *Livid* didn't really sum it up, either.

I barely spoke to Dad all weekend, lest I give in to the temptation to murder him in his sleep. Dad was a gruff man who didn't do diplomacy well, but the way he treated Ellia crossed the "rude" line and dove deep into are-you-kidding-me? territory. I tried calling her and got her voice mail all weekend. There was no guesswork involved this time—she was flat-out avoiding me.

By Monday, my mood hadn't improved. I drove to school in a manner that could be called outrun-the-cops driving. Wade sat in the passenger seat, struggling not to choke on his breakfast burrito through the turbulence. His hands braced the door, ready to jump out in case I chose this moment to go through with my murder-suicide pact.

When we pulled into the school parking lot, he tore out of the car, threw himself onto the ground, and kissed the concrete with religious zeal. "Land! Oh, blessed, solid land!"

I left him to his worship and stepped through the back entrance of the school where hellos went unanswered, friends and teammates were ignored.

And . . . it was Valentine's Day.

Paper hearts and flowers hung from strings on the ceiling. Candy hearts and lollipops were taped to lockers by secret admirers. Couples kissed in the halls and made promises of forever with a twenty-four-hour shelf life. I hated them all, and though it wasn't Christmas, I wore the title of Grinch with pride.

A junior girl named Casey Basset stood by her locker showing her friend the half-dozen balloons her boyfriend gave her. I unhooked a button from my backpack, straightened the fastener into a point, and stabbed two balloons as I strolled past. Onlookers jumped at the loud *pop*, and I heard Casey yell, "Hey!" but I didn't break my stride.

This chubby band kid named Blake Glover sat on a stool in the hall dressed up as Cupid and serenaded the kids with his guitar. He would be there all day between classes and at lunch, and even took requests for two dollars. I gave him ten bucks to play "She Hates Me" by Puddle of Mudd and "Cry Me a River" by Justin Timberlake, which set the perfect mood to unleash my wrath upon the student body.

Brian Matheson and Tiana Daniels, his arm candy of the week, were cuddled up by the bathrooms. I stopped and back-pedaled until I was standing next to them. At first they didn't see me. They were too busy cooing baby talk.

"I love you," he said as they nuzzled noses.

"No, I love you more," she replied.

"No, I love—"

"Dude, you know she's sneaking around with your boy Travis, right?" I cut in.

Finally realizing I was standing next to him, Brian yelled, "What?"

"It's not true, baby, I swear." Tiana shook her head vehemently.

"She's lying. Check her phone. They're always texting each other in Biology."

"Shut up, Liam!" she spat.

"You're hooking up with Travis?" Brian accused her.

"Don't listen to him. He's just jealous," Tiana pleaded, but Brian wasn't convinced. The seed of doubt had been planted and my work was done.

I walked away, looking for my next victim. As a quiet observer, I'd accumulated a load of dirty laundry and spent the entire morning airing it out for my peers. Cute and sweet, they'd call me. Shy and unassuming, they'd say, but now they were getting a glimpse of what bottled rage looked like. And it sure wasn't *cute*.

By fourth period, my streak of mayhem had reached the four corners of school. What was once laughter and good times was now a gripe fest of the brokenhearted and betrayed. It was music to my ears. If misery loved company, then I wanted to throw the party of the century. I'd promote the event with flyers that said,

SINGLE-AWARENESS SOIRÉE

FREE ADMISSION, NO DRESS CODE.

BRING YOUR OWN TEARS!

The warm weather allowed students to eat at the tables outside, and given my behavior, it wasn't a surprise that I sat alone at lunch. My thirst for anarchy had been quenched and now I just wanted a quiet place to write. Too bad that didn't happen.

"Hey, nephew, what's up?" Wade sat next to me and leaned his back against the tabletop.

"Not much," I returned with a smile that felt painful.

Elbows on the table, he scanned the perimeter under dark sunglasses. "Fair warning, you might wanna steer clear of the band kids and any cheerleaders. They're plotting revenge on you. I didn't catch all the details, but from what I heard it's not pretty."

"Bring it. There's nothing they can do that I—AHHHH!" The sudden downpour overhead was a shock to my nervous system. My muscles locked, my back stiffened from the avalanche of ice chips sliding inside my shirt.

I wiped my eyes to find my entire body covered in red slush. Cheers and whistles quickly followed, and I watched in frigid horror as kids stood up in applause.

"That'll teach you to butt in and ruin people's dates, you jerk!" a random sophomore girl yelled behind me.

I turned around and saw Brian's now ex-girlfriend and four other girls holding jumbo-size cups in their hands and high-fiving each other.

"You tell 'em, girl!" Wade joined the chorus with three finger-snaps in a Z formation. "The no-good bum."

I turned to my traitorous uncle, who now sat at a safe distance from the spray. "Whose side are you on? Ow!" A plastic cup bounced off the back of my head, which brought on another round of laughter as the girls stomped away.

"The side that keeps me dry," he replied. "What did you expect? We don't take kindly to bullies and party poopers 'round these parts."

"Right." I swiped my tongue around and caught the wetness on the side of my cheek. Cherry flavored with a splash of cola. Nice.

Wade handed me a napkin, though it would take a towel and a mop to clean up this mess. "So . . . what did we learn?" he asked in his best teacher voice.

"Not to trust you to give me a decent heads-up." I wiped my face and then chucked the balled-up tissue at him.

He dodged the blow, and then began fiddling with his phone. "Listen, I get that you're not in the Valentine's mood, but you can't take it out on other people. When I got dumped by the-chick-who-shall-not-be-named, did you see me trying to sabotage other people's relationships? No."

"No. You just curled up in a ball, refused to shower for three days, drowned in a tub of ice cream, and stalked her online. *So* much healthier." I held up my notebook and shook off the melting slush. Thankfully, only two pages had suffered flood damage.

"Maybe so, but I'm much better now—thanks for asking. The cloud is lifting and I'm slowly coming out of my funk."

I did a double take at the gray T-shirt and blue jeans he wore. That ugly maroon sweatshirt he never washed was nowhere in sight and he had actually bothered to shave.

"What made you decide to lose the hoodie?" I asked as I ripped the soggy pages from my notebook, crumbled the wad, then threw that at him, too.

He tilted his head to the left, causing the ball to fly past his ear. "It was time to move on. Might be a good idea that you do the same," he replied. "I can get why you're still pining for Ellia, but you're in a sea of eligible females. I mean, they kind of hate you right now, but . . ."

I shrugged. Even if a girl found my mood swings appealing, I wasn't interested in a rebound, which was all it would amount to anyway.

Wade peered at my wet clothes and dripping hair. "You might want to change so you don't attract ants."

I couldn't even find the strength to care. The mess seemed to reflect my mood, which couldn't get any worse at this point.

"Hey, Hemingway!" Stacey called out as she approached us, her knee-high boots clacking on the pavement.

I spoke too soon.

That freakishly large handbag swung from the crook of her arm and whacked a boy in the face as he stood up from his table. But it would take more than a possible concussion to break her stride—she looked determined. And ticked.

"Whoops! That's my cue to leave." Wade stood up and left, but not without taking a picture of me on his phone. As he chuckled and walked away, I had a sneaking suspicion that my soggy state would go viral within the hour. And he wondered why I kept certain parts of my personal life a secret. Anyway, I had bigger problems at the moment.

That bigger problem took a seat across from me then slapped a thin stack of papers on the table. "A B-minus? Is that the best you can do?"

I inspected the English essay that I rewrote last week and noticed the red ink scattered on the document. This report focused on feminism in *Jane Eyre*, which confirmed that Stacey was a closeted Brontë fan. "You said to keep it authentic. It couldn't be perfect," I explained.

"Yeah, but my teacher marks off for grammar, Liam. I know how to use spell-check. I expected more from you. You don't strike me as one who would settle for mediocre."

I sighed. "So how is she?" I asked.

Stacey rolled her eyes at the familiar change in topic. "She's fine."

"Come on, you can do better than that. 'Fine' is just so . . . *mediocre*," I fired back.

"She's still trying to remember things, and asking a lot of questions. Some of them are about you."

That got my attention. "Really? What did she say?"

"She asked about how you guys met and what you saw in each other. Oh, and also she thinks your dad is a racist."

Of all the outlandish remarks to fly out of Stacey's mouth, I hadn't expected that. "A *what*?"

"*Raaaaciiiist*," she repeated slowly. "Ellia said that she went to see you and your dad came out of nowhere and started yelling about how *her kind* wasn't welcome or some mess like that."

I kept perfectly still because I needed all my energy to think. I replayed the discussion in my head and couldn't find anything offensive other than Dad's lack of decorum. Then it hit me.

"*My son's in enough trouble dealing with the likes of you people*," he'd said. "*So hop on your bike and don't come back.*"

Without the proper context or backstory, that statement could easily be misconstrued as something else. My Dad was a lot of things, but a bigot wasn't one of them. "That's not what he meant," I told Stacey.

"You sure about that, Mr. Blond-Haired, Blue-Eyed, All-American Hero?

"Stacey, I—"

With a flippant wave of her hand, she said, "No need to explain it to me. It's Ellia who needs assurance."

I reached for my phone in my pocket. "I need to clear this up."

"You need to do something 'cause this thing right here is not gonna work." Her finger swung between us. "Don't get me wrong, I enjoy the perks, but our arrangement is getting on my nerves. This back and forth, passing messages between people too stubborn to hash it out for themselves—I do enough of that with my own parents. So this is the part where I bow out gracefully."

My thumb paused over the keys in midtext. All of the humor and snark that was there a moment ago had vanished. Stacey was dead serious. "Where's all this coming from? Is this because of the B-minus?"

"No, it's been a long time coming, actually," she said wistfully. "See, I've been doing a lot of thinking—"

"Whoa, careful now," I interrupted. "Did you at least stretch first?"

"Shut up. Anyway, it didn't really hit me until I went to see Ellia last week. I was wearing this sexy nurse uniform . . ."

"This sounds like the beginning of a dirty joke—"

"Oh my god, shut up!" she snapped. "I was trying to pinpoint where her blank spot began. We were going through pictures and skipping down memory lane and she couldn't remember the Decades Celebration. But she could remember the layout of the hallways, our Spanish One teacher, and crab soccer in gym class. Ellia's memory loss stretches exactly two years—from October of freshman year all the way to her accident this past December."

"Okay," I said, eyeing the students getting up to leave and dumping their trash. There was a point to this somewhere, I just knew it. As weird as Stacey's ramblings got, it always led to something. But man, did she love to drag scenes out for dramatic effect.

"Isn't it funny how that time frame lines up perfectly with your dating history?" she asked. "It makes you wonder if her brain is trying to block you out completely. You said that you had nothing to do with her accident, but you avoid her like you have something to hide. And now your dad doesn't want her around to cause trouble. Now what kind of *trouble* would that be, huh, Hemingway?"

I didn't like her accusatory tone. The conversation had taken a dark turn and caused my knee to bounce under the table. "I didn't hurt her."

She gave me a cold stare. "You were there."

"It doesn't mean I'm responsible," I argued, and even as I said the words I knew they were a lie. "If I'm guilty then why haven't the police arrested me yet? Why did you agree to help me if I was so dangerous?"

"Because there's more to the story than what you're telling. You're not exactly going out of your way to get her memory back. Unless you did something that you don't want her to remember?"

Ah, so my hired spy was spying on me. Stacey was much smarter than she let on. And unlike the rest of the kids in school who just wanted to get the dirt on what happened, Stacey genuinely cared for Ellia. That may well be the reason why I haven't strangled her yet.

"It's just a coincidence," I said through gritted teeth.

"Really? Why haven't you gone to see her? Why haven't you called her? Her phone works now, and I'm sure her cell is number one on your speed dial. Why am I stuck answering questions that only you can answer?"

"Or maybe you're jealous," I argued. "I'm competition for you, someone who knows her better than you do. I'm someone who she shares secrets with, deep secrets that she won't share with you."

"Yet *I'm* the one she can remember."

Her words cut deep and I had to take a breath to reel in my composure.

Struggling to keep the anger out of my voice, I finally said, "I can't see her, all right? I'm not allowed to go anywhere near her."

Stacey reared back at my confession. "So you did have something to do with it—"

"No!" I slammed my fist on the table, the loud impact making those within earshot jump, including Stacey. I didn't want to frighten her or have her see me as an unstable freak, but she needed to get a few points straight so as not to jump to the wrong conclusion.

I leaned close to her and spoke in a softer tone. "Her parents didn't want us together from the start and the accident was a perfect way to keep me out of her life. Every time I visited her at the hospital I was turned away. I've tried calling and emailing, but her phone was locked and she never got my messages. I've done all I can, so don't tell me that I'm not doing enough."

Stacey sat stunned for a long moment, her eyes growing larger with each blink. "Why don't you ever talk about the accident?"

"Because it's not worth mentioning and we're not exactly close," I replied nastily.

"Maybe." She shrugged. "But you need to find some type of closure for yourself. Whatever's going on with you is eating you alive and you need to talk it out. If you can't go to her place and she can't go to yours then you have to meet up on neutral turf. You can't use me because she'll know it was a setup." A sly smirk appeared at the corner of her mouth. "Hmm. I think I might know a place."

She rubbed her hands together, giddy at her own brilliance. She only needed to stroke a creepy cat on her lap to finish the look of criminal mastermind.

Tired of the suspense, I asked, "Where? Just tell me."

"Consider this a parting gift. It's the last piece of info you're getting from me. Anything else you'll have to find out on your own," she warned while relishing my desperation for every crumb of detail.

"Hold on to your knickers, Hemingway." She leaned in and whispered in my ear. "The Great Ellia Dawson is going to therapy."

CHAPTER TEN

ELLIA

s usual, I woke up with a pounding headache and an acute sense of *Where am I?* My sleep pattern was all over the place and I kept waking up before dawn for no apparent reason. This could've been some residual trauma from being shaken awake every hour by a cheerful nurse. In the hospital, everyone and their mother wanted to check on me and make sure I didn't die in my sleep or something.

It always took a minute or two to get accustomed to the layout of my room and the strange decorations. I turned to the nightstand and groaned at the time on my alarm clock.

5:29 A.M.

I rolled over and threw the covers over my head. I applied the breathing exercises my therapist taught me and focused on a quiet, peaceful place. My mind drifted to the sound of crashing waves and seagulls in the sky and imagined the soft give of the sand under my feet. That thought seemed to give me the most comfort, but it also caused a slight pressure just behind my left eye.

I rolled over and peeked at the clock again from under the covers.

5:34 A.M.

"Are you kidding me?" I threw the covers off and crawled out of bed, giving into the fact that I wouldn't go back to sleep until I looked out the window. It was like some sort of compulsion I couldn't help. There was a kid who went to the same counseling session as me who had to wash her hands seven times and click the light switch twice before leaving the bathroom. Maybe this morning routine was some latent OCD that was slowly breaking out.

And surprise, surprise, Liam stood across the street under the lamppost, doing stretches and looking up at my window. I was careful not to disrupt the curtains so he wouldn't know I was there. As I watched him watching me, I dueled with two courses of action: call him and cuss him out or go outside and cuss him out. He made the decision for me by leaving for his run.

I turned around and nearly screamed at the figure standing by the closet. It was Vivian, the mannequin that I should've trashed weeks ago, but didn't. It seemed like a waste of a perfectly planned heist, and leaving her on the curb might incriminate me somehow.

As of late, I'd been in the habit of dressing her up and

talking to her. She was a pretty good listener, but now she seemed to be watching me and judging me with her blank stare.

I crawled back into bed. My day didn't start for hours. That was one good thing about being homeschooled—I didn't have to get up early. When I finally awoke at noon, I squashed all thoughts of Liam McPherson and focused on my academic future.

I signed up for the online course my counselor recommended and I was starting to get into the rhythm of my work routine. Every lesson came with a new assignment and daily quizzes that would be sent to my instructor at Serenity Health. I swear, I spent more time in that building than in my actual home. My tutoring periods ran three hours every Tuesday and Thursday, followed by an hour therapy session with Dr. Kavanagh each Friday. Juggling appointments with a neurologist, a psychologist, and a personal instructor—I needed to install an app on my phone just to keep track of them all.

As for schoolwork, all I had to do was roll over, open my laptop, log in to my student account, and watch the online course of the day. If I had a question, I would just rewind the tutorial video. No books, no pencils, just a keyboard and high-speed Internet service, and I would be caught up in no time. Hauling bulky textbooks around like a pack mule wasn't something I missed about school. But I did miss the activity, the chatter between classes, outrunning the bell, and the mad dash to finish last-minute homework. Public school left plenty to be desired, but it gave you a reason to get up in the morning. It gave you someone to talk to.

On the up side, I could do all my assignments in bed without brushing my teeth or fretting about wearing the same outfit to school two days in a row. I could eat during the lessons, even though the menu selection in my house was grim, and I could work at my own pace. I wondered why my parents didn't have me homeschooled before—it definitely had its benefits.

"What do you mean I'm failing?" I shrieked, slamming my hand on the table in outrage.

Denise, my instructor, consulted the printout of my weekly report and frowned. "Well, it says here you scored poorly on the reading comprehension and math section. Now we need to assess if you're able to attain knowledge or if you have difficulty with test taking in general," she said. "Relax, Ellia. We'll figure this out."

We were in the learning center on the fifth floor, which was basically a large gray room full of cubicles, computers, and tables. The area stayed packed in the afternoons, each round table occupied by the autistic, dyslexic, bipolar, and learning deficient patients with their assigned tutors.

Denise was a blond, twenty-something grad student who was working on her PhD in child psychology. All dimples and smiles, she had the bright-eyed optimism that none of the counselors here seemed to have. She didn't treat me like a number, so I liked her.

Denise handed me a worksheet. "I'll give you thirty minutes to complete the assignment and we can work from there. I'll be back in a bit." She stood up from her seat and left for her routine coffee refill and smoke break.

The entire facility was nonsmoking, so she had to get her fix in her car. I wasn't sure if that sort of thing was prohibited by the staff, but whatever. She didn't baby me or hover, and I appreciated the freedom to do my own thing. If I needed help, I'd just text her to come back.

As the minutes crawled by and my attention began to lag, I was tempted to do just that. Equation solving was not my thing and I could only register the letters and symbols on the paper. The hypnotic blur of text weighed my eyelids down. Top it off with my complete disinterest in word problems, and my brain was out to lunch.

I put my head down on the table and let out a heavy and very loud sigh.

"What's wrong now?" A familiar voice came from my right.

I turned around and saw Cody sitting at one of the cubicles, his chair balancing on two legs as he leaned back. Placing his hands behind his head, he reclined with a sandaled foot draped over his right knee and his headphones hanging around his neck.

I pointed an accusing finger to my worksheet. "This! This is what's wrong. It's sorcery, I tell you, with tricky wording and numeric voodoo."

"Uh-huh." He stood up and came to my side. "Want me to help?"

"Sure." I scooted toward the window to give him room.

He pulled out a chair next to me, searching the area for prying adults. "Algebra One."

"Yeah. It might as well be Sanskrit or some other dead language," I griped. "Why do we have to learn all this stuff anyway? How will this benefit me in the workplace?"

He scratched the stubble on his chin. "Well, rumor has it that a high school diploma comes in handy during job interviews, so . . ."

"I mean the classes," I clarified. "High school should be about real life. Teach us stuff like how to pay a bill, or how to write a resume, or how to fold laundry. You know, something useful."

"I think that's what college is for." He snatched the pencil from my hand and began to jot digits on the page. "It's pretty simple, but the way the instructors tell you isn't always the best solution."

His explanation went in one ear and out the other. I was more captivated by his enthusiasm than his math skills.

Cody's recovery was fascinating to not just me but the entire staff here. His issue was with declarative memory, dealing with events and fact collecting. He was able to learn quickly, acquire new skills and do complex tasks, but would have *no idea* how he did it.

Last week, he showed me videos of him playing classical guitar. His fingers strummed in perfect harmony, yet he was clueless about whether he'd ever took a single lesson, or what the chords meant, or the name of the song. Doing the same thing over and over again made his actions habitual, an instinct that didn't require deliberate thought. This was what he meant by *repetition*.

Cody relied heavily on his phone to keep track of info. He had several ringtones and beeps to remind him of when to take his medication or when to call his parents. He was even allowed to drive with the aid of an interactive GPS. He also had organizing software on his home computer that gave him hourly updates. Everything had to be preprogramed and scheduled ahead of time in order for him to function in daily life. Aside from the hourly recap, he was just a kid, fully aware of what was going on, but not knowing how things got that way. Then again, weren't we all?

Which was why I asked, "What does it feel like to lose your memory?"

He paused to look at me. "I don't know what you mean. What is it supposed to feel like?"

"Well, what's the last thing you remember?"

He searched the ceiling for insight. "I remember the ocean water and the sound of the waves and the feeling of being dragged down and not being able to reach the surface and then . . . I'm sitting here doing math problems with . . ." He looked at me.

"Ellia. We have the same tutoring times every Thursday. We've been in this room for about an hour. And we've been talking for about ten minutes," I explained, knowing the drill already.

Cody frowned as he processed the new information. "Really? What are you here for?"

Another thing I'd learned was that his short-term memory didn't zap out completely, but gradually dissolved within the hour, like a waning dream that you could only remember the tail end of. The problem for Cody was that he kept "waking up" about twenty times a day. The mind was a scary and fragile thing; I couldn't imagine living my life from minute to minute the way he did. Cool in theory, but a complete mess in practice.

"Check your notes. Filed under: therapy session, patient, hot girl, Jason Bourne."

We'd hung out for two weeks and I already knew how he organized the notes on his phone. Instead of repeating the story all over again, I'd just direct him to it and he could catch up on what was happening. He had about two pages' worth of data on our interactions—the questions he'd asked before and little inside jokes.

As more details about me piled up on his phone, I'd assembled a mental fact sheet of my own. Cody was a Gemini, a music nerd, and an avid fan of flip-flops and vintage tees. The boy practically had gills, so a near-drowning experience wouldn't keep him out of the water or from following his dream to become a marine biologist. He worshipped his older brother, who was a kickboxing champion who tried to get into Hollywood stunt work.

"Okay, so it says here that you have a boyfriend, but not really," he reported while scrolling down the list on his phone.

I cut my eyes at him. "Seriously? That's the first thing you ask me?"

"Hey, I'm an amnesiac, not dead," he replied in his defense. His brown eyes twinkled with a humor that I found contagious. "So tell me, what is this guy like?"

My focus drifted to the window, not really seeing anything but the image of Liam in my head. One had to be blind, deaf, and dumb to find him unattractive, and I held the same admiration of him as one would for a Van Gogh painting. It's beautiful, weird, and made a great conversation piece, but there was no way I'd take the real thing home. And since I didn't know much else about Liam, appearance was all I had to offer for discussion.

"He's tall, cute, smart, athletic . . ." I paused at the sound of snoring next to me. I looked over to Cody, who pretended to nod off.

"*Boring,*" he sang.

"*Jealous*," I sang back.

"A little," he admitted. "But I want to know real stuff."

"Like what?"

"Does he make you happy?"

"I guess." I avoided Cody's dubious look and said, "We're taking things slow."

"You don't seem like a 'take it slow' kind of girl. You come off as a girl who would jump in with both feet."

"How would you know what kind of girlfriend I'd be?"

"Wishful thinking, I guess," he said. "Am I wrong?"

I had to think about that for a second. "The sad part is that I can't even answer that. I've never had a serious boyfriend before so I don't know what to expect. I haven't even kissed him and the only play I've gotten since I woke up was making out with a snack machine." I chuckled to myself.

Cody seemed thrown off by the comment. "What?"

At first, I thought he was joking, but he seemed genuinely confused. "The snack machine in the hall. That's where we met." I referred him back to the notes on his phone.

"Really?" He broke into a fit of laughter. "Wow! And I thought I had issues."

I glared at him as he poked fun at my expense all over again, or in his case, for the first time. I could've given him a fake name and spared myself the repeated embarrassment. I could've been several different people throughout the day and he wouldn't have known the difference. But I hated being lied to as much as he did. Trust was a hard skill to master as an amnesiac because you had to rely on it so much from others.

Cody kept looking at his digital notes. When he reached the section about my likes and dislikes, he nearly leapt from his seat in rage. "What do you mean you don't like roller coasters?" He showed me the passage, demanding a reason for such blasphemy.

I shrugged. "I just don't."

"But why?" he whined. "They're awesome."

"The same reason I don't like scary movies. I'm not going to pay hard-earned money for someone to give me nightmares. There are enough scary things in the world—why provoke fear? Same goes for books that make me cry. Can't do it. It's best to not even go there."

He watched me carefully. "Sounds like you don't want to feel anything."

"I just want to control how much power emotions have over me, be it other people's or my own. It's like chain letters. Bogus or not, there's that little twinge of doubt that wrecks your whole mood, just because you're aware that it exists."

"So ignorance is bliss with you, huh?" He sucked his teeth in disapproval. "I can't live my life with my head in the sand. I'd have to do something."

I shook my head and frowned. "Some actions can get you in trouble, as you probably know."

"Part of the fun," he offered.

"Is it? Let's say you witness a violent crime. What do you do? If you try and stop it, you could get hurt. If you report it, someone might come after you. If you do nothing, someone else could get hurt and you're now an accomplice to the crime. I don't want to be held accountable for someone else's reality. Sometimes it's best not ever knowing."

He searched my face for a long time. "As an expert in 'I don't know,' reality is a luxury item. Knowledge is like money. You only need a little bit to survive, but you should always strive for more. And at one point, whether you want to or not, curiosity will make you greedy. It's what makes us human. It's what makes us alive."

Though I didn't agree, I admired his conviction and I found myself leaning close to him until our elbows touched. "You're a very interesting person, Dory," I said.

A smile appeared at the nickname, but it quickly fell when Cody spotted something over my shoulder. "Oops! Grown-up alert." He shot up from the chair and hurried back to his cubicle.

"Okay, thanks. I'll meet up with you after I'm done," I called after him.

"Sure," he said, then vanished from sight.

Only half of the worksheet was done when Denise returned, but at least I felt better than when the session started. I still had no idea what I was doing, but I was comfortable here. No one knew who I was, and, most of all, no one cared who I dated or what I did that one time at band camp and so on. I was anonymous. I could be anyone.

Another hour and a folder full of homework later, I met up with Cody by the elevators. He was once again zeroed in on his phone, so I snuck up on him from behind and tickled his rib. "Hey, you."

"Hey, yourself." His lips pulled into an awkward and timid grin. "You coming or going?"

"Definitely going," I said, and stepped inside the elevator with him. And for the third time today I repeated my name and directed him toward his notes.

I was sure this ritual would drive anyone else crazy, but it proved to be a much-needed exercise in patience and understanding. It could take months or even years, but these trivial short-term memories would eventually become long-term for him, and I enjoyed being someone who was worth remembering.

I waited for Cody to get rebriefed on our past before asking, "You good?"

He nodded. "So Jason Bourne, huh? Makes me want to watch the movies again."

"Did you know there are almost a hundred movies based on characters with amnesia?" I asked.

His brows lifted in surprise. "I didn't know that. I know

they do it a lot in soap operas. That and the evil-twin-switched-at-birth thing."

"I know, right? It's awful. You would think they would know what amnesia was really like. So anyway, there was this one movie I saw on Netflix last week about this vigilante with amnesia, like the kind you have, and he goes on this killing spree to avenge his dead family then comes to find out he was the one who killed them," I said as we stepped out of the elevator.

He grimaced. "Heartwarming."

"Yup. A time-honored tale of family dysfunction and mass murder."

He shook his head, but at least he was smiling. "There is something seriously wrong with you."

I was about to respond when I saw someone waiting.

And once I recognized who it was, I stopped walking.

CHAPTER
ELEVEN

LIAM

My history with hospitals ran the gamut of uncomfortable to excruciating. No happy memories accompanied glaring fluorescent lights, the snap of rubber gloves, or the smell of alcohol wipes. Just restraint, pain, and an absurd amount of waiting.

My earliest memories involved restraint—my mother's hands pulling me back to my seat or pressing my arms to my sides to keep me from reaching for something breakable. Dad's arms would hold me still while needles pricked my chubby arms and threaded seams into my torn skin.

The pain portion of my doctor visits came in various flavors for a rambunctious child who loved to climb. I had so many skinned knees, sprains, and bloody noses, it was a wonder my parents weren't reported for child abuse. I'd carried every strain of flu known to science and the number of doctor visits rivaled my school attendance.

But waiting was by far the worst. Waiting to get called to the back room, for the doctor to show up, for test results to come back negative. Waiting meant standing still, and it's been established already that that wasn't something I did well. That impatience, that reflexive need to act was what brought me here in the first place. And now I was in my least favorite setting in the world doing my least favorite activity. Waiting.

The theory was simple: This was neutral territory. This wasn't Mercy General, where she was taken that day, so I was spared from reliving that trauma. This was something else altogether, though the antiseptic white floors and ceiling still applied.

The space was open with a bunch of windows, a showroom for rare tropical plants and boxy modern furniture. A giant water fountain greeted visitors as soon as they entered the building. The sharply dressed lady at the front desk seemed better suited for a modeling agency than a hospital. If the lobby was this swank, I could only imagine the layout on the upper floors.

According to Stacey, this was where Ellia spent her Thursday afternoons between 2:00 and 5:30. I didn't know which floor she was on and the wall directory looked like a map of the Pentagon outlined in braille, so I decided to sit in the lobby.

The plan was to catch Ellia on the way out, maybe give her a ride home if she needed one, though given the way her family had her under lock and key, that wouldn't be an option. It was high risk just being here.

I hadn't quite worked out what to say to her yet, though I knew a great deal of groveling would be involved. Making it to *this* part of my plan had been my key focus, but now I had to face the real challenge. My words, my tone of voice had to be both sincere and direct, leaving no room for misinterpretation. Rehearsing all the reasons for us to try again kept me occupied during the wait, but did nothing for the flip-flopping in my stomach.

At 5:30 on the nose, I saw her emerge from the elevator. She was wearing her lounge-around, be-happy-I-bothered-to-show-up yoga pants and a blue sweater that hung off her body in a way that made me worry about her diet. Was she eating right? Was she taking care of herself?

But immediately I had other concerns. Like: Who was the guy walking with her? And why were they laughing like they'd been buds for years? The guy was skinny, average height, with brown hair that did that swoop thing so I couldn't see his eyes. He had a natural tan, so he wasn't allergic to the outdoors. He was probably in a band or something equally obnoxious, and, more importantly, he seemed way too interested in whatever Ellia had to say.

Somehow, seeing them together made my visit that much more inappropriate. But I hadn't come this far to back out now. So it made perfect sense, at least in my mind, to step in and break up this little powwow.

My approach could use a bit more work, though. They barely made it past the front desk when I swooped in on the scene. Ellia jumped back a step and got out a "Liam, what are you—" before I pulled her to me, cupped her face in my hands, and brought my lips to her mouth.

Maybe it was my inflated ego that assumed a single kiss from her prince would break the spell and her memories would suddenly come flooding back. But the simple need to kiss her, just one more time, had my brain on autopilot again.

Her lips were as soft as I remembered and as she kissed me back, she tasted like Sprite and Sour Patch candy. Her hands slid up my arms, not to push me away, but to hold me in place. In that moment, nothing else mattered—not the memory loss, not the people standing in the lobby or the boy at our side taking pictures on his phone. Holding her again made me realize just how long we'd been apart. I'd missed her in all tenses: past, present, and future. And now that she was in my orbit again, I wasted no time showing her how the separation affected me. Privacy was out of the question and breathing was simply an afterthought. It was about us, just as it was before and just as it should be. Whatever the reasoning I had before the kiss no longer mattered, and I regretted nothing.

We pulled apart and stared at each other. Her eyes were half-hooded and sleepy as she whispered the rest of her question, ". . . doing here?"

"It's pretty obvious, don't you think?"

She must've remembered where we were and what we were doing because she leapt back in a start. "You mind telling me what that was?"

"A greeting."

She frowned. "Most people just say hi."

"I know. I, um, wanted to go for something a little more personal."

She frowned, and I could feel the magic of the kiss fading. "By invading my personal space?"

"By doing something I should've done weeks ago." My words poured out in a ramble. "I kept my distance and gave you time to adapt to everything around you, but I can't just sit around and wait for you to come to me. I had to do something."

"Why come here instead of just going to my house?" Ellia demanded. "You obviously know where I live—and how did you know I was here?" She began looking around for witnesses.

"Stacey told me," I confessed with embarrassment. "Don't be mad. I practically begged her to give me the information."

"I can't believe her!" she raved, throwing up her hands. "I didn't want anyone to know about this and she goes running off at the mouth to you, of all people."

I reared back. "What do you mean 'of all people'?"

Before she could answer, the boy stepped in and touched her arm. "This guy bothering you?"

"Now why would her *boyfriend* bother her?" I stressed the word.

"Really subtle, bro," he murmured then turned back to Ellia. "So this is the guy?"

She nodded.

I got right in his face, my mind busy with ways on how I could rearrange it. "You got a problem, man?"

He didn't even flinch. "No, but she apparently does."

Ellia stepped between us. "How about we not do this here? Go on, Cody. I'll catch you later," she told the boy next to us.

The guy's name was Cody? Really? Where's the surfboard?

"You sure?" he asked, ready to step in if needed. He had about five seconds to leave before my foot made contact with his solar plexus.

"I'm fine. I'll see you next week." She waved him off.

When he walked away—at a glacial pace, I might add—she turned to me. I tipped my head in the direction of the other guy. "What's up with the Code-meister? You guys look awfully chummy. Is it serious?"

"I'm not even gonna dignify that with an answer, so I'm just gonna turn my back to you and walk away. Observe." She headed toward the main doors, but I caught her by the arm.

"Look, I know what my dad said was messed up, but it's not what you think."

She snatched her arm back and rounded on me in fury. "Just stop, okay? I'm not your little revenge pawn!"

I came equipped with a litany of "I'm sorry" and "it'll never happen again," but the comment threw me into left field. "What are you talking about?"

Ellia crossed her arms and pushed out her hip. "Were you going out with me because of your parents?"

I still wasn't tracking. "My parents?"

"You're bitter about your parents splitting and you wanted to hurt your dad by dating someone like me."

"No, that's not true at all. I went out with you because you were awesome, and because you were kind enough to let me," I replied. "My dad has nothing to do with us."

She searched my eyes, seeking honesty, but then gave up. "I'm getting two different stories and I don't know what to believe anymore. I have enough on my plate as it is. Just leave me alone and don't show up like this again. Oh, and one more thing." She grabbed a fistful of my shirt then pulled me closer until we were nose to nose. "I wasn't here. You didn't see me."

At first glance, her eyes were brown, almost black. But up close, undertones of red filled the irises with a warmth that had always reminded me of a luxurious dessert. Barely an inch of air separated my lips from hers—pillow-soft and stripped bare of gloss, they held a sweetness I could still taste.

Wait, what were we talking about?

"I'm not going to tell anyone," I said once it dawned on me.

"You better not or I swear . . ." She sucked in a long breath, conjuring composure. Finally, she let go of my shirt.

I noticed that the rumpled material in the center of my chest still held the shape of her fist. "Why do you care who sees or doesn't see you?"

"Because I'm not a freak!" she gritted out. "You should see some of the people that come here. The third floor is for recovering drug addicts and you can hear them screaming from the elevator. The fourth floor is for the regular crazy and the second floor is for the *old* and crazy."

"Are there people here who paint the walls with their own fecal matter?" I asked, amused and more intrigued than I probably should be.

"No. Those kind go to the psychiatric hospital across town. This place is for people who can function in society but need a little help."

"I'm still not seeing why this needs to be a big secret."

"Because few people know the difference!" she snapped. "And now you know, and there's no telling who else in school knows that I'm a nutcase who can't remember how to do algebra."

When she tried to step around me, I blocked her path. I held her by both of her shoulders and stooped down to look her in the eye. "Hey, hey. Calm down. I'm not going to tell and neither is Stacey. I promise."

That seemed to give her some relief. She nodded, the muscles in her shoulders loosening under my hand.

"Don't let the therapy get to you. I had to go as a kid," I confessed. She knew this already—well, the old Ellia did. But obviously, this new Ellia didn't remember.

"Really? Why?" she asked.

"I was hyper. Had to take a ton of Ritalin. Anyway, this one doctor was a total windbag. He thought I had some sort of Oedipus complex because I was closer to my mom than my dad, and I was like, 'Dude, can't I just have a favorite? I relate more to her because she's nicer and she does my laundry. Don't read too much into it.'"

Ellia wrinkled her nose. "So this guy thought you had the hots for your mom?"

I nodded. "Yeah. The whole Oedipus thing is kind of misplaced," I said, thinking out loud. "I mean, according to the play, King Oedipus was real cocky about his epic wisdom, yet it took a team of advisors to figure out that he was adopted. He also didn't know that the guy he killed years ago was his real dad or that the woman he married afterward was his mom. He didn't take the news well, what with the whole eye-gouging thing and all. So the *real* Oedipus complex isn't freaky family issues. It's claiming to be wise when you don't know the first thing about yourself."

"In that case, I think we all have that," she said thoughtfully. "Do you normally do this?"

"Do what?"

"Go off on tangents and spit out random information."

I smiled at that. "That's how I got you to go out with me."

"Oh yeah? Do tell."

"Maybe some other time. So, back to you and your school-work," I began. "If you need catching up, I can tutor you."

Her eyes grew wider and shimmered with hope. "Really?"

I felt a rush of hope myself. "Sure. We can meet up at the public library after school. What subjects are you having trouble with?"

"Math, History, and English."

I looked skyward and laughed to myself. It still wasn't a song with our names, but fate was definitely at work here.

"What's so funny?" she asked.

"I happen to be in advanced placement classes for all three of those subjects. So I'm perfect for you." The statement came out with more meaning than I intended it to, and that fact didn't go unnoticed by Ellia.

She made a face at me then began a slow stroll to the exit again. "Okay, we can try and do something this weekend. Let's say Saturday at one. You can pick me up."

Whoa! Bad idea. I had to think fast. "Um . . . better yet, why don't I pick you up at Stacey's house?"

"What's wrong with my house?"

Oh, nothing. It's a lovely home—except for the grown-ups who live there. "I don't want to upset anyone by showing up."

She waited for a follow-up to that answer. When none came, she asked, "My folks don't like you, do they? They know that we dated, but they never talk about you."

I nodded. "Yeah, well, there's a reason for that."

"Why? You saved my life."

"Because they still hate me. Our dads had it out the one time we stayed out late and your dad threatened to call the cops if I came near you again. And then after the accident, *my* dad freaked out and that's why he doesn't want me around *you people*—as in, *your family*."

"Oh." Ellia paused, biting her lip, and then her mouth dropped open. "Oh my god! Are we in some secret forbidden romance that our folks don't approve of? The Montagues versus the Capulets? Crips versus Bloods? Vampires versus werewolves?"

"Not that bad," I said. "Your parents thought you could do better than someone like me."

"I'm sure I can, but that's up for me to decide, not them." She stared off for a moment, as if debating about what to do next. "Let's meet up at the park instead. I don't want to be cooped up inside. They've got picnic tables so we can work."

"Sounds like a plan. So do we have a date or what?" I asked, fighting a smile.

"I wouldn't go that far. It's just work. No touching, no kissing, no funny business. We'll see where it goes from there." I nodded, and she said, "I'd better go before my mom comes inside. Later."

"Was the kiss bad?" I called after her.

Her head whipped in my direction. "I didn't say that."

I did a little victory dance in my head. "So it was good?"

"Good or bad, it was unwelcomed. Don't do it again."

The demand was sharp, but lacked the sting that came with her anger. She could deny it all she wanted, but the kiss had been potent. Still, I didn't want to scare her or risk losing the ground I'd gained.

"I promise. From now on, I'll let you initiate the kissing and anything else you have in mind. You don't even have to ask. Just go for it."

She held my gaze for a long time, gauging my sincerity. "Good to know." She waved and made her way to the main doors.

I spent the rest of that afternoon in my room, tapping away at my computer. Seeing Ellia again left me oddly inspired, and I had to ride that wave of creativity before it passed.

Unfortunately, Wade busted into my room without knocking. I could've kicked myself for not locking the door.

"Hey, Liam! Your mom called," he announced.

"Tell her I'll call her later," I replied without looking up.

"I wouldn't have to do that if you answered your cell phone," he said.

"Whatever. Too busy to chat. She should know what that's like."

Wade didn't bother to touch that one, so he got to the real reason he entered my room. "You using the car tonight?"

"Nope. Go ahead." I waved him away, hoping he would leave.

"Whatcha working on?" he asked.

"Something for school," I lied. "Make sure you fill the tank back up when you're done."

"Don't I always?"

The idiocy of the question was enough to force me to stop typing and turn around to shoot daggers at him. I immediately regretted it, because he stood in the doorway wearing nothing but a very small towel. "Jeez, man! Put some clothes on, will ya?"

"What? I like to air-dry." He grinned and wiggled a Q-tip into his left ear.

He was going hardcore with the hygiene and aftershave, so I assumed he had a date. It was good to see him competing in the dating Olympics again. The problem was that Wade wanted the real deal, not just some fly-by-night fling like he had with what's-her-face. He'd never admit it, but back before the accident, I'd see the longing in his eyes whenever Ellia and I were together. My girl wasn't what he coveted, but the relationship itself.

"Who's the unfortunate victim?" I asked him.

Wade flicked the Q-tip into my trash can next to my bed. His perfect aim was the only reason he was allowed to keep breathing. "If you must know, it's Kendra Bailey. We hit it off at the Valentine's dance, so we're gonna hang out tonight on the promenade; maybe see a movie."

I did a double take. "Really? *Kendra?*"

He stood up straight at my response. "What? She's cute."

"Adorable," I agreed. "But so are puppies and five-year-olds. And no offense, but you don't seem like the nurturing type."

"So what advice can you give me?" He leaned against the door frame and crossed his legs. "What's it like dating a black girl?"

"The same as any other girl," I replied with disparagement. "You'll have differences, but don't make it a mission to point them all out. Don't undermine her social views simply because they don't line up with yours. Ask questions, listen and learn, but most of all: Be *yourself.* Don't act fake or talk in a certain way to be 'relatable.' You'll just look stupid. And switch colognes. You smell like a tire shop."

To my surprise, he was actually listening. And if my eyes weren't deceiving me, he appeared nervous. He'd been rubbing sweaty palms onto his towel and fidgeting with his wet hair through this entire dating seminar.

"So I should just be . . . *myself?*" he asked.

"Yeah." Why was this such a hard concept to grasp?

Although, I acted the same way when I started crushing on Ellia. I spent an entire weekend watching movies and TV shows so we'd have stuff to talk about. That Monday, I went to her locker, excited to share what I discovered. It took three days and numerous unanswered phone calls to realize just how stupid and out of touch I really was. It was a painful lesson I learned quickly, and if I could spare someone else that kind of embarrassment then it was worth it.

"Just be yourself, Wade," I told him again. "Adding anything else insults you both. Trust me."

He nodded. "All right. But if this date tanks, then I'm coming after you."

"Oh no. I have soiled myself for fear of your impending vengeance," I replied in a flat tone, then turned back to my desk. "Now would you please put some clothes on? I'm going blind over here."

"Jealousy is an ugly emotion, nephew," he said before a damp cloth landed on my head, blocking my view from the computer screen. Roguish laughter drifted out of the room as the door closed behind me.

Shuddering at the thought of where the towel had just been, I plucked it off with the tips of my fingers and flung it across the room. I pushed my plot for revenge to the side, and dove back into my story. Without meaning to, Wade had actually reminded me of something I'd wanted to write about: my first date with Ellia.

UNTITLED | Page 40

It was times like these I wished I owned a car. Granted, one newly fixed, thirty-year-old relic waited for me in the garage with my name on it, but I couldn't legally drive it for another year. This didn't help in the dating department. As I rode shotgun in Dad's Blazer to

Cape Plaza, I considered cancelling all social gatherings until my sixteenth birthday.

Everyone hung out at what was locally known as "the Plaza" on the weekends. It was one of those town centers that just popped up out of nowhere with shops, cafes, and a cool laser tag arcade. I was to meet Ellia in front of the multiplex. Since I spent most of the homecoming dance people-watching by the wall, we hadn't had much time together. Her countless friends kept pulling her aside to talk and I kept stepping on her feet whenever she dragged me onto the dance floor. Staring at a giant monitor in the dark would cause the least damage, and she agreed on meeting up alone. No chaperones. No third wheel.

"So what time does the movie end?" Before I could answer, Dad said, "'Cause I expect you to be standing out here by eleven thirty."

I pointed to the ice cream parlor on the corner. "Can you drop me off here?"

The shop rolled past my window as he asked, "Why? They've got a drop zone right in front."

"I know." I sunk down in my seat. The man couldn't have been this out of the loop. Apparently he was, because he not only pulled up in front of the movie theater, he leaned over my seat to peep at my date.

"Is that her?" Dad pointed to the girl sitting by the water fountain. "She's pretty." He had the audacity to wave.

"Yeah, that's Ellia." If I sank any lower in my seat, I would've been on the floor. I had to make a run for it.

I opened my door and barreled out of the truck, unaware of the automatic seat belt across my chest. My legs kicked from under me and I fell flat on my butt. My hands tugged at the killer strap at my throat while I sprawled halfway in and out of the car. Worst of all, Ellia was staring right at me. She looked concerned and rose to her feet to assist in my humiliation.

No, don't help me; just let me die here on the curb.

"Real smooth, son. You've definitely got the McPherson swagger." Dad chuckled menacingly behind me, and for a brief second I thought he was going to take off with me halfway in the truck. Finally, I was able to wiggle free. I stood up, straightened my clothes, and smoothed back my hair just as Ellia approached.

She wore tight blue jeans and a matching fur-lined jacket. She regarded me and then the death trap on wheels. "You a'ight?"

"Yeah. I'm good. Childproof locks, you know?" I glanced behind me and saw Dad still parked on the curb with the engine running. I tried to shoo him off, but he kept grinning and gave me a thumbs-up.

"Is that your dad?" She stooped down and waved at the lunatic in the window.

I turned away from the Blazer, denying its existence. If I didn't see it, the vehicle wasn't still sitting there. Very simple logic. "Nope. That's, um, someone else."

"Such a terrible liar." She smirked. "My dad dropped me off like five minutes ago. You just missed him. Relax, Liam. Stop trying to try. You just look silly." She hooked her arm in mine and I smiled. I

expected her to crack jokes or call me a loser, but she clung to my arm all the way to the ticket booth.

While waiting in line, I skimmed the movie titles on the screen behind the clerk. There was only one movie out that I was interested in seeing, but I decided to let Ellia take the lead. "So what movie did you want to see?"

"I was waiting on you," she replied.

"Oh. Okay." I scanned the list again. "We can see Mama Big Ton's Reunion.*"*

She unhooked her arm from mine and stepped in front of me. "Before this goes any further, there are some things you should know about me. I don't do lowbrow. Just because it's a black film, doesn't mean it's a good *black film. I'm not about to watch a guy in a fat woman suit making stupid fart jokes. I'm not that chick."*

This was useful information because I was flying blind, and last time I tried to be "down," she ignored me for a week.

"What about the one with the bank robbers?" I suggested, and I was floored by the smile on her face.

"Sure. I'm known for a little scheming myself." She winked at me then inched up the line when it began to move.

"Wait. It's an R-rated movie. We can't see it without an adult."

"Says who?" she said then stepped to the guy in the ticket booth. He had straight, blue-black hair that covered one eye, a lip and nose piercing, and tattoos running along his arms. He looked in his early twenties, maybe a college student.

Ellia smiled at him. "Hey, Squid."

"Hey, El." He tipped his head. "I'm still waiting for that date."

"And I'm still waiting for that to be appropriate," she quipped and slid the money through the ticket window. "Two for The Counterfeit Game, *please." When he started to protest, she added, "Come on. Just this once."*

"You said that the last three times," he grumbled then printed out the tickets anyway.

I had a ton of questions and I was more than certain Squid wasn't that guy's real name, though his name tag suggested otherwise.

With a smile and a wink to the clerk, Ellia collected our tickets and headed toward the theater entrance.

I dashed in front of her to open the door. "Who was *that?"*

She glanced back at the booth then replied, "That was Danny. He graduated from León two years ago. Everybody calls him Squid."

"Why?"

"You didn't see all the ink on his arms?" she asked then slipped through the opened door.

It took a minute, but it finally dawned on me. "Oh! I get it. Tattoos. Ink. Squid."

I shouldn't have been surprised. Even people who didn't go to León had at least heard about Ellia Dawson, and I found all the hype to be a bit intimidating.

"So he's a friend?" I asked her on our way to the lobby.

"Yup."

"You have a lot of those," I noted.

"I know," she agreed then paused to look up at me. "But very few remain that way."

There was something kind of sad about that statement, but she didn't elaborate.

A giant bucket of popcorn and two fountain drinks later, we claimed a pair of seats in the middle row of a semipacked theater. By the time the trailers appeared on the screen, I came to the sound conclusion that I was falling for this girl. Ellia didn't do the dainty thing with her food; she shoveled handfuls of popcorn in her mouth. She took charge of the drinks selection and had the Sprite/fruit punch ratio down to a science. Her scent alone—clean and fruity—had me seeing stars.

The plot of the movie was pretty standard: The ex-con who tried to go legit was pressured to do one last job to save his kidnapped girlfriend. The dialogue was atrocious, the acting was even worse, but the stunts were top rate. It was an R movie, so I knew there would be some sort of love scene thrown in for no reason.

When the soft music played and the actors got that look in their eyes, I suddenly found the walls and floor particularly fascinating. Unable to take the tension, I headed for the bathroom.

My butt had barely vacated the seat when Ellia whispered, "You do that, too?"

I paused mid-row scoot. "Do what?"

"Mush dodging," she whispered, then took a sip of her drink. "Whenever you're watching a movie with other people and a love

scene comes on, you take a bathroom break, fast forward, or mess around with your phone—anything to avoid the awkwardness."

So true, but what did a person say to that? I went with, "Umm."

"Don't feel bad. I do it, too, especially when I'm watching a show with my parents. Come sit back down. I got an idea."

I couldn't just stand in the middle of the row, blocking the screen, so I slowly and reluctantly obeyed.

She dug in her pocket then pulled a ten-dollar bill from her wallet. "We're gonna sit and watch this entire scene. No flinching, no looking away, and the first person to break out in laughter loses ten bucks. Deal?"

"Deal." I settled back into the seat and waited for the movie to do its worst. I didn't wait long—as I said, the plot was standard.

The couple kissed on screen. The music swelled. And the awkwardness climbed to new heights. From the corner of my eye, I saw Ellia bunching her lips together and shuddering from suppressed amusement.

"Why is this so weird?" Her voice sounded strained as she tried not to giggle.

"I don't know. It just is."

Out of nowhere, her hands took hold of my face and pulled it to hers. The next thing I knew, our mouths collided in an atomic blast that scattered all the molecules in my body. Her lips, soft and full, pulled me in. Our heads turned, our noses mashed together as we tailored our mouths to that perfect fit.

When we pulled away, the scene had ended, but I was more

interested in the one offscreen. Ellia's eyes shimmered in the dark as she smiled back at me.

"You cheated," I whispered.

"I'm a sore loser. Sue me." She pecked my nose.

We laughed nervously, giddy and uncertain of what to do next. This time I took the lead. I pushed the armrest aside and scooted closer. Her arms wrapped around my neck and her lips met mine with an impatience that took my breath away.

I'd lost all interest in the movie. I had no idea how it ended or who died. We had our own show playing out and we made it just in time to catch the beginning. I didn't want to miss a single minute.

ELLIA

Pacing the floor, biting my nails, and changing my outfit for the third time did *nada* to preoccupy me. I was supposed to meet Liam in twenty minutes, and this countdown to doomsday had me sweating bullets and applying an extra coat of deodorant. I searched around my room for a solution, an exit, a weapon, but the only options were discarded clothes and art supplies.

I glanced at Vivian. I'd dressed her in a peasant blouse and skirt with a beaded emerald sash around her waist. I was going for a gypsy fortune-teller look, but she couldn't predict how this day would go, either. I looked away.

I grabbed a backpack that was gathering dust in my closet and shoved folders and all of the notes I would need inside. With my stuff packed, I went downstairs and found Mom in the living room surrounded by magazines and swatches of black-and-white fabric. Her latest clients were really into *Alice in Wonderland* and they wanted their living room to resemble a chessboard. Mom was up for the challenge. She once remodeled an entire house to be an exact replica of that ship from *Star Trek*. The woman had mad skills.

"And where do you think you're going?" Mom asked.

She also had eyes in the back of her head. I couldn't prove it, but I knew they were there underneath all those curls. Her voice stopped me in the foyer, my hand wrapped around the doorknob. I was so close.

Once I set foot into the living room, the interrogation began. Where was I going, and why? Who was I seeing, and why?

I replied with my carefully rehearsed answers. Liam wanted to keep our study session a secret, and the way Mom and Dad clocked my every move, I agreed that was a good idea. Stacey was my go-to alibi and I'd already texted her about the situation in the event of Mom checking up on me.

Yes, I had a brain injury. Sure, my parents loved me and worried about my safety. Okay, my migraines could flare up while I was riding my bike and I could get run over by a garbage truck and die, but . . . could I at least *breathe*? I was fighting not just for my freedom, but for my sanity, so a little white lie was a small price to pay. I wasn't completely irresponsible—I packed extra pain meds and bottled water just in case.

Five minutes and a rundown of safety measures later, I was in the fresh air on my bike heading to the park. As I approached the end of the street, the layout of the playground came into view. Cape Park hid under a shade of trees, designed like a rustic 4-H club. Everything was made out of wood, iron, and dirt and bordered by lined-up logs. Most days the park was packed with young'uns exploring the swings and jungle gym. Today was no different and the sight helped me to recall my own hatching season, back when I was small, fragile, and ignorant of the dangers that came with knowledge.

Liam arrived a few moments after I did and apologized for being late because he had to borrow a bike from a friend. After we docked our rides in the bike rack, I marched across the sand toward the seesaws. I had hoped to get some swing action while I was here, but all four sets were occupied by urchins who hadn't yet been introduced to the notion of sharing.

Liam followed behind me and didn't speak until he took position on the other side of the seesaw. He swung a leg over the metal plank, dropped down, and adjusted his weight. As he gripped the handle, an image of a cowboy riding a mechanical bull popped into my head. He pushed the sandy hair from his eyes and squared his shoulders, determined to stay on this wild beast for longer than eight seconds.

He began the ride with a light spring of his feet. "I thought you needed help with schoolwork."

"I do, but I want to play for a few minutes first. It's been forever since I've done this and I kinda miss it."

"Me too," he agreed. "Nostalgia is good sometimes."

"In moderation."

He waited until I was airborne before saying, "Are you okay? You seem to have something on your mind."

"Why do you say that?" I asked.

"Other than the fact that you're still wearing your bike helmet? No reason."

My feet touched the ground and locked in place, stopping all motion. I patted the top of my head and sure enough, the dumb thing was still on. Mom wouldn't let me leave the house without wearing it. It was one of those "too little too late" safety precautions, as far as head injuries were concerned, but at least it covered my hair.

"I'm just making a fashion statement." I sucked in my cheeks in a pouty supermodel pose.

He offered a smile, not buying my reasoning at all. "Let me guess, you're self-conscious about your scar?"

"A bit," I admitted and was lifted to the air again, my stomach jumping a little from the takeoff.

"Well, FYI, you're drawing more attention wearing that thing than anything else." He saw me flinch then checked himself. "I'm sorry. I didn't mean it to come out like that—"

"Yeah, you did," I cut him off. "But whatever. I need to get used to people looking at me funny, right?"

"Hey, don't do that to yourself. You had an accident. It's not your fault."

"Who cares about fault? As my dad would say, *Blame is like your rear end and reflection. Seeing either always leaves you looking back.* I'm more worried about what's in front of me. And right now . . . the view is all messed up."

"How so?"

We seesawed in silence for a while as I worked up the courage to say what had been on my mind. I'd come to him last week for a reason, and I believed I'd get an honest response from him.

His sea-blue eyes watched from above and then from below, our gazes never meeting in the middle. Up and down. Up and down. No boy had looked at me with so much open and honest concern and it made me dislike the imbalance even more. We both carried enough weight to support the other, but one of us had to let go in order for the ride to continue. Up and down. Give and take.

Sick of the stalling, I drew in a breath then finally asked, "When we were together, did I ever tell you about Babette?"

Liam surveyed the playground for the answer. "Your first pet. Your only pet. She was a cocker spaniel, right? She died when you were fourteen."

"Yeah." It shouldn't have surprised me that he knew, but it did. "She was old and her heart grew too big for her body, and the vet put her to sleep so she wouldn't suffer. Seeing her sick hurt me more than her actual death. She was sluggish with a black tongue and too weak to eat. Dad wanted to buy another dog, but I couldn't do it; it was like I was betraying her memory.

Anyway, I woke up this morning and just started crying all over again." I swallowed hard. "That's been happening off and on for a couple weeks now and I'm not sure why. I loved that dog, but I should be over it by now, and I was wondering if I was still grieving before the accident?"

Liam shook his head. "You showed me pictures and you mentioned how sad it made you, but you seemed over it," he answered. "I never had a pet, so I wouldn't know how long the grief period should last."

"I figured as much." I noticed a little girl getting off the swings, and thoughts of climbing to new heights distracted me. I hoped Liam didn't mind waiting until another swing was available, because that one was mine! I got up from the seesaw—a bit too fast. Liam slammed to the ground with a loud *oomph*.

"Oh! Sorry. You okay?" I went to help him up, but he got to his feet on his own.

He slapped the sand off the back of his basketball shorts. "Yeah. Some warning would've been nice."

I walked backward toward the swing set. "My bad. Come on, let's get on—" I turned around and saw that my swing had been hijacked.

A chubby little boy sat smugly on the swing.

"Hey! I was next!" I snapped.

The kid cut me a look as if to say, ". . . and?" then kicked out his feet to gain momentum, spraying sand everywhere.

"I don't see your name on it," he retorted. Trash talk could be added to the brat's many charms as he was so kind to point out, "You look stupid with that helmet on."

"Well, you look stupid with that face on," I shot back.

"Ellia!" Liam called behind me, but I ignored him.

I had to step back before the kid kicked me, which was what he was aiming for. "Oh yeah? You're so ugly, you make onions cry."

Oh, it was on now. "You're so ugly, you have to trick-or-treat by phone."

"Ellia!" Liam yelled.

"What?" I snapped at him.

He watched me in abject horror. "The kid's like eight years old."

"He's gotta grow up sometime," I replied in my defense. "I'm just saying—what ever happened to respecting your elders?"

Liam grabbed my arm and led me to one of the park benches. "Come on. We'll just wait."

I was about to say something along the lines of "he started it," but that would only support Liam's case. I was being petty and lashing out at the wrong people, but that kid had it coming. So I plopped down on the wooden bench and sulked instead.

Liam sat next to me, the proximity making our height difference neck-strainingly obvious. "So what is this stuff about Babette? Why are you bringing her up now?" he asked.

"I think that's the point. I *should* be over it by now, but the pain feels fresh, like it just happened. The amnesia removed my memories, but it also removed the time it took to heal from that grief, and now I'm back at square one." I glanced at Liam. "Does that make sense?"

He nodded slowly.

"Kinda like with you," I continued. "You have all these fond, happy memories of me and you're back at square one, too. I gotta ask—were we in like-like with each other, or . . ."

"Madly in love?" he finished. When I nodded, he said, "I like to think we were."

That confused me. "You're not sure?"

"I know how I felt on my end, but . . ." His words trailed off and soured the air like a breeze at low tide. And best believe there was something awfully fishy about that answer.

I would never string a guy along and it's not because I was a good person. I was just lazy. Why act fake for months when it only took three seconds to say, "I'm not feeling you like that. Swerve." Seeing as I'd been with Liam for two years, we had to be on that what-would-our-babies-look-like? stage in our relationship. That alone was reason enough to explore this connection and see if there was anything left to salvage.

"Did I ever tell you that I loved you? Out loud? To your face?" I asked him.

Thankfully, he didn't have to think too hard about it. "Yeah. A few times. In fact, you were the one to say it first."

I felt my heart jump. *Oh.* "Then I meant it," I said softly. "I don't go flinging that word around willy-nilly. That word's a weapon that should only come out if you intend to use it."

I saw the smile that he tried to hide. This guy would suck at poker. "But that was then. How do you feel *now*?" he asked.

I battled with a combination of emotions: fear, confusion, anger, frustration, bereavement over a dog that died two years ago . . . but instead of going through all that, I grumbled, "I dunno."

"What do you want to feel?"

That was a strange question, refreshing even, and I gave him the best answer I could. "Safe."

My reply had him leaning closer. "So . . . you feel safe with me?"

"Ah, I wouldn't go that far," I was quick to let him know. "You're the same guy who conducts stakeouts in front of my house every morning. Yes, I watch you watching me. You're not slick."

He scrambled for an excuse. "I-I'm sorry. I wasn't trying to scare—"

"Liam, if I honestly thought you were a psycho ax murderer, I would've called the cops weeks ago and I wouldn't be sitting here with you now. I'll admit it was creepy at first, but now I get it."

His confused expression told me I needed to elaborate.

"When they put Babette to sleep, I closed myself off," I began. "I wouldn't talk about it to my parents, or even to Stacey.

But I turned the dog collar into a keychain. It jingled whenever I unlocked the front door, and I'd pretend it was Babette running to meet me when I came home. You watching my house is *your* dog-collar keychain, so I figured you could relate. Somehow I knew I could talk to you about this and you wouldn't over-analyze or give me stank-face."

"Not unless you actually stink, then we'd have to have a talk about hygiene." He leaned in and took a whiff. "You smell good though, like some peach lotion or body wash."

"I can't believe you just sniffed me." I playfully shoved his shoulder.

He playfully shoved me back. He wasn't a pushover and gave as good as he got. I liked that. I also appreciated his attempt to lighten the mood.

"Tell me something about us," I said.

His smile remained. "What do you want to know?"

"Let's start with something simple. Your birthday, your middle name, your shoe size, what our first date was like; who asked out who. Stuff like that."

Liam reclined in a way that was primed for a long discussion. His elbows rested on the back of the bench, his long fingers draped over the side and tapping absently on the wood. I noticed that he fidgeted a lot, a nervous sequence of knee bouncing and hair stroking.

The tapping picked up speed as Liam stared out into the yard. "Well, my birthday is January thirteenth. My middle name is

James. I'm a size eleven shoe, and *you* asked *me* out because I was too chicken to do it myself."

My gaze lifted from his twitchy fingers to his face. "Really?"

"Yeah, I was in P.E. running the mile and you ran up to me on the field and tackled me to the ground in front of everyone. You pinned me to the grass and said, 'Homecoming Dance. Friday. Be there. Wear something sexy.' Then you got up and left me lying stunned on the ground. I'd never been accosted by a girl before. It was awesome," he said with a far-off look in his eyes.

I drank in the information with a critical ear. "Yep, that sounds like something I would do."

"The weirdest part of all was that you didn't even have gym that period. I guess you got tired of waiting and sought me out," he added. "You're a straight shooter and you're not shy around boys."

That was true. I never really saw the point. It's not like boys were a different species.

"Well, thanks for answering my questions," I said. "It's weird. You're telling me things, but I can't even imagine them. It's like a punch line to a joke that everyone gets but me."

He tilted his head. "Would you feel better if I asked you questions?"

"You mean questions to stuff you already know?"

"Maybe I do and maybe I don't. But at least it'll feel like an even exchange of information."

It was worth a shot. I shifted on the bench so we were facing each other. Our knees touched and we underwent this strange dance where neither of us wanted to move away or else acknowledge the physical contact.

"Okay, let's start with a speed round of questions. Don't think—just answer as fast as you can," he instructed. "What's your favorite color?"

"Black. It's slimming and goes with everything," I answered.

"Mine's blue," he supplied. "What's your favorite ice cream flavor?"

"Vanilla. It's boring on its own, but you can mix it with anything and make it awesome."

He nodded in approval. "I'm a Cherry Garcia fan. What's your favorite book?"

"*Matilda.*"

"*The Shining* for me," he said. "Favorite school subject?"

"Lunch."

That got a chuckle out of him. "If you could live anywhere, where would it be?"

"The UK. It's foreign enough, but with no language barriers."

"I'd like to travel around the whole U.S. Each state is like its own little country." His eyes went to the top of my head. "Can I see it?"

The question came out of nowhere. "See what?"

"Your scar. You keep it covered up and I figured maybe if you showed it to someone you'd feel more relaxed."

I glared at him. "You just wanna see if it's as bad as people say."

"You say that as if that would scare me off," he said with a sincerity that could be both heard and felt. "Show me. Please?"

With shaky fingers, I unhooked the chin strap and lifted the helmet off my head. Next came the silk headband. I watched him cautiously, waiting for the first flinch of shock or scrunch of disgust in his features.

The hair on my left side was coming in nicely, although the few centimeters surrounding the incision may never grow back. The wound had closed and the stitches had begun to dissolve, leaving a crooked pleat of purple skin and dry scabs. When fluid needed to be drained from inside the skull and an inch of bone had to be reconstructed ASAP, aesthetics were the last thing on a surgeon's mind, so the scarring would be permanent. I might look like a comic-book villain now, but I had a family-size tub of cocoa butter at home that would be put to good use.

None of that seemed to faze Liam, though. His eyes roamed my face in quiet wonder. He reached out to touch my hair, but then stopped himself. "May I?"

I gestured for him to proceed.

Slowly, his fingers drew up to the bald side and traced the puckered skin. "Does it hurt?" he asked.

"No."

"Good." He continued to trace the scarred area down to where it ended at the top of my eyebrow. "It's not as bad as you think. Even if you wore an eye patch and had a peg leg, you'd still be beautiful. But that's just my shamelessly biased opinion."

I snickered but I couldn't deny that what he said made me flush. "Beauty is subjective."

"Tell that to a sunset," he argued. "No human can see one for the first time and not be mesmerized. Some beauty is unattainable, some beauty is deceptive, and some beauty is intimidating. But yours . . ." He paused to look at me fully. "Yours is inviting."

His eyes lowered to my mouth and lingered there. I found myself leaning in a bit. His lips were thin but well shaped, with a sharp bow at the top, and I knew from recent experience that they felt as soft as they looked. His head tilted slightly. I could feel his breath on my cheek, a warm sweetness that I could almost taste.

Something large and red came flying toward my head at frightening speed. Instinct forced me to duck away from the blow, but Liam's hands shot out before it made contact. I observed the red ball the size of a grapefruit in his hand. It was just air and thick rubber, but it could be dangerous with the proper aim and intent.

Liam stared out to the playground, his jaw tight and his eyes promising vengeance. I followed his line of vision and saw the rotund swing stealer pointing and laughing at me.

"Ew! Look at the freak!" the brat called from the sandbox. "What'd you do? Comb your hair with a chainsaw?"

"Shut up, tons of fun!" I yelled and retied the scarf on my head.

Chubs McGrub did a giggly dance in the sand as he chanted, "Hatchet face! Hatchet face!"

I shot to my feet, but Liam pulled me back down.

"Just let it go," he said softly.

"You know what? I'm going home. I can't do this." I sprang off the bench.

"Come on, don't let that kid get to you." Liam tried to reason, but I wasn't having it.

"It's not him. I'm just not ready for all this yet."

With his head low, Liam muttered, "If you keep being afraid of stuff, you'll never be ready."

"Maybe. But I'm not going to get any studying done here. Thanks for hanging out." I was about to turn away when he glanced up at me with a look so broken and lonely that I couldn't take another step.

In a voice full of eleventh-hour despair, he asked, "If I found another place to study, would you stay?"

What a simple request for such a sad face. It revealed the toll our separation had taken on him. My conscience wouldn't allow me to leave him hanging like that. And if we were ever going to find some common ground, I had to be open to communication.

"Sure. What do you have in mind?"

Oh. Good. Lord! That smile could melt ice caps! He may

well be the cause of global warming. Was there anything non-hot about this guy? No wonder I jumped at the chance to ask him out. Literally.

"Well, come on then. Stop making googly eyes at me and let's go." I went to my bike before I made a bigger fool of myself. There was something about him that made me feel comfortable and nervous at the same time.

"Ooh, what? You gonna go home and cry now?" the kid taunted in the distance. "Look at the big baby. Wah! Wah! Wa—" His mocking wails were cut off by a loud clunk.

I turned around. The boy lay in the sandbox, covering his head. "He hit me! He hit me!" he cried as a red ball rolled to a stop beside him.

Liam was standing by the bench, glaring triumphantly down at the boy.

Wow. He'd never get a babysitting job in this town.

Liam joined me on the curb and untied his black ten-speed from the bike rack. When he hopped on, he said with a sigh, "I now appreciate being an only child."

"Me too." I slid on my backpack, hopped on my bike, and rode away with my helmet tucked in the front basket. No point in wearing it now. The damage was done and it was nowhere near as bad as I'd thought.

CHAPTER THIRTEEN

LIAM

I had no intentions of taking Ellia to a new spot today. Her re-induction into society needed to occur gradually. I knew that much. I also knew that she probably shouldn't operate moving machinery such as a bike, but she steered hers like a pro, circling around me with broad dips and turns, hands and no hands. There were some actions you just didn't forget and were able to perform on instinct. Like when I'd kissed her in the hospital.

Now I tried to focus on the road as we pedaled the two miles to Wade's house.

Everything in Quintero was within biking distance. Tourists and vendors crowded the main artery of Cape Street all year round. Palm trees lined the sidewalks like lights on a runway, pointing us toward the roundabout where a bronze statue of our county's namesake stood in the center. The junction served as the city's compass, dividing east from west, residential from commercial. With the ocean at our backs, we navigated through the long strip of boutiques, bistros, and brick storefronts covered in bad folk art.

"Okay, when you said you wanted to take me somewhere, I didn't know you meant someone's house," Ellia commented as we stopped at the crosswalk. It could've been the ride uphill or the shirtless guy singing behind us with flowers and Christmas lights in his beard, but she looked annoyed. I couldn't blame her either way.

"Not just any someone. Technically, it's Wade's house," I said. "My—my uncle," I added awkwardly. "My grandpa left it to Wade when he died, but he only stays there when his mom comes to town. I doubt he'd mind us hanging out. I have to return his bike anyway."

"His mom?" she asked, frowning. "Wouldn't that make her your grandmother?"

"Step-grandmother, yes, but she's the same age as my *dad*. Her son, Wade, is sixteen and goes to León with us. Well, with me." I braced myself for the impending questions. There was no way to get around them.

Ellia lifted her scarred eyebrow. The words "you gotta be kidding me" were written all over her face. "So you're older than your uncle? What kind of *Jerry Springer* mess is that?"

I returned the look with what I hoped communicated my extreme offense. "Not everyone has a picture-perfect family, El. I gotta work with what I got."

"Trust me, my family isn't perfect," she replied.

"I know," I said dryly. "But don't let anyone tell *them* that."

"Oh, you're gonna talk smack about my parents?"

"Why not? They do it to me all the time," I argued. "You've seen where I live. It's not the ritziest neighborhood in town. My entire house can fit in the bottom floor of your house. My folks are divorced, my dad's blue collar, and my grandfather married a younger woman and had a kid my age. As far as your family's concerned, I'm poor white trash. Good for reality TV, but not a proper suitor for their daughter."

She opened her mouth to respond, but closed it again. It was hard to contend with the truth. "I'm sorry. I didn't mean to judge you."

I gave a curt nod and stared straight ahead. When the crosswalk sign turned green, I gestured for her to go first. I was annoyed, but I was still careful to monitor our surroundings and ride curbside to block her from traffic. In truth, I wasn't mad at her, but at the tiny voice in my head that asked, *Why would she want someone like me?* This blaring alarm, this dripping faucet, nagged me with its ceaseless noise. It never really went away, it just lowered in volume.

I reached the end of the block as Ellia rolled next to me, her expression contrite. "I really am sorry, Liam."

"I know. We all have our pressure points, El. That one's mine."

Another ten minutes of cruising brought us to Wade's

neighborhood, a terra-cotta suburb that reminded me of a soundstage from a 1950s TV show. I expected to see a paperboy on his bike route or a milkman delivering door-to-door. It was that quaint. It was that sickening.

The cherry-red Mustang parked in Wade's driveway was a bit of an attention grabber, which was undoubtedly his mom's intent.

We climbed off our bikes and rolled them the rest of the way to the porch. "Is this Uncle Wade person cool?" Ellia asked.

"Sometimes. You've known him almost as long as you've known me."

"Okay." The way her thumbs hooked into the straps of her backpack as she scanned the yard made her look like a shy new girl in school.

"Low-key, though? Meeting new people freaks me out," she admitted. "Even when they're not *really* new. And then it's awkward because they know all this stuff about me that I don't even know. Then you add more people to the mix and it's like system overload."

"I get it. Don't worry. I'll be here," I assured her. "You have his number and a ton of pictures of him on your phone and you have my certified safety seal of approval. And I won't leave your side for a second. I promise."

"Does he know about me?" she asked as I knocked on the door.

"That you have amnesia? Not exactly. He knows you were hospitalized for head trauma, but he doesn't know the full extent of the damage." She was about to turn around, but I latched on to her shoulders and spun her back to the door. "Relax. He's cool with it. He's my best friend and family, and I had to talk to someone about it."

Ellia nodded her understanding at the same time that the door flew open. My grandfather's widow posed in the threshold in a black bikini and a sheer white robe. She had the face of every basic white girl on the coast: bronzed, airbrushed, augmented, and fresh off the assembly line. Batteries not included. Originality sold separately. Neither the house, the sports car, nor her Botox came from hard-earned money, but from a gullible old man who forgot to update his will.

"Liam!" she squealed.

"Grandma!" I returned with fake cheer.

Her smile dropped, though the taut skin around her face held a permanent look of surprise. "I told you not to call me that." Her dark eyes settled on Ellia. "And who do we have here?"

"This is my . . ." I balked, unsure what we were exactly. "My friend, Ellia Dawson. Ellia, this is Wade's mom, Jupiter."

"It's *Juniper*. Like the flower." Her upper lip twitched in her effort to keep things classy in front of company. "It's nice to meet you, Ellia. Please excuse my attire. I was heading to the beach to work on my tan. The entire state of Illinois is covered in eight feet of snow—I kid you not. And I thought, 'Hey, you have a house in Cali. Why don't you take a few days off and catch some rays?'"

"Or maybe hang out with your son," I suggested dryly.

Her response was an awkward laugh. Grandpa bought this house six years ago and moved Wade cross-country so that the entire McPherson clan lived in the same state. But the woman treated their family home like a friggin' timeshare, and so did Wade.

"Anywho, if you're looking for Wade, he's out back doing something with the grill." She sashayed back inside, her robe and brown hair floating behind her. The open door was as good of an invitation as we could expect, so I allowed Ellia to enter first.

Wait, had she said *grill*? Wade could burn a bowl of cereal with how few culinary skills he possessed. And where did he get a grill?

Juniper crossed the living room, pushed back the glass patio door, and stepped outside into the smoky yard. We followed her. Wade stood with his back to us, manning one of those wheeled charcoal kettle grills with a dome lid. Next to him sat a trash bag and a milk crate of miscellaneous items: a water hose, a fire extinguisher, lighter fluid, and cooking utensils.

"Wade, honey! Liam's here!" Juniper called out to him, but he didn't turn around. "WADE!" she called again to no avail. "Ugh! I can't do this right now. He's in one of his moods again.

Maybe you can talk to him. I gotta run." With a wave, she went back into the house.

"She seems nice," Ellia said once we were alone.

"Yeah, like a Siberian tiger. Real nice," I sighed as we strode across the grass toward Wade. I tapped his shoulder.

He spun around with a jolt, revealing a chef apron that said LICENSE TO GRILL on the front. He pulled the buds out of his ears. "Hey, Liam. You back already?"

"Yeah, I'm done with the bike, but we need access to the guesthouse."

"We?" Wade wiped the smoke from his face then locked eyes on Ellia. "Hey, Ella-Bella. What's up?" He scooped her up in his arms and squeezed. Ellia giggled at the unexpected flight.

He set her down and studied her face. "You sure you're okay? You seem a little off."

Ellia snuck a quick look to me before saying, "Nope. I couldn't be better, Uncle Wade." She gave him a playful punch on the arm. "How've you been, buddy?"

Okay, she was overdoing it. To ward off suspicion, I steered Wade's attention to the inferno raging behind us. "What's the story with the cookout?"

"Oh no!" Wade rushed to the grill and used a large spatula to poke at the charred mass inside.

I squinted at the grill, realizing it looked familiar. "Does Dad know you snatched his grill?"

"Define *know*," he said with air quotes as he scraped off a blackened piece of plastic. "As for what I'm doing—I'm undergoing a personal cleanse, if you will. I blocked her from all my accounts, deleted all of her pictures from my phone, and melted the CD she made for me. I mean come on, who plays CDs anymore?" He showed us said CD, which was now a wad of tar bubbling on the gridiron.

Ellia leaned in and whispered, "Who's 'her'?"

"His ex, Natalie. She broke his heart months ago and he's just now getting over it," I explained quickly.

"And now the *pièce de résistance*." Wade squatted down and pulled that ugly maroon sweater from the trash bag. It reeked of lighter fluid, which the flames devoured as soon as it hit the grill.

I let out a dramatic gasp, but the shock was genuine. "Oh wow. Not the hoodie!"

Wade flipped the sweatshirt over with the spatula and folded the sleeves for an even broil. "Yes, my friend. It is time. I have worn this shroud of heartache and shame for *far* too long. I have spent days with no sleep, no sunlight, or a decent shower." At this point in the rant, Wade turned over the milk crate and stood on top of it. "I have eaten my weight in baked goods and shed rivers of tears watching those sad commercials for battered animals. But no more! Today, I stand against the oppression of the power ballad. Today, I cut the shackles of the adulterous she-beast. I am a strong, independent man. Hear me roar!"

I assumed more was coming, but Wade stood locked in a victory pose on the crate with the spatula pointed to the sky. Ellia seemed at a loss, too, then began a slow clap.

"So anyway, Ellia needs a quiet place to study. Can we use the guesthouse?" I asked.

"Sure. Go ahead. The door's unlocked." Wade pointed to the small cottage at the edge of the backyard. "If you need help with anything, let me know."

I thanked him and left him to his barbeque when Ellia let the words slip: "It was nice meeting you, Wade."

I nudged her arm in warning of her error, and she quickly followed up with, "The new you, that is. It's about time that you reinvent yourself. Find out who you are outside of that relationship."

Wade nodded and returned to his work.

"Good save," I whispered.

She smiled brightly as I led her to the guesthouse.

The cottage had white walls, a shag carpet, and not-so-modest décor. The showstopper was a mega plasma TV that covered the back wall of the house.

"Okay, so the bathroom is across the room and the kitchen is right behind you." I didn't need to move around to give the grand tour; a quick turn of the head captured the full vista of the guesthouse.

Ellia circled the room, gracing random items with timid fingers. She'd been in this room a thousand times, kicked off her shoes at the door, napped on the couch, and helped clean up after every party. Now she was a sightseer in what could be considered a second home.

I picked up the remote from the coffee table and turned on the TV. "Do you want to watch a movie while we work?"

"Sure," she called back and wiped debris from the small dining table.

I scanned the movie menu. Wade had over a thousand movies in every genre. He even had an automatic setting so one movie would play after another. "What are you in the mood for?"

"Nothing too heavy; just something buzzing in the background."

I selected an Adam Sandler movie, then joined her at the table. She had already unloaded her books and for all intents and purposes was determined to study. I pulled up a chair across from her.

"You think you're funny, don't you?" she asked.

I froze. "Huh?"

Her head tipped to her right toward the screen. "*50 First Dates*? Really?"

I wasn't getting it. Then I remembered the plot. I shot to my feet and changed the movie to *The Wedding Singer* instead. "Sorry."

"It's okay. I'm not as sensitive about it as you might think. Let me stop lying—I am, but I'm getting better, I swear. And just so you know, that type of amnesia that Drew Barrymore has in the movie doesn't apply to me. Now Cody, on the other hand . . ." She bit her lip.

"Yeah. *Cody*." I tried to keep the malice out of my voice, I honestly did. "You guys are getting along pretty well."

"Uh-huh," she hummed, not giving one inch of detail.

I was sure she could feel my knees bobbing under the table. "So, his memory is erased every day?"

"Every hour or so," she affirmed.

"Are you kidding?" I laughed out the words, but then snapped my lips shut at her unamused expression. "I'm sorry."

"You say that a lot."

"I'm hoping it'll stick."

She leaned forward and slid her hand across the table to hold mine. Staring into my eyes, she said, "Don't make this weirder than it needs to be. We're just friends, so you can let your inner caveman go back to sleep. Now let's start with this absolute value business." She let go of my hand and picked up her pencil.

I followed her lead and got to work. Within the hour, my chair had somehow migrated to her side of the table. I had to hand it to her, she was all business and she used the time to its full advantage. She was serious about learning, not just letting me do all the work like other kids who asked for my help. I watched her fingers dance across the page and found it cute how her brows furrowed and how her tongue stuck out the side of her mouth when she concentrated.

This might sound completely sappy, but I was an avid neck person. The delicate bone and the dip between the clavicle and the slope of the shoulder would give me chills every time I thought about it. Ellia had a beautiful neck, swan-like and thin, and I followed the path upward to the curve of her jaw.

My mind raced with memories. I remembered my hand cupping around her ear to whisper a secret, smelling her orange-scented shampoo. Each second within her vicinity made it harder to keep that promise not to kiss her. It was fine outside in the fresh air; however, with two people, four walls, one closed door—

"Biggity-bam!" Ellia cheered in triumph, shattering my trance. She dropped her pencil and turned the notebook around to show me her work. "Nailed it!"

Thankful for the reality check, I zipped through the problems and was surprised she only got two wrong. "Good job."

She batted her lashes and fanned herself in false modesty. "I try."

After three more practice drills, we decided to take a break in time to catch the tail end of the movie. All of the love and singing must've gotten to Ellia because she once again said, "Tell me about us."

I tried to answer her as best I could but the words were difficult to say. I was writing the book for this exact reason.

"What book?" she asked from her side of the couch.

My head whipped in her direction. I must've said the last

part out loud. Clearing my throat, I laid everything out on the table. "I'm writing a book about us. That way you can have all your questions answered without odd segues and distractions."

She remained still for a moment, then asked, "Can I read it?"

"When it's done, yeah. It's like half finished."

"So you write? Can I read some of your other stuff?"

"Again?" I asked, and her annoyed look told me that it was a stupid question.

"Yes. *Again*," she said.

I shifted on the couch to face her head-on. "Okay. But on two conditions."

She rolled her eyes. "I promise I won't laugh."

"Wouldn't matter if you did," I assured her. "Condition one: You agree to hang out with me again—outside of tutoring. We can chill here or somewhere else. Agreed?"

She nodded. "And condition two?"

I moved slowly to her end of the couch, not wanting to scare her. If she wanted to break away, she had every opportunity, but she didn't take it.

With my face mere inches from hers, I made my request. "For once and for all, let's make the matter plain so there're no further misunderstandings. You answer one simple question: Is there any chance of us getting back together?"

CHAPTER
FOURTEEN

ELLIA

couldn't answer that question. Not yet. But for the next two
weeks I kept to his first condition. We went back to the park a
few more times and rode bikes on the promenade. As we
roamed around different parts of Quintero, Liam told me
about his parents and why they split up. He let me read some of
his poems. Some were pretty good; some were *really* good. When
I told him that, it was the first time I'd ever seen a guy blush.
Adorable.

One afternoon, Liam invited me to sit in on one of his
practices after school. The track encircled the football field. Just
being out in the sunshine among yells, cheers, and whistle
blowing made me ache for the real high school experience. Ah,
the smell of teen spirit: cheerleaders doing kicks and waving
pom-poms, and guys in tight uniforms chasing other guys in
tight uniforms. I was missing out on the action. As for

short-distance running, well, it was about as riveting as watching car races on TV.

I sat on the grass around the thirty-yard line, my laptop rested on my crossed legs as I did my best to stave off the boredom by doing homework.

The team had a big meet in San Luis Obispo this week for what was supposed to be the smackdown of the decade. I listened to the coach trash talk the competition, stating that León was going to *crush* them, *pulverize* them, and other demolition terms on the field.

I felt compelled to show my support from the grass. "Um, yeah. Kill 'em! Go, Conquistadors. Rah. Rah."

Between drills, Liam would run over and try to entertain me and help me with my reading assignment. My grades were improving thanks to his tutoring and even now he offered useful study tips.

"The key is to read a chapter three times—once," he said as he bent down to touch his toes. "Most people remember the beginning and end, but forget the middle. So read from the beginning to middle. Take a break. Then go back to the quarter mark and read to the three-fourths mark. Take a break. Then reread the middle and keep going all the way to the end. Works like a charm."

I tried to follow his instructions, but it was hard to focus. I won't lie; Liam looked scrumptious in his running shorts.

He knelt down and faced me. He had a clean, aquatic scent with a hint of sweat, and I wanted so badly to kiss him. But that might send the wrong message.

"So are you going to answer my question?" he asked.

I blinked. "What question?"

"You want to be my girlfriend, or *nah*?"

I tugged on a blade of grass. "Do we have to put a label on things?"

"Table salt and sugar don't need a label to know their own flavor. It's for the rest of us so as not to confuse the two."

I rolled my eyes. He was forever spitting out parables. "Look, I'm not seeing anyone. Cody and I are just friends with special needs and I spend all my free time with your crazy butt, so what does that tell you?"

"It tells me that the question is even more relevant," he countered. "You got any idea how frustrating this is?"

"Look, I'm gonna be real with you. I can't give you an answer because I don't have one. And seeing as I just got my outdoor privileges not even a month ago, I don't think I need to. If I *was* in the boyfriend business, you'd be first on my list, but right now I need a friend more than anything else. If this is a problem for you, let me know." I waited.

He seemed to understand my explanation, but his frown stayed put.

"For what it's worth, I think you're sweet and cute, especially when you wear your hipster glasses," I added in an effort to make him smile, but I soon found out that was the wrong thing to say.

His hands balled into fists, his face tight. "What did you call me?"

"Cute?" I guessed.

"No. A hipster. A *hipster*? Those are fighting words. Do you see me sporting a Paul Bunyan beard and plaid? I listen to metal, punk, and underground hip-hop. I don't knit, or whittle, or grow my own food. I wouldn't be caught dead in skinny jeans. I'll have you know, madam, that I only wear my specs for reading. They're prescription glasses for farsightedness. I'm not trendy. I'm just visually impaired."

Wow. I definitely hit a nerve. I'd have to make a note of that. "All these flavors in the world and you choose to be salty."

"I'm not salty!" he yelled, further proving my point.

"Is that why you're turning red? 'Cause your sodium intake is sky-high. They've got anger management classes for this kind of thing."

"I just. Hate. Hipsters," he said. "This town is infested with them and their arts and crafts and ukuleles. There are more bike racks than there are parking lots. If I see one more dude with a fedora and vest, you will *truly* see what salty looks like."

I leaned back with a gasp and clutched my invisible pearls. "You know, you're rather dashing when you're mad. So aggressive. So virile."

"Again with the flirting." He threw up his hands in frustration. "You can see how a guy can get mixed signals, right?"

A whistle blow came from the track. We turned and saw a boy heading toward us. Two weeks ago, Liam had introduced, or *re*-introduced me to his uncle Wade, along with an origin story that gave me a newfound appreciation for my own family. Standing a few inches shorter with dark hair, Wade was the night to Liam's day. However, once their relation was brought to my attention, it was hard not to see the resemblance.

Wade trotted over and rested his hands on his knees to catch his breath. "Hey, you're up, man," he told Liam.

When Liam left, Wade claimed his spot on the grass next to me. "Ella-Bella. Oh man, are you a sight for sore eyes. So, is it true that you're part bald?" he asked.

The question was spoken with a childlike curiosity that made it hard to take offense. "Yeah. Mostly in the front, though."

"That is so cool. You should wear it out." He lifted his hands, but stopped. "I probably shouldn't touch it. I know how black girls feel about their hair."

A wise move. "Who told you that?"

"*You* did," he replied with a hint to fright. "I tried it once and you nearly broke my wrist. But, why is that a thing, though?"

"The same reason you don't just walk up to a pregnant lady and start rubbing her belly. How would you feel if somebody mistook you for a petting zoo? You don't know where their hands have been. I'd spend hours setting a style and one stroke, one splash of water will ruin the whole thing. *No me gusta*," I explained, though I had a suspicion there was a reason for this conversation. When I called him on it, he poured out his heart all over the Astroturf.

"I've been hanging out with Kendra Bailey a lot and she has hair like yours, but straight. I think she puts stuff in it to make it that way. We went to the beach a few times and she won't put her head in the water and she'd freak out and run whenever the waves got too high. Weird."

The dreamy glaze in his eyes made me smile. The last time I saw Wade, he was honoring his ex with a fiery send-off and he now showed signs of a heart on the mend. "You like Kendra Bailey?"

His body tightened up, taking the defensive. "You got a problem with that?"

"Not at all. She's really nice. I think she's just a little on the naïve side, but sweet."

"Naïve? Oh, it's much worse than that," he said. "She asked Liam one time why astronauts couldn't travel to the sun and it shouldn't be an issue if they went at night. She said that with a straight face, El."

I whistled. "Wow."

Wade kept going. "She's into philosophy, right? She's reading all these famous quotes and stuff about life. She was telling me about this Greek philosopher named Aéropostale."

"Oooh." I curled inward. "Okay, fine. She's not the sharpest knife in the drawer, but she's cool people. Don't pick on her."

"I'm not! I'm taking her to the movies tonight. I dunno, I just like her. She's fun and . . . wait, there's a word Liam uses a lot to describe her." His face scrunched up in thought. "*Cloying*. That's it. Sickeningly sweet. That's Kendra."

"Which says more about you than it does about her," I said.

He shrugged. "I can use some sweetness in my life. Wash down some of this bitterness."

When he didn't unpack that ominous statement, I asked, "You wanna keep going with that thought or just let it float away on the breeze?"

"Let's just say that I don't have the best luck with girls," he began. "That's why Liam and I are so tight. The women in our lives don't stick around very long. Sometimes they forget we exist."

He didn't elaborate and I knew at least *part* of it was about me. But Wade had to be referring to Liam's mom as well as his own. Liam would talk about his dad and the divorce, but the other half of that severed union was barely mentioned.

Not that Liam's family was the only unconventional one around. I'd recently learned that Trish Montego's dad was involved in some insider trading and had been "vacationing abroad" for the past five years. Stacey's parents fought like heavyweights to the point where divorce was one of her frequent prayers, yet they insisted on staying together for her and her little brother's sake. My family was on that low-key crazy and for them to come off normal by comparison brought a chill to my spine.

That evening's struggle meal with the parents left me irritable. So after the dishes were cleaned, I locked myself in my room and talked to Liam on the phone. While he finished up his homework, we discussed my recovery, and he encouraged me to keep hope alive. I tried to do some sketches, but they all turned out cartoonish and god-awful. I tossed sheet after balled-up sheet in the trash.

"I gotta ask you something. It's been killing me for weeks now," I began.

"Shoot."

"What is *Lessthanthree*? I see it on every email and old texts. You wrote it under our Facebook pictures. What *is* that?"

He laughed. "You know how the less-than sign and the number three make a heart?"

"Ohhh," I said. "Yeah."

"So yeah," Liam echoed. "It's the written-out version of that. Also, the next number that's less than three is two. As in, a couple. A couple, as in me and you."

Silence filled the line for a long time before I broke into laughter. "Seriously? That was our thing? Why couldn't we do the name mash-up like normal couples?"

"I guess we weren't really a normal couple . . ." Liam said, but I detected humor in his voice.

"Was I a bad girlfriend?" I asked.

"What do you mean?"

"You know those girls that walk all over their boyfriends, make them carry her purse and make a scene."

"No—wait. Yes. You were definitely known for making a scene." He chuckled.

"Did we ever get into fights?" I asked.

"All couples get into fights."

"Yeah, but what was our nastiest one?"

"Me being jealous over another guy. You getting jealous over another girl. Me being obnoxious and clingy in public. You sneaking off to a frat party and not telling me."

"Oh! I heard about that," I jumped in.

"Uh-huh. I had to sneak out of the house and come get you and Stacey in the middle of the night." Liam sighed. "It's all explained in the book."

"For real though, are all the stories true?" I asked.

"Depends on what you've heard."

"Let's see. There was one where I snuck into LA Fashion Week and punched out a model on the runway?"

I wasn't sure if he laughed or coughed. "LA? You wish. It was a model search competition here in Quintero. And you didn't throw a punch. You threw a folding chair." In the stunned quiet that followed, he added, "The other girl pushed you and made you trip on the runway, and you—in your special way— made your objection known. You're a bit of a firecracker, El."

I frowned. "I think you mean a violent psychopath. I'm getting tire-slashing, rabbit-boiling, crazy ex-girlfriend vibes here, Liam. Or maybe I had a death wish. I read one post about me riding around with a dead homeless guy in the trunk of my parents' car."

"Nope. Not true," he said.

I lifted my head to the ceiling. "Oh thank God—"

"He was alive in the trunk."

"*What!*" I sat straight up in my bed.

"You felt sorry for the guy and offered him a ride to the bus station, but he smelled *really* bad. It was his idea to ride in the trunk." He tacked that on as if this was just another day at the office.

My brain was about to explode. "You were in the car with us?"

"Uh-huh. We had a fight about that little caper, too. Anything could've happened to us. Like I said, you'll have to wait until the book is finished for the gritty details."

I groaned into my pillow. "Why can't you just tell me?"

"That's what the book is for," he replied. "It's like that thing you told me about Cody's phone. He reads a few notes to get caught up so you don't have to repeat yourself. Same concept; just a longer read."

This was killing me. I blew a raspberry at him through the phone. "You're such a tease."

There was a long stretch of silence on the line, and I thought he'd hung up.

"Liam? You there?"

"Yeah. I'm here," he spoke up, though he sounded distracted. "Just thinking about stuff. I've had a lot of wild moments with you. Some good, some bad, some made me question your sanity, and others made me question my own. In all those things, my heart never stopped racing."

"You really are a romantic, aren't you?" I teased.

I expected Liam to deny it or crack a joke. Instead, he went the straightforward route with a reply that hit me right in the feels. After we hung up, I stayed awake for hours obsessing over his answer.

All of a sudden, I was thirteen again, hugging my pillow and pretending it was a boy, my first kiss made of cotton and feathers. This boy felt too soft with no arms to hold me back. But behind my eyelids, imagination filled the gaps and my fingers searched the bumps in the pillow for his cheeks and mouth. His fabric lips would part with a smile. His breath would push out a whisper and repeat Liam's words in my ear. "I learned it from you."

CHAPTER
FIFTEEN

LIAM

My Saturdays were sacred—everyone knew this. I didn't run, walk, or anything that involved me getting up before noon or leaving the house. If friends wanted to hang out, it had to happen on a Friday or be planned days ahead of schedule. You didn't just spring stuff on me on my special day. Calling me four times in a row wouldn't make me answer the phone if I had no desire to speak. Recruiting relatives to break into my room and drag me out of bed to attend a secret meeting would only incur my wrath. But then I wouldn't expect anything less from Stacey Levine.

At the queen's behest, we gathered at Wade's guesthouse. Various school pranks had been devised here, including the department store mannequin abduction, and a car wash fundraiser that nearly got the football coach fired. Either Stacey or

Ellia was always at the helm of these escapades. Sometimes, if the job was really big, both would lead the charge, equipped with blueprints or dioramas.

The usual crew was in attendance. Nina Hahn—the skeptic who always appeared bored, even while laughing—sat in the armchair to my left. On the sofa's arm sat Trish Montego, a cantankerous redhead and drama magnet. At my right, Kendra Bailey was parked on Wade's lap; they were officially dating. Lastly, Ellia slumped beside me on the couch, no doubt wondering why we'd assembled in this small dwelling like some random goon squad.

I knew the purpose. Posters had been plastered on every wall in school for a week. The guy who did the morning announcements wouldn't shut up about it.

Next week would begin the proceedings for León High School's annual Decades Celebration. What started as a means to bridge the generation gap between teachers and students had now turned into a battle among the classes. Alliances were formed, loyalties were tested, ethical lines were blurred in the quest to win the best costume award. The grand prize: exemption from a final exam of your choice, and a $100 Amazon gift card. Those who participated in the death games had to submit their costume idea to the main office by Monday to prevent students from showing up with the same outfit.

I had hoped to avoid the madness after last year's fiasco.

Stacey was determined to keep the tradition alive and was now disclosing her plan of attack through an elaborate PowerPoint presentation.

"Now, I know we had a few setbacks last year. I take full responsibility for the glue-gun incident, and the principal already sent out a notice that there will be no hair spray or flammable hair products on school property," Stacey announced as she paced in front of the TV.

Ellia leaned close to me and asked, "Hair spray?"

"Eighties Day. Glam-rock hair bands. Pyrotechnics. Fire marshal," I whispered.

"This year, we'll have to play it a bit safer but still be awesome. The grand prize is next to impossible to win, so it's best to go for the class prize." When the groans died down, Stacey continued, "I know, I know, but we have better odds this way and we all get a piece of the pie. I, for one, could use a free homework pass. How about you?"

While the other girls bickered among themselves, Ellia leaned in and whispered, "Homework pass?"

"It's like a get-out-of-jail-free card. If the juniors win this year, each student is allowed one per class subject. That boring book report, that tedious class project, that stupid take-home quiz—boom! No work, no penalty."

"Wow," she whispered in awe.

"Stacey didn't tell you about the Decades Celebration?" I asked.

"Yeah. But I didn't know about the prizes. Makes me want to compete."

"You just might win." I winked at her.

She gave me a slight grin, causing the apple of her cheeks to plump up. She shied away from my gaze and began playing with her hair. Her customary scarf wrapped around the front of her head, leaving a cloud of curls to tumble past her shoulders. With the exception of the fading bruise on her forehead, no one could tell that she'd had an accident, and her headbands always matched her outfit. Today it was green.

Our heads turned as the argument around us escalated in volume.

"That's not gonna work," Trish singsonged. "The rules state that there can only be five students in a group theme, and they all have to be in the same grade." She turned to Ellia. "Since Ellia doesn't go to our school anymore, she can't participate this year."

"She doesn't have to compete, but she can still participate, especially at the dance," Nina chimed in.

"The Nineties Dance on Friday, sure, but no other school activity. Do you really want to risk being disqualified? *Again?*" Trish arched a brow at Stacey in defiance.

"That's the least of your problems." Wade dislodged his lips from Kendra's long enough to join the discussion. "The sophomores already stole your idea for Eighties Day. I heard a couple of girls talking about it on Thursday during the fire drill. The Bangles are off the table."

This was the rare occasion where Wade's nosy side came in handy. If this were a heist movie, he would be the intel guy that waited in the van with headphones.

The room erupted in a gasp, and I rolled my eyes. Nina glanced around the group as if in search of the leak in our operation.

"No!" Trish wailed. "I ordered my Egyptian costume a month ago and I am not about to lose this year to a bunch of underlings."

"Everyone, just calm down." Stacey brought the meeting back to order. "We still have two days to come up with something for Eighties Day."

"What about *The Breakfast Club*?" Kendra offered.

"The seniors did that freshman year. It's too easy. The judges will expect that." Stacey stroked her chin in contemplation. "We may have to ditch the group theme altogether. I can pull off a quick Cindy Lauper. With the right makeup, Wade can be Boy George and Liam can be George Michael." She turned to me. "How fast can you grow a five o'clock shadow?"

"Actually, I wasn't planning on participating this year."

Silence. Six pairs of eyes gaped at me in astonishment.

"What?" I shrugged. "I'm just not into it this year."

"But we need you for one of the guy roles," Stacey whined.

"Don't worry—he'll do it." Trish snickered. "Ellia only needs to bat her eyes and he'll be right on board."

Ellia shifted in her seat and shielded her face with her hands. What made this situation even worse was that no one argued the point. It was a forgone conclusion that I would just do whatever Ellia said. Was I really that predictable? Was I really that weak?

"Hold on. Why do I have to be Boy George?" Wade piped up.

"Is anyone else going to touch that one?" Nina asked the group.

"You got a problem with my man?" Kendra slid from Wade's lap then squared off with her rival. How those two had stayed best friends for this long remained a mystery.

The meeting fell into complete chaos after that. Names were called, threats were issued, and this was just a preview of the Decades madness. The celebration itself wouldn't start for another week.

Ellia, who had been a silent observer until this point, leapt to her feet. "Hey!"

The room went quiet and all eyes landed on her.

"I've been doing a little research of my own. Your ideas are good, Stace, but you don't have to stick to just movies or musicians. What about cartoons?"

Nina removed her hands from around Kendra's neck and listened with intrigue. "Go on."

Ellia pulled out her phone and after a series of clicks showed the image to the group. "Four words. *Jem and the Holograms.*"

A wave of *oohs* and *aahs* echoed, and the girls huddled around Ellia's phone.

"It's pretty simple. Kendra, you'll need a purple wig, but you can be Shana on bass guitar. Nina, with a blue wig, you can be Aja. Trish, your red hair would make you a shoo-in for Kimber on the keyboard. And of course, Stacey would be Jem. There's even a boy character for Wade, too." Ellia scrolled down whatever web page she found, and the girls squealed and clapped in delight.

"Okay. I can take care of the hair and makeup, but outfits are gonna be tricky." Stacey looked at Ellia, fear and worry etching lines into her forehead. "I know you can't participate this year, but do you think you're up for the challenge?" she asked.

Ellia stood straight, her chin up. Her face hardened with determination as she snarled, "Bring it."

The meeting wrapped up around three. I wanted to talk to Ellia alone, but I had a feeling she was avoiding me. She promptly left the cottage with Nina and Stacey and they disappeared into the main house. Finally, I found her outside the front porch, leaning against the railing.

"Hey, do you need a ride?" I asked her.

"Nope. I'm good. I caught a ride with Stacey."

I figured as much, but Stacey and promptness didn't run in the same circles. I glanced inside the main house, where I could hear Stacey laughing with Nina and Kendra about some reality show. "It doesn't look like she's leaving anytime soon. Come on,

I'll drop you off." I trotted down the steps, expecting Ellia to follow, but she remained standing on the porch.

"That's okay. I'll wait," she said. "Today's the first time I've seen you and Stacey interact," she added. "Hilarious. Are you two close?"

"I plead the fifth. She tolerates me and I do likewise," I replied.

She nodded but looked clearly bugged by something. When I asked what was wrong, she dismissed me with a fervent head shake.

"No, seriously. What's wrong?" I pressed.

"I just . . ." Her head turned toward the house then back to me. "Are they right about you? Do you let me boss you around? I don't like the idea of having that much power over anyone."

"Ellia, I don't do anything I don't *want* to do. Being with you happens to be one of those wants."

Ellia strolled along the grass with the grace of a dancer. "Listen here, Liam James McPherson," she said when she reached my side. "You live life on your own terms. Don't let anyone—not even a girl—keep you on a leash. I don't care how fabulous and awesome she is, *no one* is worth forgetting who you are."

I grinned at her humble self-assessment. "What if she helps me remember who I am?"

"Then your memory is worse than mine." She laughed, and I did as well. When we were quiet again, her warm eyes peered up at me. "What do you really want, Liam?"

We stared at each other for what felt like days, standing toe-to-toe, face-to-face. Our chests rose and fell with synchronized breaths. I could grab her and kiss her. I could. My lips felt raw and parched for something water couldn't quench.

I closed the space between us. My thumb brushed her cheek then tilted her head toward mine. She watched me, curious and a little anxious, but she didn't pull away when I leaned in. Her body relaxed as my lips landed on her forehead and lingered a moment just over her scar.

When I pulled away, she wore a stunned expression. Little did she know that I was just as shocked as she was. I should have given her a real kiss, but I knew she wasn't ready.

"Good luck with the costumes," I said, walking away. "I know you'll do an awesome job. Talent outlasts any memory." I climbed into my car, leaving her standing and staring on the pavement.

At home, Dad was in one of his home improvement moods, which usually led to more destruction than refurbishment. The sawdust on the kitchen floor and the absence of cabinet doors were the latest casualties. The band saw whirred as I quietly climbed out of the car, crept past the garage and into the house. Then I dashed upstairs in case Dad decided to put me to work.

I sat down in my swivel desk chair. I could still hear the buzz of the saw but suddenly it inspired me. The world ended at my locked door and began at my fingers on the keyboard. Death metal raged through my earbuds and words chased the cursor on the screen and gathered the outpouring of memories . . .

UNTITLED | Page 199

I woke up to a buzzing sound by my ear. I cracked my eyes a sliver and tried to follow the sound. After clumsy searching, I found my phone tangled in the covers, but whatever moron was calling me at eight in the morning on a Saturday had hung up.

There was a notification that I'd missed two calls and had three text messages. They were all from Ellia. I sat up and immediately called her back. "Hey, where are you?" she asked before I could even speak.

"In bed. Like normal people. Where are you?" I asked.

"I'm pulling up to your house now. Come outside. I don't want to wake everyone."

The request posed a dilemma for me. Fulfilling it meant getting up, leaving my warm, cozy bed, finding jeans and a shirt, brushing my teeth, and going downstairs to open the door. None of these things appealed to me.

"Stop thinking about it and come down. This is important."

"Fine. Give me five minutes." I hung up, did a roll-crawl combo out of bed, and headed to the bathroom.

Five minutes later, I opened the door to see Ellia, perky and bright-eyed, standing on my porch. I invited her in, but she declined.

Whatever she wanted to tell me had to be serious, considering how she kept pacing back and forth in front of the door. I braced myself for the worst.

"Okay, here's the thing." She checked her phone for the time. "It's 8:02 on a Saturday and I'm in love with you."

I stared blankly at her, uncertain if I was dreaming this or not.

"So yeah," she continued, still pacing. "I love you. I'm telling you now because at exactly 5:28 this morning, I woke up with that awareness and I knew I had to tell you. 'Cause honestly, I never felt . . . It feels weird and exciting and I'm scared and it's okay because that's how people act when facing a phenomenon, like a UFO or Bigfoot. But I can't capture this on film. I have to tell someone or else it doesn't exist. And who better to tell than the person it's about, so . . . there it is. It's out there in the ether. Ignore it, reject it, or explore it, but you are now accountable for that reality, too." She checked her phone again. "It's now . . . 8:04 and I still love you. And I don't think it's going away."

"Did you rehearse this before you came here?" I asked her.

"Just on the drive over," she confessed. "So what are your thoughts?"

"My—my thoughts?" I stammered. "My thoughts are that . . . I love you, too."

And then I pulled her to me and kissed her. I wrapped my arms around her waist, pressing her close as her fingers tangled themselves in my hair. After a minute, I leaned back, but not too much because distance hurt. Her expression mirrored mine, and the question in her sleepy brown eyes was the same one I asked aloud. "So, what happens now?"

I leaned back in my seat and read the last line three times. That question was much more of a mystery now.

But it wasn't for me to answer. Ellia had set the rules, and I promised I'd abide by them to my best ability. She had to be the one to make the first move. If that look on her face after the forehead kiss meant anything, this tug-of-war raged on from both sides, not just mine.

CHAPTER
SIXTEEN

ELLIA

ell, Vivian, what do you think I should do?" I
glanced up at her. A red flannel shirt was tied at her
waist, exposing her flat stomach and frayed cut-off
jean shorts. The braided, pigtailed wig finished off the cowgirl
look I was aiming for. Hands on hips, she remained locked in a
vacant daze that reached across the room.

I surveyed my wrecked bedroom. Patterns and cloth lay
everywhere in a mosaic of chaos. I may have bitten off more
than I could chew. The Jem costumes were indeed "truly outra-
geous," but they were also a pain to replicate. I uploaded every
picture I could find online and watched old episodes of the show
to get inspiration and I still felt overwhelmed. I'd been sewing
since I was eight years old. I never thought I could make a career
out of it, but now the idea held more possibility. Hours of my day
had been eaten alive by this project and I hadn't even noticed.

My gaze landed on the clock by my bed and I jumped. I was late for my tutoring session.

"Mom!" I raced out of my room and into my parents' bedroom down the hall.

Mom was sitting on her side of the bed with the phone to her ear. Whatever was making her giggle like a schoolgirl lost its humor once she saw me.

She covered the mouthpiece with her hand. "What is it, baby?"

"My tutoring session starts in twenty minutes. Who are you talking to?"

"Just a friend from work" was her instant reply. "What on earth are you wearing?"

I looked down at my outfit. Getting in touch with my inner eighties girl, I wore black tights, neon-green leg warmers, and a ripped blue shirt that hung off my shoulder. Maybe I was being extra with the theme, but I thought I looked cute.

"Mom, I'm gonna be late. Can you drop me off, please?"

She covered the phone again and leveled me with the "mom stare," which had a built-in heat ray. "Ellia, do you not see me on the phone? Go ask your father."

"Whatever," I murmured under my breath.

"What was that?" It was a challenge rather than a question.

"Nice sweater," I said, then went downstairs to search for the man of the house.

Ambling through the kitchen, I snatched a banana from the

fruit bowl on the counter and moved to the door leading to Dad's home office. Sometimes I wouldn't see him all day, only in passing on the way to the kitchen or to the bathroom.

No one was allowed to even cross the threshold of Dad's sanctuary. I poked my head inside and found him seated behind his drafting table by the window. "Hey, Daddy," I called out.

He spun around in his chair and smiled. "Hey, sweetie. What are you up to?"

"Class. Can you drive me to my session?"

"Ask your mother."

Oh my god! Every time. *Every time* I wanted to go somewhere or do something, I got the same runaround. Could I for once get a straight answer from someone? I drew in a deep breath to reel in my frustration. "Mom's busy on the phone. I really want to get there sometime this week."

He eyed me carefully. "You take your medicine?"

Uh-oh. I totally forgot. I showed him the banana in my hand. "That's why I got some food. Can't take it on an empty stomach."

He didn't buy that excuse for a minute. "Ellia, if you ever plan to get better, then you need to keep consistent. Your medicine is too expensive for you to take whenever you feel like it. I know you hate the side effects, but this is for your own good."

Isn't everything for my own good? I wanted to say, but that would kick off another argument that I didn't have time for. "Daddy, I'm gonna be late."

Thankfully, Mom came to my rescue and we set out five minutes later, but not without a ton of shade thrown by both parents. This led to me having more questions than I knew what to do with, so on the drive to Serenity Health, I started with something simple: "Are you and Dad okay?" I asked.

Mom glanced at me from the corner of her eye as if it was a stupid question. "Of course. There are a few rough patches that need ironing out, but we'll be fine."

Denial. Dr. Kavanagh mentioned something about that in therapy a few weeks back. Though she was referring to me accepting permanent memory loss, it might apply here, too. "Mom—"

"It's all right, Ellia. The moment it isn't, you'll be the first to know," she said, rendering the subject closed.

I knew things were strained between my parents, but the unknown reason behind the tension had me thinking the worst. My medical bills were hurting their wallets and increasing the hours Dad spent working. That picture-perfect image wasn't looking so flawless anymore, and nothing broke up relationships quicker than money.

I decided to postpone my freak-out until the custody trial. I prepared for another session of math I'd probably never use after high school. Anything was better than being stuck in the house with two stiff shirts. They sucked all life out of the room.

But Denise had no luck keeping my attention for longer than five minutes. The lesson didn't even penetrate the brain—it went in and out the same ear as I drew doodles in my workbook. I told her about the Decades Celebration that started next week, and we spent the last hour of the session discussing nineties nostalgia. She was really into some chick named Blossom.

After my session, I left the learning center and found Cody nestled into one of the beanbags in the sitting area. He stared blankly out the window.

"What up, Dory!" I plopped down on a beanbag next to him.

He looked at me, his dark eyes canvassing my face in re-collection. "Well, if it isn't Jason Bourne. How's it going?"

"Good." I told him about my session with Denise, but he seemed distracted. His stare kept veering toward the window. "What's wrong?" I asked.

"Just came back from the doctors for my test results."

I waited for more details, but none came. "And?"

"I still have amnesia," he replied on a flat note.

"For real? Say it ain't so!" I gasped in fake surprise. "Is there any improvement?"

"Nothing I haven't heard before. My hippo is repairing itself. It's gonna take a while to recover. Yadda, yadda."

Among the many technical terms I'd learned, one of them was a thing called *hippocampus*, the hub of both of our problems. It was this seahorse-looking gland inside the bottom-middle part of the brain that turned short-term memories into long-term ones. From what Cody told me, his "hippo" looked like a dried-up piece of shrimp, so any word of improvement was hopeful. He could try to have a normal life, but it would take some time. That was another thing I discovered about my condition—the brain did its own thing and would not be rushed.

"You're making mad strides, Dory. You can recognize my face and my name and not once this week did you ask me if I had a boyfriend. This is progress! This is revolutionary!" I cheered.

A smile peeked around the corners of his mouth. Cody had a great smile, childlike and sweet, not like the pearly white blaze of swoon that Liam boasted. God, just thinking about it made me sigh, but I didn't want to compare and contrast the two boys in my life.

We talked for a few more minutes before I had to leave. I told him about the Decades Celebration and my struggle to assemble the best costume.

"You tried the thrift store?" Cody asked. "You might find something that's already made. I got this awesome T-shirt there." He stretched the front of his shirt so I could see the caption. It was a drawing of a boxy Japanese robot that had hearts for eyes. The words I'M JUST A LOVE MACHINE stood out in big sixties sci-fi movie font. Cody collected T-shirts the way some guys I knew collected sneakers.

However, the thrift store idea was a good one. Stacey and the girls had put me on a tight budget, and hitting the bargain rack could save money on fabric. "I think I'll do that," I told him.

"Be sure they don't try to stiff you on the prices," he warned me. "Vintage stuff is mad trendy these days."

"Yeah, all the hipsters around town have taken over." I slapped myself on the forehead as soon as the words escaped. Did Liam have to leak into every conversation I had? What was wrong with me? I needed a new topic. Fast.

"Why don't you come to the dance with me next Friday?" I blurted out. "It's going on at my old school, but my friends can get us tickets."

He placed a hand over his chest as though scandalized. "Are you asking me on a date, Jason Bourne? I gotta tell ya, this is all so sudden. Why, I wouldn't know what to do. Will there be dinner before the dancing?"

I gave him the best annoyed stare I could muster. "Are you finished?"

"No," he replied, and then fanned himself with his hands. "Oh my god! What am I gonna wear? Should I wear my hair up or leave it down?" He pulled the brown waves from his forehead and gathered them in a ponytail at the back of his head. "How's it look?"

"Boy, you stupid." I walked away and headed to the elevators.

He caught up with me when the doors opened and joined me inside. "So, should I meet you there? Or do you need a ride?"

"Nah, I got a ride," I said.

"You still can't drive?"

My head whipped in his direction. "How did you—"

He showed me the entry on his phone. His finger pointed to the note:

Jason Bourne's written driving exam = epic fail typed in bold with a row of crying emoji faces next to it.

I rushed to defend myself. "That wasn't my fault. I got played! That DMV lady had nothing but attitude as soon as I walked through the door."

Cody cut his eyes at me. "Uh-huh."

"Now I gotta wait two weeks to take it over again. Two weeks!"

Cody shook his head. "The nerve of some people."

I bumped him with my hip. "Anyway, back to the dance. It's happening next Friday at León High School. You should come. It'll be fun. There'll be cute girls there and food and a ton of nineties references. Do you own any flannel shirts?"

His smile came into full bloom, and I could tell that he was warming up to the idea. "So when does this shindig start?" he asked as he typed notes on his phone.

He walked with me to the lobby, and I gave him all the vital info, including my number. We passed through the revolving door and stepped into blinding sunlight. It was then I realized that all of our encounters ended at the curb. This wouldn't do at all.

"Don't go flaking out at the last minute," I told him. "We never see each other outside this stuffy building. I don't like those limits."

"Agreed. We must hang. Hanging must happen." He used his hands to block the sun from his eyes. "You said something about a boyfriend. Is that still a thing or what?"

I should have guessed that was coming. "I don't have a boyfriend. I have complications. Trust me, you don't want any of this." I gestured to myself.

"So you're damaged goods, huh? Pity. We could've had something special." He wiped an imaginary tear from his eye. "Anyway, I'm off to the beach."

"You better not be surfing again," I called after him. "That's how you got here in the first place."

"I gotta live life, chica. I can't let this stop me. Besides, if not for my accident, how would I've met you?" He turned around and walked to his car parked in the handicap spot in front of the building. His easy stride spoke of a light mood, which meant his earlier upset was probably fading from memory.

A black town car pulled up next to me on the curb, and it took several blinks and a double take to realize that it was Dad's car. Mom usually picked me up after my appointments, so something had to be wrong. I climbed in to the passenger seat.

Before the door shut, I asked, "Where's Mom? What happened? Is she dead?"

Dad recoiled. "What? No. Sweetie, I'm picking you up today."

Dad was starting to gray around the ears and sideburns, but not one wrinkle marked his dark skin. The man was in his late forties yet he looked ten years younger. Grandma had a saying for that, something along the lines of *black don't crack*. The motto was true, in my family at least. It didn't crack; it just sagged and got a lot of moles. These thoughts kept me entertained as I stared upside Dad's head, waiting for him to come clean.

When we pulled out of the parking lot, he asked, "What? Can't I pick up my daughter from her doctor appointment?"

"You were never involved with my sessions before. Mom did all the therapy stuff with me."

He lowered his head and nodded. "I know. And I'm sorry. It's been brought to my attention that I haven't been very supportive with your recovery."

Translation: Mom had told him off for spending all his time locked in his office.

"The last thing I want is for you to feel ignored or feel that you have to deal with this alone," Dad went on solemnly. "So I promise from now on I'll be more involved with everything going on with you."

Whoa. That would actually make matters worse. His involvement meant a complete and hostile takeover, and I didn't need any more micromanagement in my life. Hopefully, this sudden motivation would only last a couple of weeks.

"So . . . I wanted to stop by the thrift store on the way home," I said, and suddenly Dad looked horrified.

"The *thrift store*? What could you possibly want at a *thrift store*?"

He stressed the last part in a sneaky whisper old women at

our church used while spreading gossip. *Oh, Sister So-and-So is back in the hospital again*—cancer. *Deacon What's-His-Name is giving his wife all kinds of problems*—gambling. *Did you hear about Gerald Dawson's girl? Poor thing busted her head wide open and has to go to therapy*—amnesia. I loved my dad, but he could be so uptight and bougie.

"I'm making costumes for Stacey and the girls, so I need something cheap and retro," I explained. "Can you take me? I'm on the clock and I really want to get this project done."

"That fashion thing you were telling me about? Not this again." Dad stopped at the red light and turned to me. "Ellia, this little hobby has been taking up a lot of your time lately. Are you keeping up with your courses?"

"Yes. In fact, my grades have improved."

He sighed heavily. "I don't think it's a good idea for you to be so distracted with these extra activities. You don't attend León anymore and there's no reason to participate in any of this Decades foolishness."

"Foolishness?" I repeated. "I'm doing my friend a favor. I'm being social and trying to put my life together. This *foolishness* gives me something to do that doesn't require an appointment. I told Dr. Kavanagh about it and she agrees that keeping me active will help the process."

That got him quiet. My folks could argue with me, but not the opinion of a professional.

When the car started moving again, he said, "I understand

that it's hard being away from your friends, but your mother and I pulled you out of school for a reason. You're doing so well lately and I don't want you falling into that bad crowd again."

"You mean Liam?" I guessed.

The very sound of his name made Dad clench up around the shoulders. It was subtle, but I definitely saw it.

"For starters, yes," he said and held a death grip on the steering wheel.

Okay, I was sick of walking on eggshells and tiptoeing around issues nobody felt like talking about. I needed to figure this out once and for all. "What did Liam do that was so horrible?"

"He's a bit too involved with you for my taste."

Vagueness: one of Dad's many talents. Oldie slow jams piped through the speakers while we cruised along the interstate in silence. Glancing out my window, I thought of all the possible reasons anyone would disapprove of Liam. The obvious conclusion made my eyes roll in disgust and glare at the driver's seat.

"Daddy? Are you hating on him because he's *white*?" Now *I* was doing the church whisper, as if Liam could hear me from across town.

"Of course not. You've seen the family photo albums—the Dawsons come in all colors, sweetheart," he said, much to my relief. "However, that boy doesn't seem to know the meaning of the word *no*."

My anxiety spiked back up again. "What does that mean?" I asked, my voice a little shaky. "Are you talking about the accident?"

"The accident was the last in a long list of rebellious behavior," he said with eyes trained on the road.

I didn't like this feeling at all. "He saved my life. If it wasn't for him, I would've died."

"True. But have you ever stopped to wonder why you were out on a cold, abandoned beach at six in the morning? He's the only one who knows what really happened. You ran, tripped, and fell on the rocks, but what were you running from? Better yet, *who* were you running from? It really makes you think, doesn't it?"

No further words were spoken for the rest of the ride home. Needless to say, my trip to the thrift store would have to be postponed. That was fine by me, because all ideas and creative passion had been sucked out of me.

I had a nagging feeling that I was being lied to. Not exactly a fib, but a lie by omission, which, if you asked me, was even worse. The other person had knowledge, leverage, that they could hold over your head or use to manipulate you. This was where the paranoia came in. Next came the fear, then the anger.

I'd dealt with this a lot when I first woke up at the hospital, so I knew exactly what to look for when someone wasn't being up front. The question was, who was withholding the truth? My parents, or Liam?

CHAPTER SEVENTEEN

LIAM

O w!"

I squeezed my eyes shut.

"If you'd stop squirming, you wouldn't get poked," Stacey told me without pity.

I dabbed my runny eye with my finger and checked for blood. Thank god, it was only tears. "It's called blinking. It's a reflex," I said over the sound of noisy gum-smacking in my ear.

The chomping grew louder as Stacey leaned over me again with an instrument of doom braced between her fingers. "You're gonna have to get over that."

Stacey and I were at the table in my kitchen, surrounded by more cosmetics than any drugstore aisle could hold, getting ready for Seventies Day at school. Stacey was going as one of Charlie's Angels. The curls of her feathered blond wig fanned away from her face and bounced with every disapproving shake of her head.

I was dead set on not dressing up this year, but Stacey and co. kept bugging me about school spirit and supporting the cause. So I was going as Alex from *A Clockwork Orange*: white shirt and pants, suspenders, and a bowler hat. The only person I trusted to do the eye makeup was Stacey, but I was praying to not go blind in the process.

So far, the first two days of Decades week had been fairly uneventful. On Fifties Day, a fight broke out in the cafeteria when the seniors showed up as the cast from *Grease*. Though the movie was set in the fifties, it was filmed in the seventies, and the underclassmen felt that was reason enough to start a riot. The skirmish and a wardrobe malfunction with a poodle skirt had disqualified the freshmen. The juniors were still in the running for the class prize, thanks to a very convincing Beatles impersonation by the drama club on Sixties Day. The only real competition was the seniors, who seemed to win every year.

"Uh-uh, boo-boo. Not this year," Stacey said with a roll of her neck. "Our nineties costumes are going to blow them out of the water."

"I think the sophomores are doing the Spice Girls," I told her.

"Oh, we changed the theme at the last minute. Ellia came up with the idea and I want it to be a surprise." She leaned forward then stopped. "I can't get a good angle. Here, stand up."

When I did, she poked out her bottom lip. "Why do you have to be so tall? Sit down again."

I did, and she spent another minute contorting into the right position with pointy tweezers hovering dangerously close to my eyes.

"Let's try this." She sat long-ways across my lap with her legs dangling over mine. "That's better. Now look upward and don't blink or you'll be wearing an eye patch to school."

She glued fake lashes on my bottom lid with the shrewdness of a surgeon. Next, she filled in the water line with a pencil shade she called The Witching Hour. It looked like plain old black to me, but what did I know?

A golden-nailed finger smudged my top lid. Her face lingered so close that I was breathing in minty air from her gum. "Artistically speaking, you really are a beautiful boy."

"Physical beauty is a perceptual bias to symmetry," I replied while trying not to move.

The chomping stopped and her eyes met mine. "Dude, can you just take a compliment?"

"Thank you." I smiled.

She released a loud breath, pushing more minty air in my face. "Ugh. You are so weird."

"And my legs are going numb, so hurry up with this makeup."

"You trying to say I'm fat?" she asked.

I grinned. "You said it, not me."

Then the hitting and threats of impalement began until we were laughing. Stacey slipped and almost fell off my lap, but I caught her by the waist. She pushed the hair out of her face and watched me thoughtfully. Her gray eyes went wide and her hand touched my cheek as if to be sure I was real.

"Will you look at this? Aren't you two adorable?" Wade stepped into the room with quaffed hair and a brown *Anchorman* Ron Burgundy leisure suit.

Stacey leapt to her feet, and by doing so looked extremely guilty. She brushed her hands along her bell-bottom jeans. "I was just—"

Wade lifted his hands in the air in a gesture of no hard feelings. "Hey, whatever. It's none of my business. Are you done with Liam? I need some help gluing on these sideburns."

"Sure." She shooed me out of the chair and waved him over. "Step into my office."

Seventies Day meant that disco balls hung in the halls, and afros, feathered hair, and polyester were on full display. The whole affair conjured up thoughts of Ellia because the seventies had been her favorite decade. We all texted her pictures and updates, since she had a doctor's appointment today and couldn't sneak in.

At lunchtime, the upperclassmen piled into the gym, which had been turned into a skating rink. I had a hard time keeping my balance, but Stacey helped me stay on my feet.

Between tumbles, I was on camera duty. I took pics of

Stacey, Nina, and Trish, who each pointed finger guns in the air while doing the *Charlie's Angels* pose. Then I took shots of Wade and Kendra, who said she was Foxy Brown, whoever that was. To avoid getting knocked down, I shuffled to the bleachers and sent the photos to Ellia. She hadn't responded to the last set of pictures and this time I also got no response from her. A sinking feeling rose in my stomach. "Stop moping and get back on the floor." Stacey skated over to me. She pulled me off the bench and out of my funk.

Holding my wrist, she shook her hips from side to side. Before I knew it, other kids latched on to me, creating a conga line on wheels. Stacey's laughter rang out, honest and boisterous.

Together, the junior class glided in a wide zigzag across the gym floor to the worst music ever bestowed upon mankind. And I actually *enjoyed* myself, and felt an appreciation for Stacey. She was a brat, but she was also loyal—a rare trait in our school—and she didn't put up with my mood swings. She was a good friend to Ellia, and as she held my hand as we skated, I knew that friendship extended to me, too.

As soon as school ended, the dark cloud returned. Ellia hadn't replied to a single text or picture I'd sent her. Something seemed a bit off and this feeling in my gut wouldn't leave me alone.

Stacey returned to my house to pick up the rest of her makeup. The tackle box that housed all her supplies was a giant

Craftsman carrier that looked a lot like Dad's tool kit, so she'd taken his by mistake. It was best that she made the switch ASAP; I was sure Dad didn't know how to lay tile with concealer and mascara.

I followed Stacey into the kitchen and checked my email on my phone, frowning at the zero messages waiting in my inbox. "Have you noticed anything off about Ellia?" I asked.

"Yeah, now that you mention it. Just between us, I think she might have amnesia," Stacey said as she retrieved her crate of war paint from under the kitchen table.

"Stop. I mean, has she been standoffish or distant to you?"

"Yeah, but she's busy with the costumes and everything."

Her response sounded reasonable, but my mind kept picking at doubt like a piece of food caught in my teeth. "But you'd tell me if something was wrong, wouldn't you? Is she really okay?" I asked.

Stacey aimed a weary stare at me. "I honestly don't know, Liam. Maybe it's that new medication she's on. I'm not an expert in how to deal with an amnesia patient, but she's making progress. She's going outside and meeting people. Let her go at her own pace, is all I'm saying. If you push her, she might break."

"If she does, then I'll pick up the pieces," I assured her. "I promised that I would that day. And I intend to keep that promise."

"What promise?" she asked.

I debated over saying more. It couldn't hurt, and her homework assignments proved that she enjoyed reading dark romances.

So, in an embarrassed rush, I told her about my book.

Her reaction was a moon-eyed, lip-quivering swoon that normally occurred while watching a cute cat video online.

"Awwww." The sound seemed to drag out for weeks. "That's the most romantic thing I've ever heard. Is it finished?"

"Not yet, and at this rate, I'm not sure when it *will* be," I explained.

"Why not?" she asked.

"The story is taking on a life of its own," I said. "And then there's the big scene. I've been writing around that morning on the beach. I wrote everything leading up to it, but I'm avoiding the major event itself. Every time I try, I clam up and work on something else."

"In other words, you're stalling," she summarized. "Just write it. Do it all in one sitting and don't stop until the last word is down. Holding everything in can't be good for you. So you can, I don't know, use this book to vomit it all out."

That earned her a sideways glance. "What are you? A shrink now?"

"Maybe Ellia's psychobabble is rubbing off on me." She shrugged. "Or maybe *you're* starting to rub off on me."

I scratched the back of my head and studied my feet. "Aw, shucks. And all this time I thought you hated me."

"I did at first," she admitted without one blink of hesitation. "You got that broody stargazer thing going on and it was annoying."

I wasn't good at keeping up with slang, but that sounded made up. "The *what?*"

"The broody stargazer," she repeated slowly. "A star is just a floating ball of gas, but you get all caught up in the pretty sparkles. You romanticize what's out of your reach and shape reality as you see fit. You turn your nose up at everything here on earth, even though you're stuck down here, too. Maybe this is the wake-up call you need and you're fighting it by not writing the ugly truth."

I had no response, no counterargument, and for a split second, she reminded me of my mother.

"Whatever you decide, I wanna read it," Stacey said as she opened the door. "You're a decent writer, Hemingway."

I smiled at that. "Yeah, okay, but Ellia gets first read. It's for her, after all."

Stacey's eyebrow lifted in the most obvious challenge if I ever saw one. "Is it?" Then she stepped onto the porch and closed the door behind her, leaving me amazed for the second time today. That had to be a record.

I went up to my room and changed out of my costume and into some baggy shorts. Fueled by new inspiration, I took a seat at my desk and flipped open my laptop.

I opened a fresh document and with a few strokes of the

keyboard, settled into that peaceful trance of productivity. Words filled the white page—nonsense at first, then slowly morphing into coherent streams of thought. Soon I was no longer in my room, but back on the beach with Ellia, running through the sand in the early morning where everything fell apart.

My sore fingers lifted from the keyboard sometime after midnight. If someone had broken into the house and robbed us blind, I wouldn't have noticed. I wonder if this was how painters, musicians, any other artist felt when they were in the zone—that high that came when their best work was no longer in their heads, but on paper.

I snatched my glasses off my face and allowed my tears to flow freely. Happy tears. Relieved tears. Tired tears. I shut down my work then passed out fully dressed on the bed. It was a deep, dreamless sleep where the changeover from night to day occurred in a blink. It was, by far, the best rest I'd had in months.

And to think I had Stacey Levine to thank for it. Go figure.

CHAPTER
EIGHTEEN

ELLIA

S o, how was your week?" Dr. Kavanagh leaned back and crossed her legs in her chair. An expensive-looking pen hovered over the yellow notepad on her lap.

"Pretty good." I sat across from her on the edge of the leather chaise, refusing to lie on my back. Doing that made these sessions way too clinical for my peace of mind.

The office resembled a hotel suite with soft lighting, beige walls, tropical plants, and framed photos of Eastern temples. A glass desk and a rolling chair went unused by the window since she preferred the cozy armchair for that one-on-one approach.

We were just two people engaged in conversation with me doing most of the talking and running down the week's events. For the past month, a raised brow and a sardonic smile were her replies to my rambles. That look remained the same today as

I discussed my friends, my hobbies, my growing playlist, and what I binge-watched online.

Unlike Vivian, Dr. Kavanagh gave useful feedback and knew how to dress herself. Her shoe game was on point and the cut of her tan power suit let everybody know that she didn't shop off-the-rack. Her light-brown hair was pulled back into a severe bun.

"That sounds pretty eventful. I'm glad you're keeping yourself busy." Her dark eyes strayed from my face toward my hand. "What happened there?"

My right hand immediately covered the bandage on my left thumb. My rush to get back into my sewing taught me the importance of hand-eye coordination. "I'm fine. I got into a fight with a sewing machine and I lost. Just so you know: Human skin and metallic-pink nylon do not stitch the same way."

"I'll make note of that," she said dryly before assessing her notes. "Your instructor said that your test scores are improving. I'm pleased to hear that. Have you noticed any changes in your learning capabilities? Do you think the new medication is helping you concentrate?"

I weighed the question for a minute. Mental health wasn't the one-size-fits-all type deal that I originally thought. There was no all-in-one magic pill, but a trail mix of capsules that handled each symptom individually. It took months of trial and error to blend the right dosage to the right compound that played nice with the other drugs in my system, all while not making me want to vomit, or fall into a deep depression. It would appear that my neurologist found the secret recipe this time around, but I still had my gripes.

"My anxiety's gone and I can focus more, picking up little details here and there that I never noticed before," I told her. "But I gotta say I'm not feeling this new prescription Dr. Whittaker cooked up for me. It gives me dry mouth and makes me moody."

She stopped scribbling to look at me. "Moody?"

I paused. Should I tell her about the morning crying jags or that I'd sometimes hear a dog collar jingling in my sleep? Nah, I'd stick to something simple. "I just get sad at random," I told her.

"I'm sure things will level out once your body gets used to it. Everyone reacts differently to new treatment. But at least you're more active now. We need to schedule an appointment with Dr. Whittaker for your three-month evaluation. Let him know if the effects become unbearable." She wrote something down then asked, "What about socially? How are you holding up?"

I bit my lip. I'd been keeping Liam at arm's length since that conversation with Dad in the car. At the same time, I missed Liam—I thought about him all the time.

"There's this boy, Liam," I began.

"Yes, you mentioned him. A lot." She flipped to a new page of her notepad. "He's your boyfriend, right?"

"Honestly, I don't really know what we are. I told him I just wanted to be friends, but he wants more."

She stopped writing and put on a stern face. "Don't let him pressure you into something you're not ready for."

"Oh, he's not. He's been really sweet and patient and I can see how I fell for him in the first place, and . . ."

"But you don't feel the same way?" she guided.

"That's the thing. I want to. All he has to do is smile and I'm weak—got the butterflies and everything. But something's not right. I don't think it's the accident, though. I'd ask him stuff about us and he'd tell me these stories about how I used to be and I can't say I like that girl very much."

She nodded. "Well, that's common with amnesia patients. It's like you can't recognize parts of yourself."

I nodded. "Also, I'm not sure our relationship was . . . healthy."

"What do you mean?"

"My parents said Liam was too intense and becoming a bad influence on me. Not abusive or anything, but like he couldn't breathe without me. That's not normal, is it?"

"Sounds like a codependent relationship. It usually occurs to compensate for something missing in one's personal life. What is his home situation like?"

I told her about his parents' divorce and how he hadn't spoken to his mother in person in nearly two years. I also mentioned the deal with Uncle Wade.

She stopped me. "Two years? And you said that you have been dating each other for two years as well?"

"Yeah. I think we got together right before Halloween of my freshman year."

She scooted closer in her seat. "Okay, let's dog-ear that page for a minute. You said that your parents thought he was a bad influence. In what way?"

"I don't know. I'm just going by what they told me. I was staying out late, running wild, and defying their authority."

"Do you remember being that way before your memory loss? Were you lashing out and rebelling then? Do you recall any hurt or resentment?"

"Not really. I remember being angry and sad about my dog dying, but that's it."

"Was that your first experience with death?" When I nodded, she leaned in even more. "Why were you angry?"

I picked at the gauzy bandage on my hand. "I guess because I was sad."

"And you're not allowed to be sad?"

I sucked my teeth. "Not in my house." I knew my response sounded messed up, so it wasn't a shock when she asked me to explain. "I mean, it's okay to cry. It's even healthy to cry, but to go on about it for months and months is overkill, am I right? It's counterproductive."

She remained quiet.

"My dad took me to get a new puppy to help things along, but I didn't want one." I paused as the memories rushed at me. Images, sounds, and long-forgotten details fused together to fill in the blanks. The deep tenor of my father's voice colored in this outlined drawing, giving it dimension.

"He said this was how people moved on," I began. "You can't let bad stuff get to you. That's a sign of weakness, and will slow you down. He told me to pick a puppy so we could go home. He seemed so impatient, like he had somewhere else to be and I was holding him up." I cleared my throat several times before speaking again. Something had stuck in the back of my throat, making it hard to swallow.

"I remember seeing the puppies in the family's living room, boxed up in the corner by one of those childproof gates. The puppies were so cute and wiggly, wanting to get picked up. But in the back of my mind the whole thing felt like a setup. Like a bribe, a way to placate me so I could get back to the program."

"What program?" she asked.

My stare wandered to the plaques and awards on the wall just over her right shoulder, but not really seeing them. "My parents are very performance driven. Dress with decorum. Stand up straight; never slouch. Behave like a lady at all times and never bring shame on your family. On sight, people will judge you, and your life must contradict their stereotypes and preconceived notions. Work harder than everyone else and get good grades. Go to an elite college. Get a well-paying job and marry a successful . . ."

"Go on, Ellia," she coaxed.

I shook my head. "I'd rather not. Let's just say there's a long list of expectations."

"That's a lot of pressure on someone so young," she said with a furrowed brow.

I nodded. So much pressure that one might rebel against it. Do the exact opposite of what they wanted. Take a different career path. Engage in sketchy behavior. Date someone who went against their standards.

"Do you think if your father wasn't there, if he hadn't organized the whole thing, you might've chosen a puppy that day?" she asked.

After some serious thought, I said, "I think I would have."

"But because he was there, you didn't. Was it because he took charge of the situation?"

"He *always* takes charge of the situation. Nothing new there," I grumbled.

"Even to the point of deciding when your grieving should be over?" she asked.

That clog in my throat was getting bigger. It was starting to choke me, and my eyes began to water. "Yes."

"Interesting."

I hated when doctors said that. It always meant something was wrong. "Are you saying the gap in my memory is because my dog died?"

"No. Temporal lobe damage is the culprit, but there may be an emotional component to explain the time frame. The dog is simply an agent to a bigger problem. We've already established that your amnesia is both post-traumatic and dissociative. So your physical *and* your psychological trauma has to be addressed. What you've explained may be a mental 'trigger event,' a catalyst to where things reach a boiling point. The last straw. I believe how your father reacted toward your grief was that last straw and you began to rebel and do things on your own terms.

"The mind is a very tricky thing. Issues we push back into our subconscious will manifest in different ways. Children lash out to cope with jumbled and unexpressed feelings all the time. That is perfectly normal. I think you should talk about this when you go home. Explain how making decisions for you and pressuring you is affecting you mentally."

I shut the idea down real quick. "They won't listen to me. I'm just a kid. That's all they'll see."

"Then I'll explain it. I'll set up an appointment and we'll discuss this in person."

I nodded. This was one of those times where adults came in handy. They knew how to talk to other adults. And she was a professional and came highly recommended by the almighty Dr. Whittaker. My folks had to at least hear her out.

"As for your friend Liam," she prompted as she checked her watch. "We'll have to discuss him next week. In the meantime, go at your own pace. Don't let him pressure you. Just focus on getting better and let the rest work itself out, okay?"

"Okay." I stood up from the couch and felt ten pounds lighter than when I sat down. I was really starting to like therapy.

CHAPTER
NINETEEN

LIAM

I dropped Wade off at home after school, and then set out on an errand that had been in the works for some time now. Of course, Wade wanted to know what I was up to, but I stuck to my default answer of "None of your business."

Wade didn't put up too much of a fuss. He had to get ready for the dance tonight, which I had no plans to attend. I knew Ellia would be there. One week prior, that would've been enough to suffer the agony of school activities, but not now.

After my mission, I returned home around five. It was dark outside and I was sure Dad had been informed that I'd recently gone rogue, but I successfully avoided him on the way to my room. I tossed my backpack in the corner and checked my phone one last time. No messages. The same as an hour ago, a day ago, and nearly a week ago. In the vain hope that she might be online, I went to my computer and logged in to my instant messenger. She wasn't there.

Stacey insisted that Ellia was just tired and stressed out from costume designing, but I knew a brush-off when I felt one. What I didn't understand was why. I crashed facedown on the bed, surrendering to the fatigue of the day and my bittersweet victory.

It was done. The Ellia Dawson Project was finally complete. I'd even come up with the perfect title, and yet typing up those last few paragraphs this morning held a distinct finality to it that left a sickening feeling in my stomach. No matter what we were now, the relationship I once had with her was truly over. The very idea of a finale just wouldn't process. So instead of the usual THE END tag at the bottom of the page, I allowed ellipses to speak for themselves.

The document was close to three hundred pages. Something this important was better left to the professionals, which sent me to the Office Copy Center uptown. The weight of the bound printout had felt strange in my hands. I'd expected it to be heavier; it seemed so much bigger inside my head. But I believed writing the story was the wisest move I ever made. It gave my misery a voice that would otherwise go silent.

Now, with my face burrowed into the jersey fiber of my bedding, I debated deleting the file from my hard drive. It would be the ultimate send-off, but pride wouldn't allow me to let all that work go to waste.

"Liam? You in there, boy?" Dad called through the door.

"Yeah," I croaked from under my pillow.

"All right. If you feel like eating, there's some leftover Chinese in the fridge."

"Uh-huh" was all I could get out through the wad of cotton in my mouth.

"Okay. I got some Navy buddies coming into town, so I'm heading out now. Don't know how late I'll be out, so make sure you and Wade lock up everything before bed. Oh, and call your mother. She's been trying to get ahold of you."

"Sure." *Please go.*

I soon heard the retreating footsteps and the front door close, followed by the roar of Dad's truck starting and pulling out of the driveway. Anything after that was a mystery because the world faded into black.

"Wake up, Liam! You coming to the dance or not?" asked the room invader and dream stealer.

I opened one eye and rolled my head toward the door. Wade stood in my domain wearing ripped jeans, a black T-shirt, and a shaggy black wig that reached his shoulders.

I studied his clothes, feeling underwhelmed, but mostly confused. "Who are you supposed to be?"

"I'm Wayne, from *Wayne's World.*" He slipped the ball cap over his head with the movie logo on the front.

"That has to be the laziest costume I've ever seen. Genius," I said then rolled back to my sleeping position.

"Come to the dance, nephew. I got a blond wig. You can be my Garth."

Bypassing how *and* why Wade happened to have a wig on standby, I politely declined his offer.

"Does this have to do with you and Ellia?" he asked.

"No." The answer came slower than I meant it to.

"Yeah, right." He sniggered. "What's going on with you two?"

"That is nowhere near any of your business," I grumbled.

"Why not?" he probed.

"There's nothing to tell."

Wade leaned in to meet my averted gaze. "What do you mean there's nothing to tell? Did something happen?"

The sudden tension in the air alerted me to a relationship talk in the works—not a good discussion to have while sleep deprived. "Just let it go, Wade."

When I heard retreating footsteps, I thought the worst was over. That was until a sharp sting ripped across my arm. I rolled onto my back to find Wade standing over me on the bed, wielding a towel as a weapon. In my hazy, half-asleep state, what left me the most annoyed was whether or not that towel was clean.

"Now, are you gonna fess up, or do things have to get complicated?" He flung the cloth again and it cracked in the air with a loud pop by my ear. "I have ways of making you talk."

"She's just confused right now and can't decide if she wants a boyfriend."

Wade lowered the towel and asked in a tone filled with horror, "Dude, you got friend-zoned? You can't be friends with someone you have feelings for. It'll just be a constant reminder of what you can't have. It's like putting boiling water in an ice-cold glass. It's gonna bust and make a mess."

"Why do you even care?" I asked.

"Well . . . I'm not just gonna sit here and let you get jerked around because a girl can't make up her mind. Don't make the same mistake I did with Natalie. There's no point in holding on to something that won't hold you back."

I sighed heavily, knowing he wasn't going to let this go. "If I agree to go to the stupid dance, will you drop it?"

"For now. Sure." He hopped off my bed then darted out of the room. A moment later, he leaned his head in the doorway and tossed the blond wig on my lap.

I realized that, deep down, I really did want to see Ellia tonight. That was motivation to shower and get dressed, and plunk on the long blond wig.

I went downstairs and found Wade on his phone. "What? I said I miss you, too!" he said. He caught me watching him and a red flush climbed up his neck to his cheeks.

"Hey, ask Kendra if she's heard from Ellia," I told him.

Wade relayed my message and the answer made his eyebrows shoot to his scalp. "She says Ellia's there with her and the girls at the dance. Ellia invited a guy with her."

My stomach fell. "What's the guy's name?"

Kendra was talking so loud that I heard her answer before Wade could repeat it.

Wade covered the phone and turned to me. "Who's Cody?"

Instead of answering, I left the house and headed to the car. Ellia wasn't allowed to travel outside of biking distance, so Stacey must've been her ride and a parental decoy. Oh yeah, I knew how that worked. She had been a coconspirator to every outing Ellia and I planned before the accident. Now the same maneuver was being used for another guy.

Around this point was when I began to see the world in a fiery red tint. I was definitely awake now, running on adrenaline and that ever-present need to act. And my slow uncle was holding up the works.

"I'm coming, man!" Wade stepped out of the house then locked the front door.

Taking all of the time in the world, he strolled over with a bottle of water in his hand.

When he reached my side, he snatched the keys out of my hand. "Now, nephew, we've discussed this before," he said in a placating tone that mirrored Dad's voice with disturbing accuracy. "What have I told you about hulking out?"

Clinging tight to the fraying threads of reason, I said, "I just wanna make sure she's safe." I reached for the keys.

"Whatever helps you sleep at night, fam. I'm driving, so grab shotgun. I've seen enough of your road rage to last me a lifetime." He lifted his water bottle in a toast. "To sanity: Let's keep some tonight, shall we?"

ELLIA

For someone who hated lies, I sure told a bunch of them these days, mainly to my folks. To be fair, they weren't all that up-front with me. Dad still wouldn't talk about the accident and kept dodging, bobbing, and weaving around the issue like a prizefighter. So no, I didn't feel too pressed about bending the truth of my whereabouts. I was going to spend the night at Stacey's house anyway. My failure to mention attending the Nineties Dance? Completely circumstantial.

Stacey picked me up right after school because it would take three hours to get ready for the event. Two of those hours involved straightening my hair and installing extensions. With a high-midriff top, baggy jeans, and Timberland boots, I pulled off a convincing Aaliyah. The hair swoop and bandanna that I'd seen in all of her pictures helped cover my scar.

Stacey's outfit stole a bit of my thunder: She wore an army-green jacket, pleated skirt, combat boots, round glasses, and a brown wig with bangs. She and the girls had taken my advice and changed their group theme. Stacey was a dead ringer for *Daria*, right down to the vacant, emotionless expression. The competition didn't stand a chance.

Around seven, we rolled up to the student parking lot of León High School. The other girls waited under the awning, dressed as the rest of the cartoon cast: Nina, in an asymmetrical black bob wig, was Daria's snarky BFF, Jane Lane; Trish was the blond cheerleader; and Kendra, in braids and a pink shirt, was the overachieving Jodi. I basked in my creative genius as the girls came over to say hi.

"You made it!" Trish cried.

"Of course she did," Stacey said. "They're announcing the winners tonight. Gotta see if all of her hard work paid off."

"I think our group is gonna win. We killed it this year," Kendra said. "I mean, come on. We're cartoons. We're alive *and* animated. It's kinda deep if you think about it, right? Right?" Her big eyes searched the group for agreement.

In a typical response to Kendra's statements, we were all silent, cutting our eyes at each other to confirm what we just heard.

Nina stroked Kendra's shoulder and crooned in a motherly tone, "So pretty. So special."

Side by side, we followed the balloons, streamers, and thumping music to the back entrance of the school. My thoughts flew back to freshman year and having to enter through the front where the buses parked. The trophies on the walls and the open space of the commons felt distantly familiar.

Stacey leaned in and whispered, "Is any of this ringing any bells?"

I nodded. "A bit."

She bumped my side with her elbow. "Hey, you wanna see your old locker?"

I perked up at the idea. "My locker?"

"Yup. It's down that hall—5118." She pointed to the hallway to our left. "Nobody's touched it. It might be haunted."

I was tempted to see the ghost of high school past, but I had other obligations at the moment. "I'll check it out later. I need to wait for Cody. He should be here by now."

Stacey reached for her purse then stopped. "I'm sorry, who?"

"Cody. My friend. I told you about him. He goes to Serenity Health with me."

She withdrew from me as if I were contaminated. "You invited him to the dance?"

I ignored her and pulled out my phone. Cody had directions to the school, but I feared he might've gotten lost.

Stacey nudged me. "Is that him?"

I looked toward the entrance, and ended the call with a huge grin.

Cody Spencer, in full punk-rock glory, stepped through the rear doors of León High School with Hollywood slow-motion hotness. He'd ditched the baggy skater attire for skinny black jeans, a black button-down shirt, and a bright red tie. His dyed black hair was spiked up with gel, and he wore thick black eyeliner.

"Look who wandered onto dry land. What's up, Dory?" I called. I ran to him, not caring who watched. He sped his pace and we met halfway with big goofy smiles and a hug. "Let me guess," I added, pulling away to admire his costume. "Green Day?"

"The one and only Billy Joe Armstrong." He spread his arms wide and then appraised my outfit. "Aaliyah, huh? Where's R. Kelly?"

"Don't even go there," I warned him, punching his arm.

He touched a piece of my hair hanging over my shoulder. "You look different with straight hair. I like it curly."

"Me too," I whispered, and led him by the arm to the gym's entrance.

Stacey hadn't moved from her spot by the ticket table and was watching the two of us with a sagging jaw. She finally closed her mouth when we strolled forward.

"Come on, weirdo. Didn't anyone tell you it's rude to stare?" I hooked her arm in my free one then escorted them both inside.

A Madonna song thumped through the speakers. The gym was packed with students and teachers decked out in nineties costumes. Balloons covered the floor and hoops of streamers hung over our heads. Steve Urkel waved and said it was good to see me. Kurt Cobain and MC Hammer pointed finger guns my way.

We found the girls at the snack table.

"There you are!" Trish called, holding up her cup of punch in greeting. "What's the hold u—" Both she and Nina went slack upon our approach, their eyes glued to the boy at my side.

I knew this was going to be an awkward meeting and I braced myself for what was to come.

"Who's your friend, El?" Trish asked.

"This is Dor—I mean Cody Spencer." I drew him into the circle that the girls formed around us.

Nina reached out her hand. "Nice to meet—"

Trish elbowed Nina aside then stuck out her own hand. "Well, hello there, Cody. I haven't seen you around school before. Do you go here?"

"No, but Ellia invited me, and I was curious." Cody shook her hand, unfazed by her hungry gaze. "You guys spent an entire week celebrating decades in history?"

"Oh no. It's far more complicated than that." Trish twirled her hair. "So how do you two know each other?"

Okay, how could I word this? I knew the question was coming, but I still wasn't prepared for it.

"We met at the hospital," Cody jumped in.

"Ohhh," the girls said in unison, then Kendra asked him, "Are you a doctor?"

"He's seventeen, Kendra," I told her.

"So?" She hiked a thumb over her shoulder to the dance floor. "There's a guy here who's a doctor and he's only fourteen."

"Oh my—I can't even . . ." Nina trapped her head in her hands and paced around in a circle. "He's a freshman dressed up as Doogie Howser, you dingbat!"

"You were in the hospital?" Trish asked Cody, her lashes all aflutter. "Poor baby. Did you get a head injury, too?"

"Among other things." Cody smiled and then turned to me with a knowing glance. I guess he figured I hadn't told my friends about my condition and he wanted to honor that decision. But that required him to act fake, and I couldn't have that.

I suddenly realized that my friends had a right to know, and if they had a problem with it, then they weren't really my friends. I was a good judge of character when it came to people. I had to trust that part of myself that I no longer knew.

Instead of lying or making an excuse, I announced so everyone could hear, "He has amnesia. And so do I. I can't remember anything past October of freshman year. And up until a few weeks ago, you were all strangers, except Stacey." I flashed her a quick smile before continuing. "Cody and I go to the same therapy sessions and he's been helping me cope with memory loss and stuff."

Not my best speech, but it got the point across.

The group fell silent for an uncomfortable stretch of time. Faces froze in shock, mouths gaped open. And during the painful wait, I stood tall with my chin high. I had no reason to be ashamed, and having Cody at my side gave me the strength to see it through.

The girls erupted in outrage. Screams and *oh my gods* carried over the music. However, it wasn't for the reason I'd expected.

"Why didn't you tell us?" Trish pulled me in for a hug and mashed me to her chest. "Are you okay?"

"So this was what you've been hiding?" Nina joined the love fest by draping her body over my back. "You've been dealing with this all alone?"

I shrugged and peeked over Trish's shoulder to where Cody stood. He smiled and watched the whole scene with pride and amusement, while Kendra gave me the side-eye and asked, "Is it contagious? Hold on—I'll ask that doctor kid."

After the group hug, we gathered at one of the round tables by the dance floor. For the next hour, I explained the intricacies of mental health. The hardest question of the night came from Trish.

"So are you two together?" Her finger swung between me and Cody. "I thought you were with Liam?"

An eerie quiet swept over the table. Everyone, including Cody, waited for my answer. What I couldn't understand was why this issue felt trickier than revealing my amnesia. I felt cornered and confused, which never went well for me. The clock ticked away in my head, and kept beat with the dull throb at my left temple. My headaches were coming on fast and I needed to take my medication.

I shot up from my seat, making my chair scoot across the floor. "I'll be back. Bathroom."

"I'll go with you." Stacey stood up, but I stopped her.

"No!" I said a little too loudly. "I'm good. I'll be right back."

After I assured everyone that I was all right, I fled from the gym to the cool air of the hallway.

It took another five minutes and several wrong turns to find the bathroom. Once inside, I took the baggie with my pills out of my jeans pocket. I tossed my head back, swallowed two capsules, and chased them down with handfuls of tap water. The aftertaste alone was enough to make me want to vomit, but I needed to get this migraine under control before it got worse.

My shaky hands gripped the lip of the sink, my eyelids squeezed shut, and all perception of time vanished in my wait for the pills to work their magic. At long last, the pressure behind my eye dissipated and clear vision returned. I delayed a few more minutes to regain my balance and then left the restroom to join the festivities.

My struggle to recall the direction of the gym had me spinning from left to right in the empty hall. I examined the doors and bulletin boards when the lockers ahead caught my attention. Double stacked, they stretched from one end of the corridor to another. The top row of lockers had even numbers.

5244. 5242. 5240 . . .

Stacey had told me my locker number. I followed the sequence down the hall.

5186. 5184 . . .

Curiosity took over and sent me running down the empty hall, turning corners, and eagerly awaiting the revelation, the pot of gold at the other end of this rainbow.

5130. 5128 . . .

My pace slowed a few feet in front of locker 5118. Mine. It had a condemned no-one's-home negligence to it. Dark smudges formed an outline against the tan surface, from where stickers had been placed. I knew it was stupid, but my hands dragged over the sticky shadows, feeling for psychic energy of my past life. Perhaps physical touch would trigger all of those dormant memories and cause an onrush of awareness. Or maybe I watched too much TV.

An emotion akin to grief hollowed out my insides. Resentment and sadness burrowed deep, growing and feeding off its host. I could feel its blunt teeth eating away at me.

This had been my life. It might not have been the best, but it was mine and it had been taken from me for reasons I couldn't understand. No matter how hard I tried to focus ahead, blame still had me looking back. Why did this have to happen to me? What purpose, what function did this two-year loss serve other than to drive me crazy?

I was once again chasing my own ghost.

"Ellia?"

The low, gentle voice sounded concerned, and I wanted to

fall into the comfort it offered. And yet, my uncertainty made it impossible to turn around and look him in the eye.

"Are you all right?" Liam asked.

"Yeah." I cleared my throat. "I'm fine."

"The others were looking for you. They were worried. *I* was worried."

"Why?" I flinched at the sound of footsteps coming closer. My hands trembled as my palms pressed against the locker door, my eyes following the tall shadow crawling up its surface. Then his large, pale hand reached out and covered mine. The contrast between our skin tones was startling even in the semidarkness of the hall.

His chest felt warm against my back, as did his breath against my ear as he whispered, "If you have to ask that, then you're in worse shape than I thought."

CHAPTER TWENTY-ONE

LIAM

A ten-minute drive and a punched ticket later, Wade
and I arrived at the dance. Side by side, we prowled
the gymnasium, squinting against the blinking
strobe lights. The Beastie Boys' "Sabotage" blared through the
speakers. The dance floor was humid with movement. Kids
jumped and threw themselves on each other like they were in a
mosh pit. Glow sticks left streaks of color in the air. This made
our search difficult, so Wade and I agreed to split up to cover
more ground. My primary goal was to get Ellia away from Cody
without a fight, but I was jumping ahead of myself. I had to find
them first.

Then I heard my name being called. I turned to my right
and saw Stacey shouldering through the masses, wearing an
ugly wig and big, round glasses.

"Don't freak out, Liam," she said before I could speak.

"Why didn't you tell me Ellia brought a date here?" I demanded.

"Excuse me? Since when do I answer to you? You need to do something about that static cling you got going on," she replied with head-to-toe attitude. "Besides, I just found out a little while ago. I don't think it's serious, Liam. They're just friends."

"Where is she?"

"Bathroom." She tipped her head to the main doors. "I was gonna go look for her myself. She's been gone awhile."

I wasted no time getting to the exit, and to my annoyance, neither did Stacey. Before my hands touched the push bar, she slipped in between me and the double doors. "Don't make a scene. You're just going to mess things up for you and Ellia." Bracing both hands on my chest, she eased me back a step.

"It's already messed up, Stace." I brushed past her, leaving the gym.

I headed for the nearest girls' bathroom but the sound of racing feet against linoleum came from my right. I followed the sound to a familiar hallway that I tried to avoid during the day. I had a hunch of who the feet belonged to and where they were headed.

It didn't take long to find her. Straight black hair covered her face as she leaned her head against her old locker. Standing with her here in this corridor triggered memories of stolen kisses between classes and walking to lunch with hands linked at the pinkie. But now everything felt dark and haunted, a sprawling estate left in ruins.

Not wanting to scare her, I called her name, but she didn't turn around. I moved closer with slow, measured steps and asked her if she was all right. She said she was fine.

Her whole body seized up as she planted her hands on the locker door.

"The others were looking for you. They were worried. *I* was worried," I said.

"Why?" she asked.

"If you have to ask that, then you're in worse shape than I thought."

I touched her shoulder and eased her around to face me. Tears and runny makeup dampened her cheeks. My hands moved to brush them away, but she turned her head.

Did she honestly think I would hurt her? Was she afraid of me? Was this why she was avoiding me? What had her parents told her?

But it was what she told me that made my blood run cold. "Liam, I'm here with Cody."

I stared at her as the words penetrated. "No."

It wasn't a reply, but a flat-out rejection of what was being presented as truth. It was impossible. She was seeing another guy.

"Uh, yeah. He's here," she said.

Clinging tight to the fraying threads of reason, I asked, "*Why?* He doesn't even go to our school."

"Neither do I, but I got an invite anyway." She looked me

square in the eye. "It's not a date. We're not a couple. We're just hanging out."

"Hanging out. Sure. If that's what you want to call it. Is this why you've been acting weird all week? You're dating *Cody* now?"

She lifted her eyes to the low ceiling and let out a bitter laugh. "I'm not dating anyone. I can barely keep track of friends, let alone a boyfriend."

"But you're willing to go to the dance with a total stranger?" My question came from a wounded and vulnerable place. I knew that. But I couldn't help asking.

"Liam, I hate to break it to you, but *you* are a stranger." She pushed off the locker and brushed past me on her way up the hall, her tan boots scuffing the slick floor.

I stood in that spot for a long time, hurt and anger swirling in my gut. How could she say that? After all we'd shared, I was still on the outskirts of her world.

I went back to the gym and allowed myself to get swallowed by the crowd. The bass pounded in my ears, pumping blood through my veins, making it impossible to concentrate. Good. I didn't want to think, or feel.

I froze when I saw *her*. More accurately, I saw *them*.

Ellia's arms were lifted in the air, her eyes closed in her private worship. That Cody guy was having a hard time keeping up with her, which wasn't a surprise. Whenever the beat dropped, it was the Ellia Dawson Show, full stop. The girl was on her own planet when she danced, moving in perfect time with the music even if she'd never heard the song before. That was when she was the most free, the most uninhibited.

Cody whispered something in Ellia's ear that made her laugh and I wanted to deck him in the face. I stood only feet away and I wasn't so much as a blip on her radar, a consideration.

Stacey sidled next to me and frowned in disapproval. A minute later, Wade joined us with Kendra attached to his arm. "So what's the deal? You gonna talk to her or what?" he asked.

"Yeah. But I need to get her alone and away from that Cody guy," I replied with my eyes glued to the happy couple spinning and twisting in the crowd.

"Cool. I can run interference and buy you some time to cut in." Wade grinned and rubbed his hands together, primed for mayhem. "How would you like to sabotage this thing?"

"We can take his phone," I suggested.

Ellia must've mentioned the importance of Cody's phone to Stacey, because she glared at me in fury. "Liam, don't you even try it. That's low, even for you. Is your love that selfish? Is it that destructive?"

Her words were the slap in the face that brought me back to my senses. Through the flashes of light, I could see Stacey's shiny round eyes grow wide. They pleaded for me to . . . I don't know, think this through or see reason. I'd crossed over to the dark side as soon as I left the house tonight and I needed to get it together.

"All right." I nodded in compliance. "Wade, just hang back

a bit. I'll go and talk to her myself—Wade?" My head spun to my left and I saw that he'd vanished from sight. I looked in Ellia's direction. "Oh no!"

Wade had cut in between Ellia and Cody. He was talking to Ellia and with each second she looked more and more annoyed. When she turned away, Wade grabbed her arm and Cody stepped in to intervene. Wade gave Cody a shove.

"Wade, stop!" I tore through the crowd, knocking people out of the way.

Cody stumbled back toward onlookers. Wade dangled what I assumed was Cody's cell phone in the air like a trophy, then got into pitching position to throw the device toward the stage. I sped up my pace, pushing through the fighting tide of bodies while calling for Wade to stop what he was about to do.

Everything happened so quickly that if I blinked, I would've missed it. Cody found his balance, lunged forward, and served Wade an uppercut to the jaw that everyone within a ten-foot perimeter could feel. Witnesses recoiled and ducked away and a collective "Ooooooh!" spread through the crowd. The impact knocked Wade clear off his feet and the group fanned out to give him room to land flat on his back. Cody's phone tumbled to the floor next to him. Even through the music and the noise, I heard the crack of the device.

"What's your problem, man?" Wade yelled as Kendra helped him to his feet.

Like a boss, Cody picked up his phone, brushed it off, and

checked for damage. "You took my phone, dude! Don't try it again."

Mr. Hicks, my old Chemistry teacher, and Coach Grady came from out of nowhere and took Cody away by his arms. "All right, son. Come with us."

"Stop! He didn't do anything wrong!" Ellia tried to run interference, but both teachers kept moving toward the exit.

"He just knocked a guy out, and you think that's nothing, Miss Dawson?" Mr. Hicks asked.

"Then why don't you kick him out, too? He started it!" She pointed to Wade, but her efforts were wasted.

Cody didn't put up a fight as he was ushered out, and Ellia followed him.

I didn't look back to check on Wade, but I followed Ellia from a safe distance all the way out.

By the time I approached the parking lot, I heard Coach Grady issuing a warning for Ellia not to return. Since neither Ellia nor Cody attended León, they could be charged for trespassing. When the teachers walked away, Ellia groaned and smoothed down her flyaway hairs. That's when she saw me standing under the awning.

I didn't even get a chance to explain myself before the yelling began.

"Did you tell Wade to take Cody's phone?"

"No, I mean yeah, I-I told him about it but I didn't expect—"

"You know Cody needs his phone, and you pull something

like this? And you're not even man enough to do it yourself, but you get your uncle to do it?"

"I didn't know he was going to do that!" I shouted back. "Look, I just came to the dance tonight to see if you were okay. You weren't answering your phone—"

"So what?" she cut me off. "Can't a girl take a breath without you knowing about it? Are you that jealous and petty?"

"Ellia!" Stacey rushed out of the entrance. "There you are. Are you okay?"

"Yeah, we got kicked out because of him." Ellia pointed to me. "Did you know he was coming tonight?"

Stacey appeared offended by the accusation. "No!"

"You sure? I saw you standing with him during the fight. Did you plan this?"

"I didn't know he was coming, I swear!" Stacey cried out.

"Whatever. Forget it. I'm going home." Ellia spun to Cody, who stood on the sidewalk filming our argument on his phone. "Hey, Cody! Can you give me a ride?"

"Sure. Ready when you are," he said, and kept filming.

"She came here with her friend; she should leave with her," I told him.

Ellia shoved me in the chest so hard that it forced me back a step. "You don't tell me what to do!" she yelled. "I am so sick of people trying to control me, pushing me to be something I'm not. I thought you were different, but it turns out you're worse! We're not a couple, Liam! You are not my boyfriend, so stop acting like it!"

I swallowed hard at her words. Her tone was sharp and succinct, like a blade.

Stacey stepped forward and spoke gently.

"Ellia, I get that you're upset, but maybe you should go home and sleep it off. I can take you; it's no problem," she offered.

"I'm good, thanks," Ellia replied with a sneer. She glared at me. "My folks are right about you. You're too clingy and intense. No wonder they don't want you around. My dad won't even let me say your name, he hates you so much."

The comment stung, but I hid it with a scoff. "So your dad finally turned you against me. I knew it would happen eventually."

"You say that like they're wrong," she said. "At least they made an attempt to tell me what happened that day on the beach. For all your talk about not trusting them, you're the one keeping the biggest secret. You were probably playing me this whole time. There probably isn't even a book. This whole 'getting close to me' thing could be a way to soften me up so you don't go to jail for what you did to me!"

Everything slammed to a halt. Stacey stood wide-eyed next to us, in a petrified state. Even Cody lifted his head from his phone at what she'd said. As a writer, I knew the power words could wield; they could both inspire and destroy. And hearing something like that from the person you loved should kill you on impact. The instant the words penetrated the eardrums, they should immediately shoot to the brain with the force of a bullet, ending all suffering.

As the shock of her words coursed through my body, my mind shifted to autopilot once again. But this time it followed a new command: CANCEL.

I couldn't keep chasing Ellia and begging her to feel something that she didn't. But my pride forced me to hold on to what little sanity I had left.

My decision made, I studied her sweaty face, her runny eye makeup, and the shimmer of body glitter on her skin. I had to remember everything because there was no telling when I'd see her again after tonight.

I pushed out my hands in appeal and spoke in a calm, even tone. "Ellia, I can't do this anymore. You're right. You deserve the whole story. You'll find it when you go home." My voice broke and it took several swallows to push down the knot in my throat. I refused to shed one tear in front of her, but I was quickly losing that battle.

Ellia looked confused. "What are you talking about?"

"You'll find out when you get home. See you around, *stranger*." I went back inside the gym, not looking back. There was nothing else to say after that—she'd said it all. Perhaps that's what she'd been trying to tell me this whole time and I just wasn't listening, or was too busy holding on to that false hope, which was both foolish and misguided. Well, I'd heard her loud and clear. The message had been received. No more calls. No more standing in front of her house. No more story. I was done. The Ellia Dawson Project was officially over.

CHAPTER TWENTY-TWO

ELLIA

M usic and flashing lights leaked through the doors of the gym, like a tease. I wished I could go back in there, but I also didn't want to explain to the others what had happened.

Stacey ambled along the sidewalk and observed the lamp-posts, the school's metal awning, the acre of parking lot behind me; pretty much everywhere but my face. Guilt always has you looking back, or any other direction but forward.

Someone inside the gym addressed the audience. Only the bass of his voice could be heard from this distance, but whatever he said made the crowd go wild. The roar of applause filled the night. The Decades Awards must've started.

I asked the question again. "What was Liam talking about?"

"I don't know," Stacey replied, still not looking at me.

I tried another question. "Why are you covering for Liam? Are you guys plotting something?"

"No," she squeaked out the word.

"*No,*" I mimicked back. "You two seem pretty chatty lately, telling him where I go and what I do. Then you try to guilt-trip me into seeing him when I'm not ready."

"Nobody's trying to manipulate you, El. But you know what would be great? If you told Liam about this"—she gestured to Cody, who was standing on the grass median, absorbed in his phone—"instead of going behind his back."

She made it sound like I was cheating. This wasn't even a date.

"We're not together, Stacey!" I snapped. Out of the corner of my eye, I saw Cody lift his head.

"Okay. Cool. You tell Liam that?" she asked. Then a shouting match began, Stacey taking the defensive and siding with Liam.

The yelling went on and on until I finally shouted, "If you think he's so wonderful, Stacey, why don't you date him?"

She reared back in shock. "What does that mean?"

"Nothing," I said. I didn't want to fight about this. Tonight was supposed to be about celebrating recovery and not thinking and now my head was starting to hurt again. "Look, you stay here and I'll go home with Cody. I'll call you tomorrow."

"Ellia." She stepped forward to try to reason with me, but I was done talking.

"Bye, Stacey." I walked away and joined Cody on the grass.

The parking lot was packed with cars and it felt weird leaving an event early. Cody seemed to sense the tension in the air and gave me a wide berth as we walked to his car.

His ride sat in the front row in the handicap space, a dirty black compact two-seater with a rack on the roof where he likely stored his surfboard. It suited him.

After we got inside, Cody spoke first. "Some night, huh?"

"Yeah, that was some punch you threw back there," I replied. "Respect."

"Yeah, my brother taught me that. Clean shot. Aim for the jaw." He started the engine and played with the weirdest navigation system I'd ever seen. He asked for my address and then typed it onto a computer screen the size of a tablet. Then a robotic female voice filled the interior and called him by name. Cody told me it was a specialized system that was linked to his phone. The automated voice worked like a personal assistant and gave him updates from the previous hour. I felt like I was in a spacecraft of a sci-fi film.

Once we hit the main road, I grew accustomed to the handi-capable tech, then settled back into my earlier funk. These little gadgets were Cody's lifeline and if something happened to his phone, I would never forgive myself.

"I'm really sorry," I told him and rubbed his arm in condolence.

"Don't be. I had a blast for the most part and I can always

get another phone." He reached for his cell and showed me the display. "It's just a tiny crack on the side. See—"

"Eyes straight ahead," the computer lady said, and we both jumped.

I looked around for cameras. "How did she know that?"

"There's a sensor that makes sure my eyes don't leave the road for longer than five seconds while the car's on." He pointed to a tiny box clamped to the visor. "So are you into this Liam guy or what?"

I was still staring at the box and its tiny camera. The topic changed so quickly, I struggled to keep up. "Huh? Oh! No way, not after what he pulled tonight."

Cody shrugged. "That's just passion. Emotions will fly and misunderstandings will happen. Then you're supposed to kiss and make up. Right?" Cody was only seventeen, but he spoke with a weary tone of someone who had seen it all. "I saw how you looked at him. There are some feelings there—don't deny it."

"Oh, please. The boy is one big ball of complication."

Cody frowned at me, clearly unconvinced.

"I . . . I just don't know what I want right now," I said.

"I think you do and you're just afraid to get it. What's holding you back?"

I was in no shape to answer that right now. "I don't know."

"An amnesiac's favorite answer." He chuckled. "And this is why it would never work out between us."

Where did that come from? "What?"

He smiled, his eyes on the road. "Look, Ellia, you're beautiful and funny, and I love how we understand each other . . ."

He trailed off and I tensed up, wondering where this was going. I'd be lying if I said I hadn't entertained thoughts of Cody before. Imagined what it might be like to date him.

"But I almost feel like we're too similar," Cody went on. "We'd both be bringing too much baggage to the table, if that makes sense. Not really what I'm looking for." He smiled and then began detailing a list of dream girl requirements. It was a long list.

"Hold up. Are you dumping me?" I asked. If it wasn't for the fact that we weren't dating to begin with, I might've been hurt. But in truth I was sort of relieved that he felt the same as I did.

Cody smiled. "I'm afraid so, my dear," he said in a voice full of old black-and-white-movie melodrama. "We had a good run, but it's time to move on. I know it's hard, but one day you'll find another."

When he stopped at a red light, he leaned in and kissed my cheek. He pulled back and added, "We'll always have therapy."

"Always, darling," I replied with equal drama. "Always."

"Eyes straight ahead," came the voice again, which made me jump like I was watching a slasher flick. Being with Cody seemed to take the edge off. He was so laid back that it made you sleepy.

"This might seem like awkward timing, given that we're

officially broken up and all. There's something I gotta know," he said after a while. "Who was the chick in the glasses?"

I turned to him. "You mean Stacey? My best friend. The one I was just yelling at?"

"Yeah. Is she seeing anyone?"

I tilted my head in curiosity. "Are you kidding me right now?"

"Nope." He shook his head. "You gotta give me her number."

"Uh-huh. I'll think about it."

"Cool." His head rocked to a happy groove playing in his head. "So, you still don't know about your accident. Why don't you just ask your parents?"

"They know the aftermath, but not how I hit my head. Liam's the only one who knows the truth."

"You sure about that?" he asked. "If Liam's the only one who knows, then why did he say you'd find out when you got home? Is there a clue there?"

I hadn't thought of that. Was there something I was missing? A note? A photograph? The fixation was real to the point where I didn't even notice we'd pulled up to my driveway until the car stopped.

Cody redirected his GPS and then leaned across the seat to peer through my window. "Nice place."

"Thanks." I followed his gaze to the house and noticed the porch light was on and Dad's car was missing from the driveway. He and Mom had probably gone out to eat. With any luck, they were having a couple's night or at least working out their differences.

I thanked Cody for the ride and climbed out of the car.

"Sorry for the drama tonight, Dory," I told him.

"Good luck, Jason Bourne." Cody waited until I got to the front door.

As I stepped onto the porch, I noticed a brown package sitting on the welcome mat. I saw that it was addressed to me, but with no postmark and no return address. It must've been hand-delivered. There were glittery butterflies and rainbow stickers on the package. Random. The odds of a stink bomb or a dead rodent waiting inside seemed highly unlikely, but I handled the package with care just in case. I waved good-bye to Cody then raced inside.

"Mom? Dad?" My call was met with silence, which confirmed they were out for the evening. Seeing as I was still wearing my nineties costume, I was glad they were gone and I could avoid pointed questions.

In the kitchen, I grabbed a bottle of water and a bag of vegan snacks then headed to my room. After changing into a pair of pajamas and washing the makeup off my face, I finally squared off with the brown package sitting on my bed. I had a good hunch who sent it. The stickers had thrown me off for a second, which I believed was the idea in case Mom or Dad found the box first.

I ripped off the paper wrapping and uncovered a thick man-uscript, professionally bound with a black cover. I flipped the cover to the title page and I didn't even bother to hold back my excitement. He'd been having trouble thinking up a name for the story, but it would appear that he finally found the right one.

LESS THAN THREE
by Liam J. McPherson

It was a good thing that my folks weren't home—my squealing would've surely woken them up. I didn't care either way. Liam had finished his story!

I lay on my back in bed and settled in for a night of binge reading. I turned to the first page.

"Either you're running from something or running to something. Whatever the case is, it better be worth all the huffing and puffing."

She told me that one night on the beach, and looking back, it seemed to be the sum of our relationship. Running. We didn't see it at the time, but that was exactly what we were doing. It was the motive behind her wild ways and the reward promised to me if I followed. It marked the beginning of what would be the most exciting time of my life. Unfortunately, it was also how it would end.

I had to pause a minute to digest the passage. Had Liam and I relied on each other to escape the messed-up parts of our lives that we couldn't physically leave? I swallowed hard and kept reading, soaking in the events and getting lost in the details and the flow of Liam's words. His descriptions of me felt like fingers on my skin and the reverence leapt off the pages to kiss me. They were completely biased and overblown, but he sure knew how to make a girl feel special.

Halfway through the fifth chapter, I heard a light tapping on my door. Mom poked her head in my room to tell me that it was midnight, and to ask why I was back from Stacey's so early. I made an excuse about not feeling well and needing to be in my own space, which wasn't a lie. I *wasn't* feeling well, and as I continued reading late into the night, the sicker I became. Not because of Liam's writing—I nearly woke up the house laughing and crying at the adventures he described. What turned my stomach was the girl featured on every page who, from all accounts, seemed sad and broken. The more I learned about her, the less I liked her.

Liam told me that the real Oedipus complex was claiming to be wise when you didn't know the first thing about yourself. I still believed that everybody had that flaw in them, some twinge of pride and superiority that always preceded a fall. It would appear that some cases were worse than others and it was hard to tell what was worse: forgetting or being forgotten.

CHAPTER TWENTY-THREE

LIAM

I only returned to the dance to find out who won the best costume award. During that time, Stacey had ignored me, Trish and Nina had given me the evil eye, and Wade had completely ditched me to dance with his girlfriend. The only good thing was that the juniors won the class prize. Thanks in no small part, of course, to Ellia's brilliance. When the cast of *Daria* stormed the stage, and Stacey began her lengthy acceptance speech, I couldn't take it anymore. I strode back outside. It was a relief to see that Ellia and Cody had left the school, but when I got to my locked car, I realized that I couldn't do the same. Wade still had my keys.

I sat on the hood of my car with my feet on the front bumper and texted him. While waiting for Wade to show up, I used the time to reflect on all the ways I'd messed up tonight.

My jealousy, my compulsion to keep Ellia safe and close to

me was on the wrong side of healthy and it needed to stop. Ellia used to call it *possession obsession* when we were dating—right around our first fight, in fact. It drove her crazy then, much like it did now. But what she never seemed to get was that I didn't exactly love that tendency in myself, either.

I swallowed hard. Thank god Dad wasn't here to see me now—he would've kicked my butt up and down the street for crying in public. This was something you did in the privacy of your home; not in the middle of a high school parking lot.

A group of kids filed out from the rear entrance of the gym, in heavy debate over what diners were still open this time of night. They walked past and I quickly swiped my eyes and checked my dying phone.

Wade still hadn't shown up to give me the keys. One would think he would've understood the urgency after text number five. I was thirty seconds from finding a brick and committing grand theft auto on my own car, when I caught Daria herself strolling up the aisle. Even from a ways off, she was hard to miss.

"You're still here? Thought you took off an hour ago," Stacey called out, swinging a tangled mass of keys in her hand.

I met her question with one of my own. "You're taking off already?"

"Yeah. Too much drama tonight. I'm gonna go home and sleep it off." One click of her key fob incited a beep and a flash of taillights from three lanes down. "You need a ride?" she asked.

I looked to my car and then back to her. "No, I just . . ."

"Wade's still dancing with Kendra, so you might be here till morning waiting for him. It's up to you, but you have ten seconds to decide." She dipped between cars, disappearing from sight as she began the countdown. "Ten . . . nine . . . eight . . ."

I was at the passenger-side door of her car by the time she made it to three.

"You really are fast. Impressive." She smiled and climbed inside.

We drove along in silence. All I could think was, *what happens now?* I couldn't imagine life after Ellia.

Eyes glued to the road, Stacey finally said, "El and Cody are just friends. They're going through the same thing so they get each other in a way that we can't. That's all."

I kept my focus outside my window. "They can do whatever they want. I don't care. I'm moving on."

She scoffed. "Worst. Liar. Ever."

"I'm dead serious. I can't do this anymore. I can take a hint, you know."

"Does this mean that you're not gonna serenade her under her bedroom window anymore? Too bad she doesn't have a balcony so you can do the whole Romeo thing."

I glared at her. "I don't do that. I have to pass her house anyway to get to the beach, so I check on her from across the street."

"Yeah, 'cause that's not creepy at all. No sir," she muttered. When she got cold silence in response, she said, "I still don't get it. Did her folks threaten to call the cops on you for trespassing or something?"

"Worse than that," I intoned. "I'd go to jail for violating a court order."

She jumped in her seat. "*What?* Ellia's parents put a restraining order on you?"

"Yup. I can't go within a hundred yards of Ellia, her house, her car—everything."

If the topic wasn't so depressing, I would've found Stacey's struggle to steer straight amusing.

"*What did you do*, Liam?" she demanded.

"I loved the wrong girl," I replied. "The odds were stacked against us, even before the accident. I wasn't good enough for their *sweet, perfect* daughter. First came the warnings to keep away. Then came blocked phones and revoked computer privileges. The restriction got tighter until we were sneaking out all the time." I paused and turned to Stacey. "Then, a day after the accident, the sheriff shows up at my door to serve me papers. My dad flipped. He went to knock some sense into Ellia's dad and they started fighting. After that, my father didn't want me near her, either." I shook my head with disgust.

"Wow, Hemingway, you stay losing." Stacey sighed as we pulled up in front of my house. "That's crazy. But why not just be honest with Ellia about it?"

I shrugged. "It's all in my book."

Stacey glanced at me. "You finished it?"

I nodded. "I printed a copy for Ellia and dropped it at her door earlier tonight."

"So that's what you meant. Liam, that's great!" Her exclamation sounded genuine. "What are you gonna do with it now?"

"Don't know. As far as I'm concerned, I'm done with it. Thanks for the ride. Night."

I opened the door and got out of the car.

When I reached the porch, I remembered that Wade had my house keys as well. Thankfully, he had forgotten to lock up the garage. I slipped under the roll-up door then went in through the side entrance that led to the kitchen. I made it halfway to the fridge when I realized that I wasn't alone in the house. I turned and saw Stacey standing in the garage doorway with her arms crossed.

"You're not gonna delete it all, are you?" she asked.

I tried to get my heart rate under control. "Wait. You follow me in here, yet I'm the creepy one?"

"Answer the question. If you plan on trashing your hard work then I want to read it before you do."

I opened the fridge and pulled out a bottle of water. This night, this conversation was sapping me dry and I needed to stay hydrated. "Stacey, some of that stuff is kinda personal."

She waved off the warning. "I'm not interested in the lovey-dovey crap. I wanna know what happened with the accident. My best friend almost died *that day*. She lost her memory *that day*, and you were the only one who knows the truth about *that day*." She stressed the words.

"How do you know it's the truth?" I challenged. "I could be lying. Creative license and all that."

"Because you wouldn't lie to Ellia. Me? Sure. The police? Maybe. But Ellia? No way."

I couldn't argue with that line of reasoning. I was done arguing, period, so I asked, "If I print out that chapter, will you leave me alone?" When she agreed, I pushed off the counter and moved to the stairs. "Wait here."

I went to my room and pulled up the document on my computer. I highlighted everything after Ellia dared me to race her to the pier and then hit Print.

Moments later, I returned downstairs with the papers in my shaking hand.

Stacey sat up straight on the couch, her eyes following me to the armchair next to her.

In the quiet of the living room, several facts went without saying as the document changed hands. *This story doesn't leave this house. Read the whole thing before you judge me.*

As Stacey began to read, I tracked how her eyes zipped across the lines.

It wasn't watching people cry that got to me. It's watching them trying not to cry—the internal battle that could be told through every strained muscle in their face. The pursed lips, the pinching of the eyes, the leaking dam of tears, the shuttered sob that they tried to pass off as laughter. It was a fight that you knew they'd lose, because you were slowly losing your own.

When she finished, she lowered the paper onto the coffee table in a smooth motion, her gaze fixed straight ahead toward the window. The look on her face conveyed pure devastation as she whispered, "I'm so sorry, Liam."

"Thanks. Are we done here?" I collected the papers.

She snapped out of whatever daze she was in and looked at me. "You didn't do this. It's not your fault. You can't blame yourself."

"Yeah, well, blame is like rear ends and reflections. You're always looking back," I told her.

She made a face at me. "Is that supposed to be funny?"

"No. It's just something Ellia . . ." I cut off that thought before it could take shape. I couldn't deal with anything involving Ellia right now. I couldn't deal with Stacey looking at me in pity. "Look, just go, okay?"

Stacey glanced at my hands. I followed her gaze to the print-out with its torn and bent edges. My fist had wrapped around the rolled-up papers so tightly that it resembled a bow tie. Add a bobbing right knee that I couldn't control and I was the image of a ticking time bomb.

"You know what?" Stacey said. "I've had it up to here with both of you. You're not the only ones who are scared and confused around here, Liam."

The brokenness in her voice put my temper in check. "What would you be scared of?"

She looked to the ceiling and lifted her hands in a helpless gesture. "Being forgotten. Losing a friend. Having all your memories amount to nothing. Take your pick."

"What are you talking about? At least she knows who you are."

"Ellia knows who I *was*. She doesn't know about the person I am now, not really." Fat droplets fell from her eyes and she slapped her cheeks to wipe them away. "She was my go-to person. I'd tell her everything. Now, all of those late-night phone calls, all the sleepovers at her house because I couldn't deal with stuff at home, all the crying on her shoulder. It's all gone. It's like if she doesn't know, then it didn't happen, and if it didn't happen then what exactly am I holding on to?" Stacey lowered her head and cried, and I just sat there at a complete loss for words.

I thought I was the only one who felt that way, the only one grieving for how things used to be. If you hated your reflection, you tended to avoid all mirrors, but I couldn't avoid Stacey. Not now.

She looked so fragile in that moment that I was afraid to touch her. I tried to get her to look at me, but she kept dodging my stare. I transferred from the armchair to the couch and held her by the shoulders. Her body trembled under my hand.

In a low, cracking voice that I couldn't recognize as my own, I said, "Stacey, come on. It's okay."

"It's not." She sniffed. "You're not the only one who lost some-one that day."

I found myself leaning in to wipe her cheek with my thumb. When she didn't respond, I lifted her chin to look at me. "I warned you not to read it."

"No. I needed to. I can't live in a fantasy world, no matter how beautiful . . ." She paused and looked up at me with that same wonder she had when she'd done my makeup in the kitchen earlier in the week.

My breath caught as my stare fell to her mouth then back to her eyes again. Then I felt myself leaning in until the next thing I knew, I was kissing Stacey Levine.

And it wasn't in the least bit terrible. In fact, it felt really good. Our faces were damp from her crying, and her lips were soft and electric. I wanted to pull her closer, but I only had two hands and my manuscript was still rolled tight in my fist.

Then clarity struck me in the gut. Its impact snatched me off the couch and across the room until my back hit the banister of the stairs. Stacey remained seated on the sofa, stone stiff. Her eyes looked dazed and she brought a hand to her mouth.

I spoke first. "That was—"

"Yeah," she finished.

I raked my hands through my hair as I struggled to think. "We shouldn't have—"

"I know."

"But I wanted—"

"Me too," she admitted, and it was a relief to not be the only one feeling . . . whatever this was. Now that the truth was out in the open, I wasn't sure what to do next. All I could come up with was, "See you at school?"

"Okay." Stacey sprang from the couch and ran to the door as if the place was haunted.

Her clumsy fingers fumbled with the locks. I went to help her, but she unlocked the bolt and swung the door so wide that it almost hit me in the face. She went from porch to sidewalk in one motion and was at her car by the time I got outside. Her Volkswagen Bug disappeared around the block a minute later, and I was too busy eyeing the skid marks left in the street to notice that I had company.

I turned to my right and saw Wade and Kendra standing on the porch with me.

My stare moved to the car parked in the driveway, and I wondered just how distracted I had to be to not hear them drive up.

"Is she okay?" Kendra asked.

"Yeah. She just had to run," I explained.

Wade craned his neck to see the end of the block, but Stacey was long gone by now. "I'll say. What did you do, man?"

Looking back toward the quiet street again, it occurred to me that an awkward week awaited me on Monday. At best, Stacey would ignore me and duck into classrooms whenever I'd walk by. At worst, there would be high-level weirdness or awkward small talk. But it was hard to dwell on the aftermath with my lips still tasting like watermelon lip gloss. I was deliriously numb and living in the moment, so tomorrow would have to figure itself out on its own.

"I let her read some of my work," I finally answered, then stepped back inside.

"Ah! That explains it then," Wade said behind me as I closed the door and locked him out.

ELLIA

P art of me just wanted to keep reading Liam's book. I felt like I couldn't stop. But another part of me needed to pace myself. I didn't want to rush. Every page contained important events of my life. I studied the text as if there would be an exam on it later. Three days after the Nineties Dance, I had about fifty pages left in the book and I didn't want the experience to end.

Liam, Liam, Liam. If I'd thought I was messed up before, I was a straight-up train wreck now. Now that he no longer stood outside my house, I felt the void. As hard as it was to admit, I'd gotten used to seeing him under the lamppost. My mornings made more sense. Getting up at 5:30 in the morning made more sense. But suddenly my internal clock had no purpose.

I hadn't heard a peep from him since the dance. The only texts I got were daily inspirational quotes from Kendra, and

Cody hounding me for Stacey's phone number. But I didn't want to give that to him until I cleared it with Stacey, and she and I hadn't spoken, either.

I'd left her two messages, apologizing for going off on her at the dance. But I got radio static all weekend. This wasn't our first fight and it wouldn't be the last, so I figured I'd give her time to chill out.

That afternoon, while I was doing homework, a new text popped up. I was hopeful it was from Stacey or Liam, but instead it was Cody again.

> **DORY:** U thought I forgot, didn't U?
> **ME:** More like hoped.
> **DORY:** R U saying I'm not good enough 4 her?
> **ME:** No! Don't want u hurt. She's messy.
> **DORY:** I like messy.

I sighed and went back to my homework. I also did some drawing. I wasn't the most talented artist, nowhere near where I was before, but I'd quickly advanced past the stick figure stage. By sundown, I'd completed a collection of one-shoulder tops and went downstairs to show Mom my progress. Kindergartners probably drew better forms, but I was proud of it and planned to tape it onto the fridge.

After a dinner of Mom's latest vegan concoction, I finally settled down for some reading. And I realized I had arrived at the scene that I'd been waiting for.

LESS THAN THREE | Page 251

Panic quickly set in as my ears strained to pick up any sign of life: a whimper, a curse, another bloodcurdling scream; anything other than the eerie quiet that made the hair rise on my arms. I begged for just one footprint, one small flash of movement to help me find her. I'd never begged for anything so hard in my life.

"Ellia!" I screamed as I picked up speed, my fear tapping in to reserved energy I never knew I had. There was no sound from her at all, and the only footsteps I could hear were my own.

I was coming up to another bend in the path when something out of the corner of my eye made me stop and double back. The bright colors seemed out of place with the rocky landscape. As I peered over the cliff's edge to the rocks below, I wished more than anything it was just a large animal. But I knew it wasn't.

If I had to guess, it was a two-story drop. I'd jumped off roofs higher than that, but there was usually a pool or a trampoline to break my fall. My girl wasn't so lucky.

I raced down the slope of the path by means of flight, levitation, or some other supernatural method of transport, because my feet never really touched the ground. I never felt the gritty give of sand, or the wind in my face. All I could feel was my heart seizing up in the worst muscle cramp I ever experienced.

The structure that gave the running path its incline was a wall of rocks and packed-in sand. At the base of the wall lay a scrap yard of small boulders that had chipped away from the siding over time. Ellia lay in the midst of that jagged debris. Her lack of movement didn't make sense to me. I could see her form clearly as the sun was rising higher over the mountains, but I couldn't grasp the stillness itself. Living things moved. A pulse. A breath. As I knelt over her, she showed no sign of any of those symptoms.

This was the one time when Mom's medical talks came in handy and I remembered what she told me about CPR and not moving the body. I pinched Ellia's nose and breathed into her mouth and pumped her chest lightly. My throat was sandpaper raw and saltwater stung my eyes.

Pinch, breathe, pump.

Again.

No response.

Again.

"Ellia, wake up! Please!"

Pinch, breathe—

Her chest jerked and air pushed back into my face in a loud cough.

Her eyes flew open and met mine with recognition; she even smiled as she lifted her hand to touch her head. I felt a rush of relief.

"What happened?" she croaked out.

"You fell over the side of the trail." I looked up at the stone wall and the height of the drop.

"I lost my keys. Dropped them . . . My keys . . . The collar."
She was fading on me. I lightly slapped her cheeks to keep her
awake.

"Hey, hey, stay with me now, Ellia. We need to get you some
help. Can you move?" I touched her arms and legs, checking for visible injuries. From what I could see, there were no broken bones—
mostly scratches and open gashes.

I searched our surroundings. My car was at home over a mile
away and the ambulance would take forever to arrive. But Ellia
lived closer with a perfectly good vehicle in the driveway. If need
be, I would hot-wire her parents' car and take her to the hospital
myself, but I hoped things didn't have to come to that.

I scooped her gently in my arms and she cried out in pain. I
asked her where it hurt and she pointed to her head. It was killing
her, she said.

This was not a good sign. I'd had a few concussions myself from
stray curveballs and bike accidents, and I knew she had to see a doctor and get X-rayed.

Ignoring the cramping in my legs and arms, I carried her off the
beach, through the promenade, and up several blocks to her house.
I kept talking to her to keep her awake; I spouted off random trivia,
like how red hair was a recessive gene, and recited some of my bad
poetry—anything to keep her eyes open.

I stumbled onto Ellia's front porch and kicked the door. I kicked
and kicked until the lights downstairs came on. The door swung
open and Ellia's father appeared, ready to yell at the intrusion at six

in the morning. His angry dark eyes took in the scene and the questions poured out laced with rage.

"She needs a doctor!" I shoved past him and entered the living room. "She fell and hit her head on the rocks and I think she might have a concussion."

"What was she doing out of the house this time of morning?" he barked.

"She was with me."

"Why was she out with you? What did you do to my daughter?" he yelled.

"I didn't do anything!" I set her on the sofa and supported her head with a pillow. When I drew my hand back, it was covered in blood.

"What is going on?" Ellia's mother came down the stairs, tying her robe around her waist. Even in sleepwear and a head scarf, she looked ready to entertain guests.

"Our daughter snuck off again and now she's gone and hurt herself," Mr. Dawson explained.

"Mom, I'm fine. I fell. Hit my head on rocks," Ellia croaked.

"You're not fine," I argued, and then turned my attention to the adults. "She needs to go to the hospital. She's bleeding."

"Why does she need a doc—" Mrs. Dawson screamed at the sight of the blood all over me and on Ellia's clothes. "Oh Jesus!" She glared at me. "What did you do to my baby?"

"Not his fault. He saved me!" Ellia mumbled with as much strength as she could.

"*The hell it isn't his fault!*" her dad bellowed. "*You wouldn't need saving if you stayed where you were supposed to. I told you this boy was nothing but trouble and you sneak off and nearly get yourself killed!*"

Mrs. Dawson knelt at Ellia's side on the couch. "*Gerald, we need to call an ambulance.*"

"*I'm fine. Just sleepy,*" Ellia slurred as her eyes began to droop.

"*NO! You have to stay awake, Ellia!*" I reached for her, but Mr. Dawson blocked my path.

"*You've done quite enough, young man. Now get out of my house before I have you arrested.*"

"*If you don't take her to the hospital, I will. On foot if I have to. I carried her this far.*" I tried to move around him, but a hard shove to the chest had me stretched out across the foyer.

"*Gerald, call an ambulance!*" Mrs. Dawson screamed.

I struggled to my feet. "*She needs to keep her eyes open until the doctors look at her!*" I tried to reason.

Mr. Dawson kept coming at me until I was on the porch. "*Get out! Do not come here again.*"

"*Gerald!*" I heard Ellia's mom wail as the door slammed in my face, the knocker clattering from the impact.

I wanted to scream. I wanted to kick the door down. I should've stuck to my plan and taken Ellia to the hospital myself. They were wasting precious seconds arguing about me rather than focusing on Ellia's injury.

I knew her dad would make good on his threat to call the police, but I didn't care. I had to make sure she was okay. I hid behind the shrubs of the neighbor's yard across the street to see if the ambulance arrived. But three minutes later Ellia's father tore out of the house with an unconscious Ellia in his arms. Mrs. Dawson trailed behind with the phone in her hand.

"Stay here and talk to the police. Make sure that boy doesn't come near this house," he told Ellia's mom.

I called Dad on my cell. He must've heard the fear in my voice because he told me he was on his way to get me. I didn't want him to come. I knew what he would say; I'd heard it a hundred times before.

I listened to Dad move around on the phone as I watched Mr. Dawson peel out of the driveway and tear up the block at breakneck speed. I wanted to run after them, sit in the waiting room of the hospital, do something other than wait here, because I knew something was terribly wrong with her. I just didn't know how bad until the police came to my house the next day. I was served papers to stay away from Ellia or else I'd go to jail. Three hundred feet. One hundred yards. It might as well have been across the country as far as I was concerned.

Of course, I didn't take it seriously, nor did I care if Mr. Dawson had me arrested. And for what? Saving his daughter's life. I loved her, and if she was hurt then there was nothing that would keep me from her.

My first attempt to see Ellia proved me wrong.

Mr. Dawson stood at the nurse's desk signing papers when he

looked up at me. "You have some nerve showing your face around here. Leave now before I call the police."

I refused to back down. In fact, I wanted him to push me again so I could press charges against him—see how he liked it. "You can't keep me from seeing her."

"No? Boy, I am her father. You don't tell me what I can and can't do. I told you to stay away from my daughter and now she's in a coma because of you." He stepped closer and spoke in a low tone.

"Ellia's in a coma?" I whispered, fear and horror shooting through me.

Mr. Dawson glowered at me and his eyes were full of pain. "Yes. My baby girl. We might lose her. That court order is ironclad, boy. And I have proof that you were there during the accident. There are cameras all over this hospital capturing your mug as we speak. It wouldn't be hard to charge you with harassment."

"What proof?" I asked, trying not to cry.

"You dropped something when you left my home the other day. It has Ellia's blood on it and no doubt your fingerprints, too. It would be an open-and-shut case for the county sheriff."

My eyes went wide. I thought of my father and his dreams for me to go to college. I thought of my future with a criminal record. Finally, I thought of Ellia and what little help I would be to her behind bars.

I took a step back and then another until I was in full retreat toward the exit. All the while I kept watching that smug look on

Mr. Dawson's face. He'd gotten what he'd wanted all along and in my own stupidity I'd helped him tear me and Ellia apart.

I didn't leave my room for a week, except for school. After finding out that I snuck into the hospital, Dad hid my car keys to keep me from returning. Wade had knocked on the door asking about the bloody clothes in the trash, but the only words I could get out were, "I'm so sorry. It's all my fault. I'm so sorry."

At some point, Dad came into my room to talk. He didn't say much at first and just sat on the bed with me and held me. He offered soundless strength, which had anchored me through every flu shot and every stitch as a boy.

"It was not your fault," he said. "It was a terrible accident. You had nothing to do with it."

But what he didn't understand, what no one seemed to comprehend, was I had everything to do with it. Blood was on my hands and it couldn't be washed away. Only now did I discover that all of our parents' warnings were true. Only now did I realize just how selfish my love for Ellia was, how dangerous. I hoped one day she would forgive me . . .

The book slipped from my fingers and landed facedown on the bed. My stare drifted to Vivian, who stood facing the window. The wheels began to churn in my brain. A healthy dose of fear had set in. That usually was followed by intense anger, which gave me enough fuel to confront them both.

I didn't care if they were working or if they were sound asleep. I snatched open the door and tore through the hallway.

"Mom! Dad!" I called out and stormed toward their room. "Where are you? Dad?"

Mom stepped out of her room in her bathrobe and looked as though she'd been ripped from sleep. "Baby, what's wrong?"

"I need to talk to you guys. Is Dad still up?" I raced down the stairs before she could answer. I passed through the kitchen, past the pantry, then stopped in front of the closed door of Dad's office.

Mom followed me. "Ellia, did something happen to you tonight? You seem agitated."

"I'm fine. I need to know about my accident." I tried to turn the knob, but the door was locked.

"Honey, we've been over this. You hit your head on the rocks at the beach and your father took you to the hospital."

"And then what?" I stepped back and saw that the lights were on inside. "Daddy?"

"Ellia Renée, you stop this foolishness right now!" she scolded, looking winded. This woman never let anything rattle her. She would slap on that plastic smile like it was a coat of arms.

Finally, the door opened and Dad appeared. "What on earth is going on here?"

Dad was an imposing figure on a good day, but he was downright menacing now in light of what I discovered. But I stood my ground and looked my father square in the eye and asked, "Where is it?"

"Where's what?"

"The dog collar. I was looking for it that day on the beach, thinking I dropped it on the path. Where is it?"

"I have no idea what you're talking about," Dad said. "Now, I need you to calm down. You're getting worked up for no reason."

More dodging. More omissions. More fibs. I wasn't listening anyway.

"You blackmailed Liam with Babette's collar. And threatened to send him to jail if he came near me," I accused.

"Don't be ridiculous."

"I'm being ridiculous? Who puts out a restraining order on their kid's boyfriend?"

"Ellia, that was for your own good," he said.

"I swear if I hear that one more time." I grabbed fistfuls of my hair and growled. "Do you even know who I am, Daddy? Do you even know why I kept that collar? Do you know why I did all that crazy stuff—the parties, the staying out late? It's because of you. Not Liam. If anything, he's the good one in this outfit. And I used that goodness to get back at you. What kind of person does that make me, Daddy?" I knew I was overstepping all kinds of bounds, but I needed to get to the truth.

Dad stepped forward. "Ellia, that is enough—"

"Let her talk, Gerald," Mom said behind me.

I turned around to her standing against the kitchen island with her arms crossed.

"It started with Babette's death, didn't it?" Mom asked me softly.

"Yeah," I said. "I guess I blamed Dad for Babette dying and not being allowed to show my grief. Or I was afraid to share anything with you because I didn't want to disappoint you. Maybe your expectations were too high and I buckled under the pressure. I don't know the answer to that, but I'm sorry anyway."

Mom nodded. "Dr. Kavanagh seems to agree."

Dad bristled at that news. "When did you speak with her?"

"During the parent-doctor appointment that you missed." Though Mom spoke in a low tone, the heat behind it could cut through steel.

"So I'm the bad guy here? I'm trying to do what's best for our daughter," Dad argued. "And that little white boy is nothing but trouble."

"My God, Gerald!" Mom pushed away from the counter. "This court business has gone along far enough. The boy is harmless. Troubled, but harmless. Why do you insist on threatening that child?"

I looked at Mom. "Did you know about the restraining order against Liam?"

"Of course I did, but that was a while ago." She said this as if it was an old song for her, but it was my first time hearing the tune.

Stunned by her nonchalance, I asked, "And you were okay with that?"

"At the time, I was," she said. "Your father and I believed that he was behind your reckless behavior and when you came home at 3:00 A.M., half-dressed and covered in feathers, it seemed like the best decision at the time. Wouldn't you agree?" Anger laced each of her words.

"The frat party," I said, recalling what I'd read in Liam's story. "Must've been pretty wild."

Neither Mom nor Dad shared my amusement. "From what Stacey told me," Mom said, "he brought both of you home from a party you had no business going to. It would appear that he's been the voice of reason throughout your rebellion."

Stacey? That was an interesting twist. "When did she tell you that?"

"She and I spoke often while you were in the hospital. Quite . . . informative." Mom arched a sculpted brow.

"Well, there you go. Liam's the good guy. What's with the three-hundred-feet restriction?" I demanded.

Now it was Dad's turn to look perplexed. "Ellia, the order lapsed over a month ago."

I blinked. "Come again?"

"It was a temporary order that only lasted until the court date," Mom explained. "Your recovery had taken up so much of our time, your father couldn't show up to court to make it permanent, so the order lapsed."

"And since you woke up with no memory of Liam, I saw no reason to reinstate it," Dad added.

I processed the words slowly and carefully. "So . . . Liam's not restricted from me or the house?"

"Legally? No," Dad replied and sounded a little tight about that fact.

"Does he know that?" I asked.

Mom's large eyes narrowed at me as if I was trying to pull a fast one on her. "He should've been served a notice by the sheriff."

"Then why is he still sneaking—I mean, why doesn't he come over to visit?" I quickly corrected myself. They didn't need to know about Liam's morning routine.

"I assumed he was giving you space," Mom guessed.

"Uh-uh. Not his style," I muttered.

Dad stepped forward and nailed me with a cold stare. "And you would know that how?"

I figured this was a good time to come clean. "I've been seeing him for a while now. Mostly tutoring stuff, but we'd hang around and talk. He's really smart and he's helped me a lot with my test scores. We're not dating or anything, so please don't call the cops on him. Please?"

"You've been seeing him behind our back again?" Dad bellowed. "I told you to stay away from that boy."

"But you never gave me a good reason why." I glanced at Mom. "What else did Dr. Kavanagh say?"

"She recommended that we have a family meeting. We've been advised to do this on a weekly basis as a part of our normal routine where we discuss our concerns in an open forum."

A family *what*? She wanted us to do this from home, without the aid of a professional? The idea just sounded weird coming from her mouth. Even weirder would be to put it into practice.

"Well, we might as well have this discussion now." Mom directed us to the kitchen table with her usual game-show model grace. She paused and pivoted toward Dad, who was still standing in the threshold. "Um, honey, will you be joining this session or do you want me to do this by myself as well?"

Oh snap! Somebody alert the burn unit. I kept quiet before they unloaded their ammo onto me.

Squaring his shoulders, Dad closed his office door and joined us at the kitchen table.

Mom started, opening the floor to anything and everything that needed to be said. And boy, did I have some grievances to voice. Since this was supposedly a therapy exercise, there was a good chance I wouldn't get grounded for it.

I let out everything I wanted to tell Dad for years, but didn't have the nerve. How sorry I was for being a bad daughter. How much I hated him and loved him at the exact same instant. How Dad's dream for me to follow in his footsteps would never happen because engineering or anything math related wasn't my thing. How he was too stubborn to see that my creative side came from Mom. How I wished he'd take over the cooking, because Mom was slowly trying to poison the entire family.

The words came in a series of stops, starts, mumbles, and shrugs, since getting all up in our feelings wasn't a family pastime. And Dad and Mom listened, really listened. And when it was their turn to speak, I was floored by what I heard. I wasn't a bad daughter. I wasn't a disappointment. Their expectations for me were indeed too high, and they both needed to start seeing me as my own person. But what had me blinking away tears was a sentiment not commonly expressed in the Dawson household. They loved me. Unconditionally.

According to the microwave clock, the discussion ran over two hours, the longest I'd ever spoken to either of these people simultaneously. By the end, Mom was wiping tears from her cheeks, which kinda freaked me out. The Dawsons didn't cry. We were doers, fixers, movers, and shakers. This sudden change in the rotation would take some getting used to.

I touched her trembling shoulder. "Mom, I'm sorry. I'm not saying you're a bad cook. You just need to ease up on the foliage."

"Preach," Dad chimed in and then rose from his chair. "I'm ordering a pizza."

"Are you okay?" I asked Mom while Dad went to get his phone.

"Yes, baby. I'll be fine." A sudden weariness crept over her smooth features as she dabbed her watery eyes. Even her tears were dainty. "I suppose you're old enough to know what you want in life."

"No. I'm not," I replied in all seriousness. "I just know what I *don't* want. And that is to be controlled or bullied or crammed into a mold that I can't fit. This goes for you, my friends, and even Liam. I can't be the girl he wants me to be. He wants us to be more than friends, but I can't deal with that."

Dad came back, his ears perked up at the sound of Liam's name. "You don't want to date him anymore?"

Why did he have to sound so hopeful about that? "It's complicated. I want to keep things simple," I replied.

Dad nodded thoughtfully. "Simple is good."

Three extra-large pizzas arrived at our door twenty minutes later and I nearly ate an entire pie on my own. After dinner, I helped Mom clean up. She didn't believe in using paper plates outside of cookouts and outdoor parties, yet she preferred to wash dishes by hand instead of using the fully functional dishwasher that sat right next to me. I wasn't sure if that was a paradox or just Mom's excuse for these quiet bonding moments, but Dad was done with the caring and sharing. He'd returned to his cave, leaving the womenfolk to the chores.

I glared at the closed door and wondered what was so important in there that kept him shut in. As a kid, I used to think that place was a spy center with all kinds of cool gadgets and government secrets locked in file cabinets. I later realized it was the only part of the house Mom couldn't decorate. She had painted, remodeled, and furnished the entire house, and had been trying to get at that room for years. No luck yet.

"I don't know how you do it," I told Mom as she handed me a wet plate to dry. "How can you love a man so . . . *him*?"

"You can't just love the good side of a person. When you see the ugly, you either love them for it or love them in spite of it."

I thought about Liam and how he went above and beyond in order to keep a promise we'd made on the beach. That was devotion. No matter what I thought about our relationship, I had to give him that.

As I dried a dish, I wondered about the restraining order. If it lapsed a month ago, then why all the secrecy on Liam's part? Unless he never received the notice. I ran the theory by Mom.

"Normally, the papers have to exchange hands. But if you're a minor, the parents can accept it for you," she explained and pulled the stopper out of the sink.

"Right."

I recalled how Liam's dad had reacted when I showed up at his house and how he didn't want me anywhere near his son.

So before I went to bed, I called Liam. I left him a voice message and prayed that he didn't hit Delete without hearing it. I owed him that much. I owed him that honesty.

CHAPTER TWENTY-FIVE

LIAM

L et me ask you something," I began. "You're so keen on the nickname, but have you ever *read* anything by Ernest Hemingway?"

Stacey sat across the table from me, both her arms and legs crossed as she stared out the café window, no doubt wishing she were anywhere but here.

I supposed I deserved the attitude getting thrown my way. After all, I did spring up at the café out of nowhere. But I needed to talk to her and settle the issue once and for all. She wasn't returning my calls and was practically a ghost in the hallways at school. We were leaving too many things unsaid.

So I had to use drastic measures, with Kendra acting as the front man. She'd arranged a coffee date with Stacey this afternoon, and when she left to use the bathroom, I slid into the empty chair. Stacey nearly choked to death on her frothy, nonfat latté when she saw me.

Of course, she made a scene and called me everything but my given name, yet not once did she get up to leave. I also noticed that, among the epithets she flung at me, *Hemingway* was not among them. Which sparked my question about the author.

"Nope. Never read him." Stacey's reply had the clipped, snotty timbre of a little girl who didn't get a pony for her birthday. She glanced out the window.

"Nothing? Not even his famous six-word story?" I pressed, eager to keep her talking.

Her face was still pointed to the window, but her eyes darted at me. "How can you write a whole story in six words?"

"It's next to impossible, but Hemingway did it.".

"Cool. Recite it to me," she said. She seemed confident that I'd know it from memory. I did, but that was beside the point.

"Right now?"

"Dude, it's only six words. I don't think I'll need the audiobook version. My tweets are longer than that."

"Okay." I cleared my throat. " 'For Sale: baby shoes, never worn.' "

That top layer of frost melted from her face. "Oh my god! That is so sad."

"Sorry," I mumbled. I hadn't wanted to upset her, but at least she was looking at me.

"You know, my mom miscarried twice before she had my little brother," Stacey said softly, her eyes filling with tears. "She doesn't believe in baby showers or buying stuff until after the baby is born. I guess that's why. But then there's no guarantee that the kid will live. There's crib death and the flu and other nasty things that take people away before their time. If you think about it, there's no such thing as a proper time to be born *or* to die. There's expectation and then there's reality, and those two never get along."

This was the most she'd ever mentioned about her family, and I rushed to drink it all in. I was getting a sneak preview of the real Stacey Levine, outside the flashy clothes and the layers of makeup that she didn't need.

"Kinda like you and me," she continued. "I *expected* to get swept off my feet or get butterflies in my stomach, but the *reality* is I feel gross. Like I've stolen someone else's identity. Like I'm a consolation prize, because even right now, you don't see me. You see *her*."

I leaned back in my chair to gain distance. "What?"

"Well, a different version of her," she clarified. "You're still stargazing, Liam. But I'll do you the courtesy of being up-front and telling you that I'm not Ellia. I need someone to see that and love me anyway."

Whoa! Where did the love stuff come from? I wasn't in love with Stacey, that was obvious, but that didn't mean I was blind to her flaws. "I *do* see you."

Her chin lifted in defiance as she asked, "What's my middle name?"

"No idea." I watched her sip her coffee. Dainty fingertips, a high pinkie, and smirking lips touched the cup as she drank to her victory.

Okay, fine. We didn't really know each other that well outside of school and our connection with Ellia, but she was missing the point. "Don't you think we need to address what happened between us?" I pressed.

"I'll admit that kiss was epic," she confessed, blushing. "We definitely have something: a spark, a buddy-cop dynamic with flirty undertones, but it's all based on *what if*. What if that baby didn't die? Would those shoes still be for sale?" She paused to look at me.

I knew she wasn't talking about the shoes in Hemingway's story. If Ellia hadn't had her accident, would I have kissed Stacey in my living room that night? Would we be sitting here now?

"No," I answered, knowing that honesty was the only way to move forward.

She nodded, and stared off wistfully. "That story. The baby shoes." She tapped her painted nails on the table. "I love shoes. In fact, love doesn't even describe my affection for designer footwear. But I'm not gonna wear someone else's, not when I know the history and the previous owner," she explained. "It's the wanting that gives me the high, not the having. All that ends once you have them in your possession and then you have nothing but a closet full of shoes that you've only worn once."

Again, it was clear Stacey wasn't just talking about shoes, but I got the message. In her weird, roundabout way, she was simply voicing what we were both thinking: We weren't right for each other.

"Wow, so you got all that from what could be considered a twentieth-century tweet," I said, hoping to alleviate some of the awkwardness again.

She gestured in a way that implied she agreed. Then she said, "I guess the name does fit you then."

"Why do you say that?" I asked.

"You managed to sum up your relationship with Ellia with half of Hemingway's word count. *Lessthanthree*. And by definition, I don't fit into the equation. No one can." She gave me a smug look.

It amazed me how someone who came off ditsy could be so insightful. It then occurred to me that all the hair-twirling, gum-chewing stuff was just an act. She didn't need to do that, but insisted on playing the role until graduation, at least. Seeing this deeper layer to Stacey had me leaning closer with my elbow resting on the table. She should show this side more often.

With my chin in my palm, I watched her for a long time before asking, "What *is* your middle name, by the way?"

Stacey looked away, embarrassed. "I don't tell anyone my

middle name. It makes me feel old," she explained. "Only my family and Ellia know. I was named after my grandmother. Vivian."

A wide, face-splitting smile spread across my face. "I really do like you, Stacey."

"I really like me, too, Liam." She smiled back.

After coffee with Stacey, I went home with the firm decision to be on my own for a while. No girlfriends. No ambiguous, let's-see-where-this-goes commitments. Being alone would be good for me, for now.

As I sat down to start my homework, I noticed that I had one new message on my phone. A message from *yesterday*. I was bad at checking voice mail. Balancing the phone between my shoulder and right ear, I let the message play, but only half listened as I rummaged through my backpack for my history notes.

The sound of Ellia's voice on the line caused a knee-jerk reaction that almost made me drop the phone. The words didn't register at first, but as the recording continued, my confusion turned into disbelief, and then rage.

I rushed downstairs and found Dad in the kitchen standing over the sink. He extended his right arm as if reaching for something down the drain. Wade leaned against the counter beside him, chugging a glass of milk. It was just a peaceful evening at the bachelor pad, but not anymore.

"The court order lapsed and you didn't tell me?" It was a question and an accusation rolled into one.

Dad turned to me, frowning.

"No, son, I didn't tell you. And before you ask why, take a minute to look at your situation from a parent's point of view then ask 'why not?'"

My fists stayed pinned to my sides to keep from swinging. "You knew how I felt about her and you kept this from me!"

Dad kept up a stoic expression, unfazed by my yelling. "It was better this way."

"For who?" I shouted. "Just because things didn't work out with you and Mom doesn't mean the same will happen to me and Ellia!"

"It's already happened to you and Ellia!" he erupted. "She can't remember who you are because you couldn't leave that girl alone and you're using her to fill some void that your mother left. I know you, son. I know how you think and feel, because I was just like you at your age. We McPhersons love hard and it can run wild if it's not put in check."

A hush swept over the kitchen, and all I could hear was my raging pulse. Wade remained catatonic at the counter, neither taking a side nor interfering. His wide eyes darted between me and Dad, his milk mustache dripping to his chin.

Dad came closer until he stood a foot away from me. His stare leveled mine as he waited for my reaction. "Well, the truth's out now. What's next? You going to see her?"

A week ago, I would've said, "Yep! Don't wait up." It was a whole other situation now, and everything, including my anger, felt pointless. I shook my head for an answer.

Dad grunted his approval, but he didn't look ready to celebrate, either. "Have you talked to your mother recently?"

"No."

"You might want to do that before you make any major decisions. I'm not a shrink or anything, but you need to get right with her before you can expect to get right with any other woman." He returned to the sink as if nothing ever happened.

I only stared, knowing he was probably right and hating him for it. Wade continued to look confused and ridiculous with that mustache, and I left the kitchen feeling half my age.

In my room, I slammed the door so hard that it nearly ripped from the frame. I grabbed my phone and earbuds then lay across my bed and draped an arm over my eyes. The world compressed into a black vacuum where my heartbeat kept in time with the death metal roaring in my ears at full volume.

Four tracks later, I heard a light tapping on my door. I told whoever it was to go away, but that seemed to translate as an invitation because the door opened.

Over the loud music, I heard a low voice say, "Ellia has amnesia."

I paused the song and uncovered my eyes to find Wade standing in the doorway. His head hung low, his manner as timid as a child awaiting punishment. After what happened at the dance, I'd kept my distance from him until I cooled down. Wade knew well enough to give me space, but he was jumping ahead of schedule.

I never told him about Ellia's condition, but I assumed he would've figured it out by now. Nosy as he was, he should've at least tapped Dad for that information. "You didn't know that?" I asked.

"No. I thought she just bumped her head." He ran a hand through his mop of hair. "Kendra told me about her and Cody at the dance. That explains a lot. Except it didn't explain why *you* didn't tell me." The hurt rang clear in his voice. "I asked you about that day on the beach. I asked about the blood on your clothes. I thought we were family."

"We are, but—"

"But what?" he snapped. "You thought I was gonna talk? Spread it around school? Alert the media? What?"

"All the above," I muttered.

"Not with something like this." He paced the floor space in front of my bed. "I know a thing or two about shocking family secrets, Liam. I *was* one. I know a little bit about abandonment issues, too."

I knew this was a sore subject for him, but that had nothing to do with my decision. "Wade, you're a part of this family. Dad accepts you and so do I—"

"I'm talking about your mother," he interrupted me. "She bailed on you like mine bailed on me. And I'm not even gonna go into that whole thing with Natalie that messed me up for months. So now, if any girl comes along, I've got my guard up, waiting for the other shoe to drop. The first whiff of drama that hits my nose—I'm out. *I* have to be the one who breaks it off."

"Does Kendra know that?" I asked.

"Yeah. But it's different when you actually want to be with that person. You'll do anything to make them stay," he said. "It's funny—you spend all this time hoping something good will come along and when it does, you're terrified that it'll be taken away from you. You're miserable either way. That's how you were with Ellia. You'd do anything to make her happy out of fear of getting dumped."

I never thought of it that way. I also never thought I'd get relationship advice from Wade.

"And you think I'm like that because of . . . my mom?"

He nodded. "I agree with Jack—you need to call her. Let her know how she hurt you but then accept the fact that it was never about you."

"I could give you that same advice," I countered.

"And I would take it, too, if my mom returned my calls." With a heavy sigh, he sat on the edge of my bed. "All I'm saying is find closure where you can get it and go on with your life. Kendra told me a good quote the other day: *Absorb what is useful. Discard what is not and add what is uniquely ours.*"

I'd never heard that line before. "Who's that from? Socrates?"

"Nope. Bruce Lee." His hands sliced through the air in a series of kung fu poses. "Now about this Ellia business . . ."

We talked for a while about Ellia's condition and I told him about *Lessthanthree*. Next came the theories on how to get Ellia's memory back, including Wade's ingenious plot to knock Ellia over the head with a barbell, as he claimed it worked in a cartoon he once saw. Now that I thought about it, he and Kendra made a good couple.

After he left, I attempted to study for my History quiz, but my mind wouldn't stick to my notes. I kept peering at my phone. So I cleaned my room, played around online, all of which led to me sitting on the edge of my bed, engaged in mental warfare with my phone. My avoidance went beyond procrastination to outright dread.

I wasn't familiar with her work schedule now, but I knew she'd still be up at this hour. She never went to bed earlier than 2:00 A.M. and was able to work a sixteen-hour hospital shift with only four hours of rest. Maybe I'd gotten my sleep pattern from her. Go figure.

She picked up after the third ring, and her voice sounded pleasantly surprised. "Hi, honey!"

"Hi, Mom," I said.

"I've been trying to get ahold of you for a while, baby. How are things going?"

I hated when people asked that because it was often a

rhetorical question. I'd rarely come across anyone who didn't use the inquiry to steer the conversation back to them. I wasn't in the mood for pretense, so I gave her options. "Do you want the Sunday brunch answer or the truth? I can work with either one."

She paused for a long beat before saying, "The truth. I'm worried about you."

"You sure? Because it's not pleasant and it might take longer than your lunch break will allow, and it may include some of that *insipid angst* that you love so much."

Yes, I was being a jerk and childish for bringing up something she said three years ago. And the fact that I could still remember every word, every pause and hitch in her speech proved why this entire phone call was necessary. I might appear taller, my voice deeper, my features sharper, but in truth, I was still that hurt little kid.

"I'm sorry. I'm just going through some stuff right now, that's all," I said, annoyed that my eyes were already filling with tears.

"Liam, like it or not, I'm still your mother and whatever bothers you bothers me. That hasn't changed." Her voice, low and soothing, threatened to break that iron hold I had on my emotions.

I told myself that it was just saltwater, but really they were the lost years running down my cheeks and neck, silence and distance tightening my throat. It was the presence of absence.

The shadow left behind held the most weight and the pressure crushed my lungs and robbed me of air. It was too much and I wanted so badly to hang up, but my hand wouldn't loosen its grip on the phone.

"I'm off the clock now, so you can take all the time you want," Mom said. "Tell me what's wrong."

Clips from the past three months played in my head like a movie trailer. So much had happened that she needed to catch up on. If nothing else, this was a sensible reason for me to stay in touch more often. It kept the updates brief.

"Oh wow." I sniffed and wiped my nose on my arm. "Where do I even start?"

Her reply held a twinge of laughter. "Start where every story does. At the beginning."

CHAPTER TWENTY-SIX

ELLIA

I sat in one of the twin armchairs in front of Dr. Whittaker's desk, struggling to process the long, multisyllable words coming out of his mouth. Why Mom thought the world of this man was beyond me. It could be the salt-and-pepper hair, the fit physique, the old-dude swagger. But this time Dad had accompanied me to my evaluation, so I was spared the hero worship.

I wasn't all that impressed with the good doctor. His vocabulary was the main source of my contempt. He honestly expected a sixteen-year-old to know what any of those medical terms meant, and he seemed put-off by having to dumb it down for the common folk.

Once my prognosis was translated to modern English, I was able to join the conversation. "So what you're saying is I may never get my memories back?" I asked.

"There's always a possibility, but seeing as they haven't

surfaced by now, it's becoming more unlikely," he said solemnly. "What I recommend now is to continue the therapy and memory exercises and see where things go in a few months."

"Thanks." I was glaring hard at him, but not because of the outcome. The sunlight pouring from the vertical blinds behind him was hurting my eyes.

Dad must've seen my expression and nudged my arm to make me behave. He sat straight in the chair next to me; chin high, hands in lap. Naturally, he was dressed to the nines in a tailored navy suit sharp enough to cut glass, with not one hair out of place. His tight jaw and glacial stare told me that he didn't seem to care much for the MD, either.

"That's not to say that it will never happen," Dr. Whittaker added. "Permanent amnesia is very rare and in most cases memories will come back on their own, but we'll have to wait and see if there's any lasting damage to the brain. The good news is that you're still quite young and only a couple years are missing from your life. Should this blank spot remain, you'll still have a lifetime of memories to make up for it."

"Yeah." I folded my arms to my chest and sank lower in my seat. For some reason, I thought of Liam, but then tried to push him out of my head.

Dr. Whittaker set my file aside and removed his reading glasses. Resting his elbows on the table, he leaned in and brought his hands together so they touched at the fingers. The whole gesture screamed *it's about to get real.*

"I've seen forty-year-olds whose entire life histories were wiped away. They have no idea who they were or when they were born or where they came from. They couldn't recognize their spouses or their grandchildren. So yes, Ellia, I believe you're very fortunate. Perhaps you could see this as a fresh start. It's a chance to reinvent yourself."

Dad rubbed my back and the contact provided a comfort I hadn't felt since I was a little kid. His dark eyes softened and his faint smile told me what I needed to hear without words. *Everything will be okay. Life will go on either way.*

I nodded. Yesterday was gone and there was no point in reaching behind me for something I couldn't even hold. Time moved in one direction: forward. And I needed to keep my eyes straight and do the same.

In the parking lot, Dad took his time starting the car. He'd slid the keys into the ignition then just stopped as if something dawned on him. The longer he stared pensively at the parked cars ahead, the more it worried me. When a few minutes rolled by, I asked him what was wrong.

Instead of answering, he reached across my seat and opened the glove compartment. His fingers sifted through papers and random junk until he found what he was looking for. My eyes bugged out at the sight of the collar dangling in his hands. The clink of tiny paw tags sounded like music from a long forgotten childhood.

"Daddy!" I cried and held the collar in both my hands.

"There's nothing more terrifying than hearing your child cry out in pain," Dad said with his eyes trained to the row of cars parked in front of us. "You have no idea what it does to a parent. It's primal, the need to protect, and kill if necessary. Rational thought is no longer a factor."

I knew he had more to say and finding the right words seemed taxing, so I waited.

"He told me to keep you awake. No matter what, don't let you close your eyes until the doctors saw you. I don't know why but I did it, just kept you talking the whole way to the hospital. You told me you needed to find Babette's collar. That's what I did. It took me twelve hours, but I found it on the running path." He chuckled, but it lacked any trace of humor. "And to think. All I'd wanted was for you to forget Babette." He paused. "And Liam. I see now that it only made things worse," he said and then started the car.

Wait. That was it? No *Sorry for threatening Liam* or *Sorry for lying about the collar or being an overbearing tyrant*? We were just gonna skip over that, huh? Why was I even surprised anymore? Dad definitely needed to work on his apologies. I should bring that up at our next family meeting. But I still smiled at the collar in my hand. I had to see this as a good sign. It gave me more hope for the future than all of my doctors combined. All was not lost, just hidden.

When I realized that we still hadn't left the parking lot, I asked, "What's wrong now?"

Dad nodded as if coming to some great decision. "You need to learn how to drive."

"I do," I agreed. My second attempt at the written driver's test scored me a perfectly good permit that wasn't being put to use. Bike riding was fun and all, but all of my friends seemed to have outgrown that form of transportation.

"Can I drive home?" I asked eagerly.

"No," he said, then took the car out of park.

I sighed.

"But we can practice this weekend," he offered with a sly curl of his lips. "In the meantime, watch and learn."

After we got home, I went to my room, prepared to curl up with the end of Liam's book.

Then I heard a light tapping on my door.

"Come in," I said absently, thinking it was Mom with one of her power juices. But when I glanced up, I discovered that it was *Stacey*, holding one of Mom's power juices.

"Uh . . . your mom told me to tell you to drink this. It looks like swamp water, so good luck with that."

"Thanks." I took the glass from her and set it on the nightstand.

She remained by the door, looking unsure whether to come any farther.

"I'm sorry for what happened at the dance, Ellia," she said. "I shouldn't have butted in like that. I shouldn't have done a lot of things."

"I'm sorry for blowing up at you," I replied. "And you're right. I was using Liam. I was using him before the accident, too, in a way. As my way to rebel and—"

"I kissed Liam," she blurted out.

I blinked. "Come again?"

"After all the stuff went down at the dance, we felt bad and turned to each other for comfort, I guess. It just happened out of nowhere and I tried to avoid him afterward."

"What am I hearing right now?" I jumped to my feet. "Because it sounds like my best friend went behind my back and put the moves on my boyfriend!"

"He's not your boyfriend!" she argued. "You made that clear. Plus, *you* told me to go for him."

"I didn't mean that. I was mad! Oh my god, Stacey, you don't date a friend's ex. That's in the Bestie Ten Commandments."

"I'm sorry. I got caught up in the moment."

"Why would you do that?" I asked, still in shock.

She shrugged, looking down. "Maybe part of me was a little jealous," she muttered. "I wanted what you two had. No guy ever looked at me the way Liam looked at you. And the lengths he went to find out about you—he did my homework, El! Just to get an update on your progress. I mean, come on, every girl wants a hot guy standing outside in the rain, throwing pebbles at her window. A guy who will carry you and refuse to leave your side and sneak into your hospital room to spend time with you. You guys had a love that few people ever get to experience."

"Maybe," I said softly. "But why'd you try and snatch up that love for yourself? In what universe would you think that would be okay?"

Stacey shrugged. "Well, it was stupid to even think I could get that from Liam, because I can't. And in all honesty, I don't even want it from *him*. I just want what he feels for you. So yeah, I messed up. And I'm sorry, Ellia."

This would be the part of the talk show where I'd get up and throw my chair across the stage and start swinging and pulling hair until the security guards broke us up. Best believe that I was tempted to throw her skinny tail out the window, but the pain in her eyes stopped me. I figured I'd actually listen for a change. I'd done a lot of reckless and impulsive things in the past, and I wanted to try on this new concept called reason.

"I don't know what to say to you right now, Stacey," I said truthfully. "Just looking at you is making me mad."

"But why?" she asked. "If you don't have any feelings for Liam?"

"Because he was my—"

"Your *what*?" she cut me off. "Your boyfriend, your exboyfriend, your standby?"

"I . . . I don't know."

"Do you love him?" she asked.

I paused. "Same answer. I mean, I want to, but I don't know what's real. Here I was wondering if I could trust everyone else's intent . . . when in truth, I can't trust my own."

"I think you did love him," she said with a confidence I wished I could borrow.

I shook my head. "It could've been an act."

"You told him all the time. That's not something you pass around like a business card, El."

"Still, though. I need something more. If I knew for a fact that I loved him before . . ."

Stacey leaned forward to look at me steadily. "Who cares about that? What do you feel *now*? Sure, you lost the first two years of your relationship, but what about the next two years or even the next twenty years? You and Liam need to stop mourning over what you lost and worry about what you still have and if it's worth saving. If not, then cut it off."

I nodded in agreement, and glanced down at the manuscript on my bed.

She followed my gaze. "Is that his book?" she asked.

Her question took me by surprise. "How did you know?"

"He told me. He was going to give up on it, but I told him to keep going. I think he needed to get it all out of his system. You know, put the old Ellia to rest."

"You think it worked?" I asked.

"I don't know."

"That seems to be the answer of the day."

"The answer to life," she said.

"Someone needs to tell Kendra that so she can stop wondering," I joked.

"I'll send her a text."

"Speaking of texts." I sat back on the bed and grabbed my phone from my nightstand. "Cody asked about you."

Stacey raised her eyebrows. "Really?"

"Yes. You want his number?" I scrolled down my contact list.

For the first time in ages, she seemed to be at a loss for words. "Um, sure. I figured he was more interested in Trish. Wait. If he has amnesia, then how does he even remember me?"

I texted her Cody's number. "Repetition," I explained. Stacey furrowed her brow, but I added, "You'll see," and I gave her a small smile. Maybe she and Cody would actually get along.

"I really am sorry, El. About Liam," she said.

"I think I know that, deep down. Anyway, I'm gonna get back to reading."

"Okay." She moved to the door and opened it. "It's a good read, isn't it?"

"It's my third read. I can't put it down," I said, flipping to the place I'd dog-eared.

"Well, maybe one day you'll tell me how the story ends."

I looked up at her, confused. "Don't you know?"

"Nope. And neither does Liam." She blew me a kiss then closed the door behind her.

I continued reading late into the night, laughing and crying, reliving the experience that was once mine all over again. Then

I came upon a passage that made me flip back. It was the moment where I told Liam I loved him.

LESS THAN THREE | Page 200

"I love you. I'm telling you now because at exactly 5:28 this morning, I woke up with that awareness and I knew I had to tell you. 'Cause honestly, I never felt . . . It feels weird and exciting and I'm scared and it's okay because that's how people act when facing a phenomenon, like a UFO or Bigfoot. But I can't capture this on film. I have to tell someone or else it doesn't exist. And who better to tell than the person it's about, so . . . there it is. It's out there in the ether. Ignore it, reject it, or explore it, but you are now accountable for that reality, too." She checked her phone again. "It's now . . . 8:04 and I still love you. And I don't think it's going away."

I closed the book then fell back onto my pillows. I turned my head toward the alarm clock—my enemy for so many mornings. It was five thirty in the morning. Of course it was.

Amnesia or not, I was just a girl, fully aware of what was going on, but not knowing how things got that way. But at least the most important question had been answered. My memory wasn't gone, just hidden. And maybe my feelings for Liam were the same.

LIAM

Double-checking the phone strapped to my arm, I reset the stopwatch then began the countdown.

Thirty seconds.

I shook my legs loose, rolled my shoulders, and got into position.

Fifteen seconds.

I knelt low—head down, back up, with my fingers planted into the sand.

Ten seconds.

Sweat ran over my nose, itching the skin, but my eyes stayed glued to the marked line spaced exactly four hundred meters away. The runner's app would automatically track the distance, but I needed a focal point, a tangible goal. In that moment, with dawn closing in on the quiet beach, that thin line was my world, my life's purpose.

The timer beeped and I pushed off the ground, sending wet clumps of sand flying in the air. Swinging arms propelled me forward, fighting traction and the reinforcement weights on my ankles. Every muscle in my body screamed in collaboration with the rock blasting from my earbuds. The bass line became a second heartbeat.

The clock stopped at the same time I crossed the crude finish line: 58.8 seconds. And that included the sand resistance and ankle weights. Good, but not great. I needed to shave off three seconds from my sprint time to make it to the state competition. If I could reach that goal on sand, I'd be a flying ghost on the asphalt. I saved the time and then restarted the stopwatch for the fourth drill this morning.

Wade said I was pushing myself too hard, but was that really a surprise? This was how I rolled—always moving, always taking things to the extreme—because that was the only way things got done. There was power in movement. That part of my nature would never change, but at least now I used that energy for something constructive.

I had my mother to thank for my renewed enthusiasm. We'd talked well into the early morning and once the serious stuff was put to rest, we had trouble getting off the phone. There were apologies all around and crying from both ends and I felt cautiously optimistic when we hung up. One phone call wouldn't erase the hurt and distance between us, but I had a better understanding of her. A little.

As much as I hated when people used the line, "It's not you, it's me," the phrase fit in her case. I was never the problem, and that truth was just now sinking in. That fear had saddled me down for so long that I'd forgotten it was there. The second that burden lifted, I went flying and hadn't touched the ground since.

When I reached the starting line again, I noticed someone jogging along the water's edge. I'd know that clumsy gait anywhere, and I froze.

It had been a week since I received her voice mail, which was the full extent of our contact. How funny was that? I saw her less now without the restrictions than I did with them.

It would appear that Ellia decided to take matters into her own hands. Typical. But I'd be a liar if I said I wasn't happy to see her.

She could pass for an active runner in black leggings and a running jacket, but I knew this was a one-time event. Memory loss or not, there were elements of a person's internal makeup that never went away.

Ellia slowed her pace and then came to a full stop a yard away.

"Ellia," I said and pulled the buds out of my ears.

"Liam," she gasped and clutched her side.

"What are you doing out here so early?"

"I knew you'd be here. You're *always* here. You're kinda predictable that way." Her words came out in short bursts as she tried to catch her breath. "I read your book. It's good. You're talented. It's a little rusty, but it's definitely there."

"Thanks," I said, and I meant it. No matter who read my work, be it a teacher or someone else, only Ellia's final verdict would make it fact.

She bent forward and rested her hands on her knees. "Ever think about getting it published?"

I shook my head. "No way. It's private. No one else will ever see it."

She smiled. "Good answer."

The writer in me wanted to know more: what she liked, what she didn't like, her favorite chapter. But I pushed my ego aside to get to the most important question. "Did it help you?"

"Yeah. It answered a lot of my questions. And I learned a lot of truths about myself."

"Me too, believe it or not," I said.

Just the night before, I'd stayed up late reading the story again. And I began to see my relationship with Ellia in a clearer light. Our relationship hadn't been perfect. We had been happy, but there'd been problems all along. It wasn't something I'd been able to understand while living it in the moment. But when read in sequence, the flaws and dysfunction were glaringly obvious.

"That's good to know. I hear that writing is therapeutic," Ellia said. She got quiet for a minute and just stared at the sand between her parted feet. She waited until her breathing slowed before speaking again.

"I know you blame yourself for the accident. I read the pain on paper, but I'm gonna need you to not do that anymore. I was out there with you that morning. You didn't drag me from my house and force me on the beach. *I* did that and *I* ran too close to the edge and fell. That's on me. It's done now."

I exhaled slowly and could almost feel the poison draining out of my system. Just like with Mom, I'd heard this line of reasoning before, but it was a whole other situation, a whole other world, when it came from the person directly involved.

Getting a bit choked up, I cleared my throat then said, "All the same, I really am sorry for what happened."

"Yeah, there's a lot of that going around. So how have you been?" she asked.

"Better, kind of," I said, kicking at the sand. "I called my mom last week."

"Oh, that's great!" She smiled. "Did you guys work things out? How did that go?"

I remembered how I'd told Mom about Ellia and her condition. Then Mom brought up a disturbing parallel that left me reeling.

"This Ellia girl sounds a lot like me at her age," she'd said. *"Disobeying her parents, running wild just because, and having big ideas with no follow-through. Your father loved that about me. Next thing I know, I wake up one day in my thirties, wondering 'who am I?' In a way, it was like amnesia of my identity, and it's taken me years to get to know the real Diane. At least you and Ellia have time*

to figure it out. The words I love you *are worthless when you don't know who the* I *is in that statement."*

It was an eye-opener to say the least, and one day I just might share that discovery with Ellia. Today wasn't that day. "It went okay," I said.

"Good." Her nod continued well into the silence that followed. Her hands fidgeted inside the pockets of her jacket and her feet spread out the sand between us.

I'd suddenly run out of words and kept busy by stretching— first the left arm and then the right. The tension between us was gelatin thick.

Suddenly, Ellia perked up. "Oh! I got an email from Wade. He asked me to tell Cody he was sorry for what he did at the concert, but Cody can't remember that part and he deliberately chose not to jot it down, so it's best to leave it forgotten, right?"

"Right," I mumbled. Cody's condition was serious, and I knew I shouldn't laugh at something like that, but it slipped out in a loud spit of air. "I kinda envy that ability."

"Don't. Trust me," she assured with the wide-eyed conviction of a person who'd seen way too much. "Good, bad, or ugly, knowledge is far too precious to let slip out of your hands."

I nodded. I didn't know what else to say. Finally I settled on, "Well, this has been nice and I'm glad you're doing better, but I need to practice."

Before I turned to leave, she stepped forward. "I was wondering if we could talk."

"About what?"

"Your bad attitude, for one thing," she said.

I stopped and glanced at her from over my shoulder. "Now why would *I* have an attitude?"

Her eyes lowered to the sand and her feet did that windshield-wiper sweep again. "You're right. You have every reason to be mad, and I'm sorry for hurting you. I can't even find an excuse for it that doesn't sound stupid or selfish."

"That's because there isn't one," I answered.

"There isn't one for you kissing my best friend, either, but I'm not getting all up in my feelings about it." The reply was pure attitude laced with arsenic. "We're both to blame, so get over yourself. You weren't exactly the best boyfriend, either."

Oh, this I had to hear. I crossed my arms and waited.

"I've been thinking about a whole lot of things," she said. "At first, I thought you dated me to get back at your parents. But now I think you went out with me to *forget* your parents. I was a distraction, something to take your mind off your real problems, your real emptiness, and you wanted me to fill that void. For you, I was an escape, an epiphany that would change your outlook on life and help you take risks and spit on the status quo. It's okay, because I think I was using you for the same reason."

If she was trying to pick a fight with me, it worked. "Okay, fine," I snapped. "Maybe I didn't try hard enough to get through to you. Maybe I got high off the nonstop thrill ride that was Ellia Dawson. Those legends in school are all people know you for because you rarely showed another side of yourself. If you had, people wouldn't have to speculate on who you are! You were unavailable in every sense of the word."

That shut her up. A remarkable feat, all things considered. I usually had to kiss her quiet whenever we fought, but this would work just fine for the point I needed to make.

"You're right," I admitted. "In the beginning, I did use you to escape my own problems. But eventually I got to see every selfish, petty, bossy, passive-aggressive flaw you had. And I loved you. I loved everything about you that mattered. Whatever you were sad about. Whatever you were afraid to tell me. Whatever thoughts that kept you awake. Believe whatever you want, but you need to know that that part was real and it hasn't changed. Love is seeing someone at their worst and sticking around anyway. That's what I've been doing all this time." I paused and took a breath. "I might wear glasses, but I'm not the only one with vision problems around here, El."

"I call that a read," she said with a wry smile, but then she grew serious. "Look. I like you. I like you a lot. I'm just starting to get to know you, though. What we had? Those two people don't exist anymore. Even if I get my memories back one day, that crazy Ellia isn't coming back. Quiet as it's kept, it was a blessing in disguise. I got past my own drama and hurt to see other people."

I nodded and shuffled my feet. I had to let go of the old Ellia. And it was an interesting idea, to think of this as a fresh start.

"Friendship is where real love starts," Ellia went on. "It's one thing to love someone, but the question is: Do you like them? As a person? Do you care enough to not be selfish?"

Rolling waves and squawking seagulls filled the air while I gave the question serious thought. The whole situation felt like a backward marriage proposal. My answer didn't help in that regard. "I do."

She grinned. "Okay. So . . ." She traced her toe in the sand. "What do we do now?"

I took a long moment to study her face. "Now . . . I guess we work on being friends. And we see what happens from there. Deal?"

"Deal." Ellia took a step back and lingered for a moment, unsure whether to go or to stay.

I realized that she was waiting for me to decide for her. I didn't want her to go.

"I was going to watch the sun come up. You want to join me?"

She smiled. "Sure."

We sat on the sand and watched the water grow lighter as the sun rose. She scooted closer to me and laid her head on my shoulder and I wrapped my arm around her back. Silence fell again, but this time around it suited us just fine. We made no plans, no promises, and had no expectation of what would happen next. The urgency that had been prevalent throughout our entire relationship was gone and the what-ifs weren't dire enough to ruin a perfectly good morning.

Sunlight and pink clouds rolled across the sky, putting a long night of stargazing to an end. The pushing, the rebelling, the fighting, the hiding, the running: It all had to go. The only thing I hung on to now was her soft hand. It was the start of a new day—a new chapter in the story of me and Ellia.

Hopefully this one would have a better ending.

ABOUT THE AUTHOR

JAIME REED is the author of The Cambion Chronicles series. She studied art at Virginia Commonwealth University. She now lives in Virginia, where she works part time as a line producer for a small independent film company. But mostly she watches 80s movies and writes. You can visit her online at at www.jaimereedbooks.com.